IN THE GREAT

The speaker on the
Changeling, Fain realized.

Him – or any of the others. The gross Alvean in the front row, the smooth-faced youth near the middle of the hall, or the wrinkled old man who appeared to be fast asleep – any one of the thirty men gathered in this hall.

And Fain had no way of finding out which one it was.

There was the joke. He had the Changeling trapped, penned, caught. And he was utterly helpless to act.

Then in a cold flash it came to him what he could do . . . what he must do.

Fain laughed aloud as he raised his heatgun. But there were tears in his eyes as he thumbed the weapon to automatic fire . . .

Also by Gregory Benford in Orbit:

THE STARS IN SHROUD
TIMESCAPE

GREGORY BENFORD
and
GORDON EKLUND

Find The Changeling

ORBIT

For Charles N. Brown

An Orbit Book

Published in the United States of America by Dell
Publishing Co Ltd 1980
First published in Great Britain in 1983 by Sphere Books
Reprinted in Orbit 1991

ISBN 0 7088 8373 7

Printed and bound in Great Britain by
BPCC Hazell Books
Aylesbury, Bucks, England
Member of BPCC Ltd.

Orbit Books
A Division of
Macdonald & Co (Publishers) Ltd
165 Great Dover Street
London SE1 4YA

A member of Maxwell Macmillan Publishing Corporation

Part
One

1

It was a sound like fingernails on tin, scraping and shrieking and filling the cabin with harsh harmonics. Fain's face twisted.

He glanced to the side. Skallon was grimacing, lines of strain carved in his young features.

If this went on—

Fain fired the retros. The sudden slam rattled his teeth. He felt a new surge of acceleration. The cowling that sheltered the nose had blown away. Abruptly the screeching wail vanished. A howling followed. *Primary skin blown*, Fain thought.

"What . . . what was . . ."

"It used a particle beam on our nose. Carved it up pretty good. I blew the retros to shake the cowling loose."

"CommCen said the Changeling didn't know how to use those subsystems."

"Yeah." Fain listened to the second skin burning away: a crisp sound, like frying bacon. He had an amped acoustic tap-in, so it came through loud and clear. Acoustics were the most reliable way to judge your entry characteristics. The turbulence-compensated airfoil scorched away at a rate dictated by the need for speed, not safety. It was a rough ride.

The shuddering roar in his aft sensors rose in pitch. High, higher—the second shell roasted away.

Fain grimaced. The entry shells peeled off and filled the sky around them with metal-coated plastaform, confusing radar, and exosense detectors. Good. Each fragmenting shell complicated the Changeling's problem.

They had damned near caught the Changeling up above, in orbit. It hadn't expected them. They had boosted out from Earth as soon as CommCen got clear word that the Changelings would try for this particular world. There had barely been time to roust Skallon and get him into gear. He was the planetary mission backup, in case they missed the Changeling in space.

Which they had, barely. They flickered out of translight just beyond missile range. The Changeling's capsule had dipped into the Alvean atmosphere. Now they had to follow the thing down, coming in fast and sleek, massing high, to try to nail the Changeling before it could touch down.

It was somewhere below, its ballistics system struggling to pick their capsule out from the shower of junk. It was quick and smart. It had found them with that ion beam, and cut away a lot of their safety margin by destroying the heavy cowling. But now it was time for a reply.

Fain thumbed in the offensive weapons systems. Below them in the murky alien atmosphere the tri-Dopplered screen showed a snowstorm of images—drifting flakes of sloughed-off entry shells, phantom debris, evasion missiles scooting sideways, luminous and misleading. One was the Changeling.

Fain repped and primed his launcher. He picked a target near the center of the metallic snowstorm. Radar could do only so much. Then you had to make a smart guess. He hit the launch command.

Thunk. "Hey!" Skallon shouted. "That sounded like—"

"It was."

"Look, introducing weapons of Class IV into Alvea's subspace—"

"Yeah, I know. CommCen ruled that out. But they're not here right now and we are. And that thing down there threw an ion bolt at us."

"I don't like it. The natives will see it and—"

"And ignore it, probably. Sit tight."

The missile spat plasma out the back, making a red image on his exosense screens. It homed swiftly. The snowflake images drifted to the right—

The A-burst flowered, bright and hot.

"Jesus!" Skallon cried. "How big was the tip?"

"Ten kilotons. Implosion-boosted stuff."

An ionized cloud spread, obliterating the triDopplered snowflakes in a blue mist. Fain looked away from the multicolored array, hoping this was the end of it. A neat, surgical job—that was what he wanted. Then they could land, call the mothership in orbit above, and boost the hell out of here on the translight carrier.

He watched the blossoming nuke burst. At the center were spikes of red, denoting objects caught in the blast. At this range they blended into a sullen ball like a bonfire. Fain thought of flame and burning and suddenly of a man spilling forward, his clothes leaping orange with licking, eating flames. The man was yelling, screaming something that Fain could not make out through the hollow roar of the flames that ate away, ate and scorched and blackened everything—the flames—the flames—

He shook his head. No.

The picture faded. He had to concentrate on the screen. He gazed deep into the cloud, looking for the telltale ionization traces of heavy metals. That would show where the capsule had been vaporized, bursting open, cracking the Changeling like an egg.

But there were none. The missile had missed.

"Shit!" Fain barked, slamming his hand against the console. Now the debris cloud itself would screen the Changeling from any further launches. They would have to follow him down.

"I've got the ribbon chutes ready," Skallon said mildly.

"Okay." Fain grimaced, angry at himself. With a rattling bang the first chute deployed. Three times Fain's weight slammed against his spine. He breathed raggedly. Somewhere a loose component crashed into a bulkhead. The capsule air had an acrid taste.

He glanced backward to check on Scorpio. The neodog was strapped in tight. Its eyes were glazed from the acceleration and its tongue lolled. "You okay, boy?"

"All. Right. Wery. Heawy." His mouth could not shape some sounds under this acceleration, but Fain was used to Scorpio's accent. They had worked together before. They had captured a Changeling five years before on Revolium, a Godawful waterworld. Fain had failed on a recent mission precisely because he didn't have a neodog with him, and he was damned if he would let that happen to him again. This job should be easier than the Revolium deal, anyway. It was easier to kill a Changeling than to capture it. A Changeling could make you look like a fool if you tried to be too subtle. A quick kill was clean and more satisfying.

"Looks like a tough job," Skallon said.

"We'll scrag him on the ground."

Fain felt the ribbon chute rip away. A second popped out; another surge of acceleration. The nuke hadn't been a total waste, at least. The Changeling was below it now, so his up-looking sensors couldn't find them in the sky. They could ride down safely. Still—

Fain fired another missile. "Hey!" Skallon cried. "What—"

"Insurance."

"But you're dropping it to within a hundred kilometers of Kalic!"

"That's the place the games theory execs said the Changeling would go for, right?"

"But there are huge crowds in the region. They'll see it. One nuke they might miss, but two— Look, Kalic is the capital, and—"

"I know all that." Fain didn't—Skallon was the Alvean expert—but he wasn't in the mood for a geography lesson. "Just can it, huh?"

"But you're running the risk—"

"It's done. Forget it." Fain hated needless talk. He phased in a search routine for the senceivers, to bracket where the Changeling could land. They would have to take the Changeling on the ground and they would have to do it fast, before the thing could get away. A messy problem, sure. But he knew how to do it.

"Shifting eighty degrees clockwise," Fain called. He stepped down heavily and his suit did the rest. He shot up thirty meters. His gyros kept him oriented to scan the area ahead and at the same time he was reading the deep scan senceivers, checking for phantom images or leakage from a power unit. The Alvean forest skimmed by below him. Vines and fronds masked the thickets, but he could make out a few trails. Nobody moving on them. No feedback from the sensors.

"Leapfrogging again," Skallon yelled.

"What? Christ, keep your voice down. I can hear you easy." Skallon was getting excited. That was bad. If he got carried away with the power suit he would start making big, dumb mistakes.

Fain watched Skallon shoot up out of the forest fifteen klicks away. The shiny suit was easy to pick out, even without the pulsing red overlay on the inside of Fain's face plate. Skallon bounded up a hill, skipping lightly over rocky ledges. He skimmed over the top, just setting down once to revector eighty degrees. Then he fell down the other face in power glide and let the forest swallow him. Fain had to admit the kid could use the equipment. Using it smart was another thing.

"We're picking up nothing," Fain said.

"Maybe the gridding was wrong. If it—"

"No, it's around here. The capsule must have its screens up, too, or we'd pick up something."

"Why assume we're even close? I don't—"

"It fits with the Changeling profile. Look, we've got to shake him up."

"How?"

"Watch." Fain clicked his Y-rack onto automatic. He stamped down and the suit reinforced the motion, sending him arcing over a tall stand of vegetation. Animals scattered away in all directions; his acoustic amps picked up their frantic scurryings. At the top of his step the Y-rack emptied two slugs sideways. Then he was down in the comparative safety of the forest. He spent two seconds analyzing the new input from the sensors; nothing. Then the slugs hit. The dual *crump* sounded heavy in the still air.

"What's the idea?" Skallon shouted. "What was in that stuff?"

"Medium H.E." Fain moved quickly around a ridge line, puffing.

"Any specific target in mind?"

"No. Get your screens up." Fain bounded down into a gulley.

"They're up already. You don't have to keep checking on me. What I want to know is, who said you could fire at random? You might hit some natives. And we're on Alvea now, remember? What I say has some weight."

"You picking up anything?"

"No, nothing. Look, we're partners and before you do something like that again—"

"Somebody has to draw fire. You want the job?"

"No, frankly. And it didn't work, anyway. You can't—"

A brilliant orange flash. A roar.

Stones rattled on Fain's armor. He hit the deck and

a blistering yellow bolt spattered over the hillside above him.

"Christ! You okay, Fain? Oh yeah, I can see your suit parameters are still norm. Where was that from?"

"Shut up." Fain lay face down in a patch of mud, studying the senceiver display rippling across his face plate. No need to move until all the score was in. The Changeling's barrage had been shrewd, with just enough delay to let him move into better visibility—or at least, that was Fain's best guess. But better visibility from where? He peered at the contour map. He called up probability distributions for the source of the barrage. They made twisted lines on the map of the hills. Blue, pink, red. Three red splotches were grouped in the same azimuthal section. Each splotch had a good line of sight toward him, if the Changeling was sighting through the narrow canyons he could trace on the contour map. He sent a squirt inquiry up to Mother. She answered in three seconds with a further analysis. He told her to weigh moderately the hypothesis that the Changeling would want to head for Kalic. The recalculated probabilities eliminated one of the high-probability red zones. Fain frowned. That was as much as he was going to get without doing something.

"Skallon."

"Yes? Everything seems quiet. I—"

"You got low-level grenades? Launch one at tree-top, max range."

"Read you. Here goes."

Fain's tally board showed the launch: green Dopplers. Fain was up on his feet and on full power before the grenades had gone a hundred meters. He double-timed it down the gulley. A bunch of vines got in his way and he went through them, cutting with a slice beam. He tapped into Mother for two seconds

and saw no situation change. He fired his Y-rack. The
high explosives *chug*ged out. Fain sprawled under an
overhang and doubled up. The Changeling wouldn't
hesitate this time; no point. But Skallon's grenades
might complicate the problem enough to throw off its
judgment.

Rock ripped open fifty meters away. Fire boiled
from the cliff face. Rocks clattered on his armored
back. But that was it.

"Skallon."

"He hit at both of us. Not close, though."

"I'm calling in Mother."

"Fine by me."

Fain squinted at the probability matrix that swam
on his face plate. Only one red site left. That didn't
mean they had the Changeling pinned, but the estimated minimax was eighty-three percent. Good. Good
enough, anyway.

Fain called for a strike from Mother. He had time
to sit up and tilt his cowling back. The tight electron
beam came slicing down through the cloud-shrouded
sky like a blue-white line scratched from heaven. It
left a bright retinal image and then it was gone, a mi-
crosecond pulse. His IRs picked up the expanding
heated region for a full second afterward. The acoustic rumble followed seven seconds behind, as Fain
skimmed over the ridgeline and ran full tilt for the
target.

Skallon appeared as a whistling blip on his port
plate. The Y-rack went *chug* and *chug* and *chug*. Fain
fanned the target area with a paralyzing beam on the
top of his fifth stride. He had seven klicks visibility.
Nothing was giving feedback for power or UV excess.
In the IR—

There it was. Heat spill.

"I make it zero five eight by two seven seven," Fain

barked. "Seepage in IR. Passive to electromagnetic probes." Skallon sent curt agreement. "Let's hit it."

The H.E. from the two Y-racks was blowing big gouts in the forest around the target. Fain sized up his sweep area and saw nothing funny. He dug in and leaped over a hill, getting max shelter. The e-beam should have taken out the whole inboard defense system, but that was a techtalk theory. Fain wasn't going to bet his neck on it.

Fain checked his flanks. Skallon was five seconds behind and to the right. He bounded forward, cutting through trees and vines and crap in the way. Ahead a big chunk of dirt went up with a bang—the last of the H.E.

The air was thick with dust; not a bad cover at all. Fain angled left. The vegetation suddenly parted. He was going better than a hundred klicks an hour and the capsule leaped up at him. He washed it in flame by reflex. Then he hit—there was no point in trying to avoid it. His armor clanged and a bulkhead crumbled. Fain stumbled into a wrecked control pod. The shiny metal and plastaform was blacked and browned by electrical fires. The e-beam had blown everything.

· Fain swiveled to the command couch, hand raised to attack.

The couch was empty.

As he backed out, Skallon crunched into the blasted clearing. Fain waved him to silence, gesturing at the couch. "Point is, how long has it been gone?"

"Could be half hour, max." Skallon was puffing.

"We'll have to search."

"Has it got a suit?"

Fain checked the smouldering capsule. "No, there's no harness for one."

"That fits with the inventory report for its ship."

"Yeah. There's room here for a skimmer, though. It could have been carrying one."

"In that case it's long gone."

"Yeah. Shit."

"Maybe it didn't have one, though," Skallon said brightly. "Let's do the search."

Fain knew Skallon was right in principle, but he didn't think the odds were good. The Changeling was thirty minutes' flight time away, probably. That meant no simple job, no early liftoff. And all the time he hadn't been maneuvering against the Changeling at all. Fain had spent valuable minutes working against a computer defense program. A good one, sure—but nothing an ordinary agent couldn't outwit. Hell of a note.

"Okay," he said.

They had been combing the area for forty minutes. Fain was getting tired of it. The damned Changeling could be anywhere in the tangled forest. Finding it here was unlikely. He was about to call Skallon when he picked up the acoustic warning.

It was a racketing noise. The clatter got stronger as he ran through his face plate situation inventory. One blip, homing on the Changeling's capsule. Was it coming back? Damned unlikely. Fain leaped above the canopy of vegetation and sighted it. "Skallon! What's—"

"Alvean military copter. Probably coming to investigate. Don't fire on it."

Fain started moving toward it. He regarded nothing as certain until he got a good look. He moved three klicks, skimming just above the trees.

But on his fifth leap the copter shot at him.

Fain tumbled and fired some retros. They flared on his ribs, driving him down into the forest. He landed on his feet and took a lateral vector instantly. The greenery behind him erupted in a cloud of twisting debris. Fain sliced through a clotted mass of vines and broke free, running at full augmentation. Ahead of him a tree withered under a flame gun. He swerved left.

"I'm on them," came from Skallon.

About time, Fain thought.

A hollow thump. Something shattered in the sky.

"Got 'em!"

Fain slowed. He would have tried a shot in a few more seconds, but it was better to have Skallon do it. Maybe the guy would settle down once he'd seen some action.

Fain took a full jump and went up for a look. Only smoke hung where the copter had been.

"Good job," Fain said, and the back of his suit blew away.

3

He woke quickly under the auto-stim. Even as his suit had died, it gave him injections to offset the impact and shock he had suffered. The gyros kept him in good falling posture. The shocks still worked on the left side, and that had been enough; he'd only fallen a hundred meters.

Skallon was there. Fain twisted around groggily. His training took hold. He worked his way out of the

ruin of the suit. It seeped fluids and buzzed and
clicked, still dying. Something sparked. The arms
jerked. The hydrasteel had lost its polish; it was pitted
and dark. A beam had hit the small of the back and
shattered the armor.

Fain groped for his rad count. No extra X ray:
good. Small level of betas and alphas, but nothing serious. He might develop a fever, but that was it. He
had been damned lucky.

"There were two of them," Skallon explained. Fain
frowned. "One must've been waiting until you exposed yourself. Then it popped up on the horizon
and—"

"Yeah. These guys don't fool around."

"They're Alvean military. I pulled one of them out
of the wreckage of the first copter."

"Let me see him." Energy was returning to Fain.
Part of it was the drugs but the rest was Fain himself.

Skallon carried him to the smashed copter. With
most of its Y-rack exhausted and the directional missiles gone, the suit could carry the weight of another
man. Skallon was getting near the end of his power
reserve, though.

The Alvean was hurt pretty badly. His eyes were
glazed. "You dope him up?" Fain asked weakly.

"No. I used the Vertil. I just breathed on him, the
way they told us. Took about a minute. He absorbed
it and now he'll do anything we tell him to."

"Yeah. Tell him to give us the truth."

Skallon turned to the big Alvean, who was sprawled
in the dry dust with his uniform burned and ripped.
"Who told you to come here? And why?"

The Alvean blinked slowly. "Gen . . . General Nokavo. Ordered us. Why . . ." His face went blank.

Skallon rephrased the question. "What were you to
do?"

"Gen . . . said . . . attack . . . anyone here. . . ."

"Where are you from? What base?"

"Araquavaktil."

"Where is it?"

The Alvean gave directions. Skallon nodded, memorizing them. Abruptly the Alvean trembled, gave a rattling cough, and went limp.

Skallon tried a spot probe at temple, arm, legs. "Guess he's dead."

Fain had been sitting on the ground. He stood up with effort. "So the Changeling's gotten that far. We'd better move."

Skallon seemed surprised. "Where?"

"Kalic. But we'd better check that base first. Correction—I'd better check the base."

"Why just you?"

"Chances are there's nobody there. A Changeling always moves fast—something mixed in with that philosophy of theirs. So it's probably going for Kalic now. You're the Alvean expert—you should move into Kalic and make our contact point."

Skallon paced nervously. His huge boots bit into the soft turf. The sliding ceramic plates of his arms and legs rasped and clicked in the pressing silence of the dense green world surrounding them.

"I guess that makes sense. But you're still groggy. I—"

"We'll need supplies. You go back to our module and get the stuff. Don't forget my gear. And bring Scorpio."

"He won't be any use, operating in the open. I've *told* you, there aren't any dogs here. Alveans will spot Scorpio at once and know exactly what's going on. You can't—"

"Right, I know that. So you take him. Into Kalic. We'll need him later."

"Me? Look, he's your—"

"No, *our*. Our dog, at least in theory. He's part of the team."

Beneath his helmet horizon Skallon scowled. "Okay, okay. But I'll have to figure a way to smuggle him into Kalic. I'm ditching this suit as soon as we get close to a town. We've got to maintain cover. That means your disguise, Fain."

Fain sighed. "Yeah, sure."

"You'll be okay here while I'm gone?"

"Drop me somewhere a few klicks away. Leave me a flamer. And call Mother. Have her scan the area. Any aircraft, she burns 'em. No cross-checks. Just hit 'em."

"You can't do that. We have no orders to just—"

"Look, it's self-defense. There are more than two copters on that air base."

"I don't like it."

"I didn't say you had to. And on your way to the module, keep down. Go through the jungle, not over it."

Skallon paced, clacking. "I don't know . . . There are so many things a Changeling could do. I mean—"

"I know how they think," Fain said harshly. "Leave that to me."

"But isn't that just it? They don't have an orderly scheme. Intelligent, yes. But not planners, not—"

"Let's get moving," Fain said, irritated.

Fain lay for hours in a cool glade, waiting for Skallon to make the trip to the module. He let the soreness and aches seep into him, relaxing the muscles with bioreg techniques he had learned decades before. His mind skittered along, fretting and picking, reviewing what had happened, and he had to give it time to work away the anxious energy, to regain its cool center.

He sensed the knotted muscles where the unavoidable shock was, and realized that getting hit had shaken him more than it should have. His emotional centers were tied into this mission somehow, deep and troubling images seeped through to him as he lay in the jungle, and the dark, sliding sense of things unknown came swirling up within him.

This Changeling meant more. Fain had captured it before, on Revolium. Then the goddamn techs had studied it for years, and tried some experiments on it, and then had started to talk about finding a way to alter the Changeling genetic material. That was the long-range Consortium strategy—patch up the right hemisphere-left hemisphere division that made the Changeling form possible and remove all the complex biomechs that let Changelings alter themselves at will. Make them back into humans again. Or rather, return the next generation of Changelings to human norm. Fixing the living Changelings was, of course, impossible.

So the techs had puttered around and tried communicating with the captured Changelings, and pretty soon word spread to the Changelings about what the techs planned, using their own genetic material—and the Changelings escaped. Most of them died in the attempt. But not all. And this one, the smartest one, had gotten off Earth entirely.

Fain started the methodical murmuring, deep in his throat, that would send him into hypnosis. He would block out the pain and anxiety and the simple, fragmenting fear. He would slip free of all that, and just stick to the facts. Facts, events, motives: hard data. The world was made up of strings and loops of hard data. As the musky damp drifted into his nostrils from

the fragrant jungle, Fain let his mind drift. Facts . . .
There were so many of them, and each could change
as you looked at it . . . but still . . . If you clung to
them, they would see you through. That was the edge
he had over the Changeling. Facts. About this planet,
for example. Facts . . .

Alvea followed a mildly elliptical orbit around an
F6 star, 1.68 AUs out. This was late summer, Fain recalled dreamily, as he began his inner chant. The natives were gathering for some festival. The vernal
equinox, that was it. Because Alvea took over two E-
years per orbit, the Fest carried more weight than it
had in the older Earth societies on which Alvea was
partially modeled.

Fain raised a wry eyebrow. More crap that would
get in the way of finding the Changeling. But maybe
that made it all the more interesting, anyway. . . .

Skallon carried him piggyback, strapped in, for
twenty klicks. Fain let himself stay in his balanced internal state, barely conscious, as the rocking, jolting,
clanging rhythm of the suit carried them through the
sweeping clutch of the forest. Snaky vines plucked at
him and Scorpio as they passed. He had forgotten
how noisy a suit was. Inside, you were insulated from
the clattering and banging. It was a wonder the exter-
nal acoustic pickups worked.

Skallon stopped in a matted mass of purple bushes.
Fain let himself slowly come up out of the hypnosleep.
Numbly, he followed Skallon's instructions for putting
on the Alvean disguise. Bulky, hot, stifling garments.
They ate some rations and talked strategy.

Fain stroked Scorpio, explaining to him what had
happened and what the dog should do. Scorpio didn't
want to go with Skallon at first. Fain quieted him.

"You know that dog pretty well," Skallon observed.

"Yeah." Fain continued stroking the dog.

"You train with him much?"

"We worked together before. And we retrained just before boost from Earth."

"Did you have time to come up to specs on Alvea?"

"Huh?"

"I mean about the culture, the—"

"I know enough."

"What about Gommerset?"

"What?"

"You know, the experiments he did, the data on immortality and the cult that—"

"What do you mean, what are you fishing for?" Fain spoke rapidly and savagely.

Skallon blinked, momentarily at a loss for words. "Well, I just meant, Gommerset was the reason people came here in the first place, and . . ."

"Oh. Oh. Okay, I see. I . . . I thought you were giving me some goddamn quiz, the way the techs are always doing Earthside."

"No, I really didn't mean to . . ." Skallon went on talking about nothing and Fain stopped listening. He stroked Scorpio smoothly, letting his sudden burst of nervousness seep out through his fingers. Scorpio picked up some of the tension, but then relaxed, panting slightly.

Skallon shed his thick suit of metal and ceramic. They hid it in the woods with a directional micro on it so they could find it later. Skallon seemed to be glad to get out of the suit. He hustled around, strapping gear under his Alvean robes. The thick folds of cloth flapped at his ankles.

Skallon peered intently at Fain's hand-held faxplate, and listened carefully while Fain laid out the route each man would follow. Mother's overlay grids changed as they watched the plate; the Alvean day

was moving into afternoon. Skallon absorbed information quickly and easily, Fain noted. That was reassuring.

They located the best paths, using Mother's finely
detailed pictures of the jungle around them. A blue
dot patiently traced Mother's calculated route of least
danger.

Skallon paused at the edge of his path. "Well . . .
see you in Kalic," he finished lamely.

"Right." Fain waved to Scorpio. "Keep your nose in
the air."

"That. My. Job." the dog said flatly.

Fain nodded in satisfaction, feeling rested. The dog
was all right. He wasn't so sure about Skallon, but
there was nothing to be done right away. He could
deal with Scorpio because there was a bond between
them. The past, yes, and something more. Not truly
understanding, just the satisfaction of jobs done together and done well. Fain didn't truly understand
neodogs; they were funny creatures, the first product
of genetic tinkering. They had neuroses and problems
and a lot of the baggage humans carried around inside of their heads. He had great respect for them,
though. Plain animals were something else entirely,
something he suspected man could never understand.
That was why he always refused to go with the high
Consortium officials who, knowing what his work en-
tailed, invited him for hunting on the company's private reserves. Fain didn't know how animals thought,
so he never killed them. He did understand people,
though.

4

It falls in a tumbling metal box. The lights around it wink and spurt patterns—constellations of the Dance. The amber crystals move and babble, clutching at numbers and lines. They sputter their truths and in the making of them give birth to lies. The liquid crystals merge and as facts are fixed, they die, becoming false as the Dance moves on.

Targets above, the dying lies say. It is so, was so, and thus will never be so again. The Changeling moves to swarm about these crystals of the Dance, to understand them in their sacrificing rhythm. They speak of the hot point of light in the sky. Fain comes, yes.

At last the moment comes, the moment rises and is consumed. As Fain will be consumed, is consumed, was consumed, as all things eddy together.

It presses against the pulsing crystals. Meaning seeps across the abyss between the metal box and the thing-of-the-Dance within the box. The thing sees, understands. Punch here, command that. Let the box do its work. *There.*

The hollow lights speak, tell of the beam which cuts air, rejoices in a sure strike. The thing knows this is but a moment passing, a locus through which it must move. The beam is not the end. It must be the beginning.

In answer, space rips open.

A fireball flares into being nearby, twin sun to the glaring purple star above. The air churns with crackling thermal death, small spikes spurting from the fire, fleeing their father, to bury themselves in the Changeling. But not enough, no. No. It will survive this. It caresses the box from inside, searching for its true center. The box must carry it to the flat plain below, deliver it to the next movement of the hunt.

The guts of this passing box are simple. Guts know nothing, do anything, sense no past or future and thus do not share the corrupt falseness of the Fain. The Changeling strokes the box, knows it, arranges it. So all will be done, when the moment decides.

Then, done, it alters. Coarse plumes encase it. Suddenly it is a great falling bird, spewing acrid odors into the stormy air. It selects not a graceful air being, but a great heavy armored bird of violent energy. At its rear something burns to slow the fall. It feels the searing throat, encrusted with excrement. A chocked tube of chemical wastes, a foul and caked stuff. And, yes, it is clogged, too, with semen. The sweet syrup fills the Changeling. Slimy, ejaculated, yellow, coating the Changeling as it lies curled in the warm bowel of the plunging bird. Semen, inside the box that is egg. For the box brings a fresh womb, falling down from the prickpoints of stars above. New birth for the fallow flatland below. The Changeling will jerk and lunge and spurt yellow into the myriad bacteria of grainy soft Alvea. Dust will give forth.

The avenging bloody bird falls. Its beak screams in the clouds. It will mate with the wind. For now.

He walked away from Fain and as the distance between them grew Skallon felt a weight lift from him.
The shooting, the death—it had rattled him more than
he liked to think. But worst of all was Fain's impassive
face and cold assessing eyes. Granted, the man knew
his work. But there was a quietly fierce way he went
about it that unnerved Skallon. Sure, he'd had training
himself. Earthbound simulations, computer-enhanced
scenarios, game therapy, the lot. But Fain had been
out here, to other worlds. He was different. And even
as Skallon pressed on, anxious to get away from his
partner, a reminder of the man skipped along, nosing
into bushes, pricking up its ears at odd noises, studying the path with slitted eyes.

Alvea. Skallon shrugged off the events of the last
few hours and stopped, neck craning, soaking it in.
Alvea. Not a sim or a roughly approximate Earthbound site, but the whole real goddamn thing.

Giant ferns nodded in a breeze. Musty pollen
pricked at his nostrils. The ferns spread great fronds
like umbrellas, magenta, leathery, shot through with
complex blue veins. Skallon heard Scorpio stop. The
dog was probably wondering why the halt. Well, let it.
Skallon had spent years studying this planet. Now he
was here. And he was damned if he was going to miss
any of it.

He turned, names popping into his head as he identified the plants. *Lugentana*, hairy ferns stirring with languid grace, so that he felt like a small mite swaying, adrift in the sea beneath a coral reef. *Bazartaeus alatan*, peacock-blue puff balls that suddenly exploded into a fog of smaller spores. *Reesjat*, rubbery stems pocked by warrens of ground animals. *Catakasi*, parasitic streamers like glittering beaten copper that clasped the red and orange trunks. A sheen of *Rutleria*, webs between jeweled blossoms. Harsh, violet light flickered through the high ceiling of foliage.

"Something. Wrong."

"No, nothing. Just looking."

"For. What."

"Never mind. Let's go."

If you were going to die, you couldn't pick a prettier place, he thought sourly. Time was so precious he couldn't take a moment to get a solid look at Alvea, and he suspected it would be this way all through the mission. No room for tourism. No time—he glanced upward again, hurrying to catch up to Scorpio, pink grasses plucking at him with wet whispers—to *feel* the place. To watch golden vines so thin a slight breeze made them swim on unseen currents. To smell the acrid, shimmering leaves that he brushed by. To *live*, for once, instead of plodding mindlessly ahead in pursuit of a career.

"Someone."

"How far?" Skallon said, blinking with surprise.

"Seventy. Meters. Closing." Pause. "Closing."

"Get to shelter. *Hide*."

Scorpio was down amid some wrinkled fern leaflets in a few seconds. Skallon decided to wait for whoever it was on the path, and then realized that would seem odd, someone just standing around in the middle of the jungle. He heard a rustle of movement. Abruptly he lurched forward, walking toward the noise. A short, fat Alvean came around the bend in the path. Skallon kept up his pace. The man's face seemed to pout beneath the fleshy folds of his cheeks. Skallon had never seen anyone so fat in his life. Slides, pictures of Alveans, yes, but the reality—He kept up the rhythm of his walking. "Hail," he said.

"Aye?"

"Do you know where I might find a small cart?"

"You are needful?" the man said mildly.

"I am a pilgrim. From the south. I have—"

"Yes, quite. I thought I spotted your drawl." The man smiled slightly, as though pleased with himself at having guessed right. "You can most probably fix upon a cart at the rail connection four kilometers onward."

"You are most kind. I shall say a prayer for you in the Transept of—"

"Yes, yes," the man muttered, losing interest. "Good journey." He stepped delicately around Skallon and went down the path. Skallon moved off, too, breathing a bit easier. He had passed his first test. The Doubluth robes seemed unremarkable to the man. They were a dull purple splotched in orange. They billowed out in the occasional breeze that whispered through the jungle.

"All. Right."

Skallon started slightly as Scorpio's voice droned out from a flowering fungoid patch. "Sure. Everything went perfectly. You'd better keep off the path, though. Follow me in parallel."

The dog disappeared again. Skallon stepped off at a rapid walk. It was already afternoon in Alvea's twenty-six-hour day and he wanted to get well into the city before darkness. On Earth the streets were deadly at night and he wasn't sure the Alvean Fests, plus the effects of the plague years, wouldn't make the same true here.

He would have to watch out for signs of the plagues. Everything he had learned about Alvea—without ever having been here—was based on the tranquil years. For several centuries the Alveans had been free of the vast, sweeping illnesses. Now they had returned, even worse than before. There were vile sicknesses that bulged the eyes out until the pressure popped a vein in the head, and diseases which gnawed away the belly, and frenzies that seized the unsuspecting and made them dance, dance frantically until their feet pounded into bloody stumps and they fell dead in the streets. All because of the slow workings of native Alvean biology. All, Skallon thought, because man would try to thrust in where he didn't truly fit, no matter what the cost.

Alvea was a seemingly placid world when mankind first found it. Its vast green oceans swarmed with life and the land was host to many plant forms. There were even a few gropings toward animal life—fish that wandered dimly along the muddy shores, awkward insects that tumbled through the air in a parody of flight. So men and women came here and mined the rare earths that were profitable. But the F8 star that Alvea circled spat out too great an ultraviolet excess. Cancers multiplied. Stock animals could not reproduce. Some breeds of cow and rabbit died first, then others, and finally men.

So the first colonists called by radio to Earth, pleading for help. This was in the earliest, expansionist phase of the New Renaissance. Earth was rich, or at least thought itself so. It sent a bioadaptant team. They studied the complex interweaving of human physiology and Alvean ecology. The problems were not obvious. It was no matter of humans digesting only left-handed sugars while Alvea produced only right-handed ones. The issues became far more subtle. Small trace elements in human cells were depleted on Alvea. Insignificant fractions of a percent in boron or indium, chemically incompatible with human biochemistry, eventually led to buildup of waste products in certain cells. Nucleotides reacted sluggishly. Contaminants compounded. The centers of some cells grew a halo of sludge. Some of this led to increased aging. Other flaws accumulated and caused the gnawing cancers. There was no cure short of either modifying the entire swarming biosphere of Alvea, or tinkering with the humans who lived there. The New Renaissance was expansive but not foolhardy; it chose genetic alteration of the few thousand humans.

But no tuning of the DNA helix has only one single effect. The chain of consequences always brings surprises. Toleration of one new element brings with it a slight weakness toward some other factor in the environment. Men were adapted to Earth because billions of tiny lives had paid the price before them. All life was engineered by the heavy hand of elimination. On Alvea, genetic research could sidestep a vast amount of sacrifice, but not all. Humans adapted themselves by delicately rearranging a few elements along the DNA helix. Phosphorus and hydrogen were nudged into new spots. But the inevitable calculus of inheritance meant that the next generation to emerge carried new vulnerabilities, fresh fears.

A beating noise roused Skallon from his wandering thoughts. Something was hammering softly, wetly. It came toward him. His head jerked up as a huge sleek bird coasted down the wind and picked up speed. A smackwing. At each upward stroke the leathery wings flapped together; its mating call. The bird casually studied Skallon and banked away into the jungle.

Another genetic adaptant. It had begun as a sea-bird, Skallon recalled. A heron or something like that. Now it was fitted into an ecological niche by a suitable trimming of its genes. A calculated creature, yes, but beautiful, too. Blue sunlight glimmered as its wings slapped together. It flitted lightly in the embracing air.

Skallon watched it go. Another sound emerged from the jungle's hush. A tinkling, ahead. He walked on. The noise rose. He crossed a brown plank bridge and looked down. Water jiggled and danced under him, dashing facets of light into his eyes.

Water. Water running open, along a kind of hole with irregular banks. Fresh water simply lying around, where it could be stolen by anyone passing by. Skallon stared at the stuff. He walked around to the edge and scooped up a handful. It was startlingly cold and tasted like a phosphorescent nerve drink, but it had no numbing effect. He drank some more. It was damned good.

From childhood memory came images: ethereal forest, humanized animals, a looming presence of man always in the background. Disney's *Bambi*, one of the great works of the past, from the latter days of the British Empire, he recalled. His friends studying the media had said it rang false, that it was obvious propaganda used to drum up support for Oversighting. Skallon doubted that. The film had an elfin quality, full of leaping stags and trembling glowing raindrops. It was unlike any propaganda he had ever seen. The real propaganda always had an earnest taste to it, as though the audience was supposed to frown in concentration. No, *Bambi* was a spontaneous product, as fresh as this jungle. And this water thing—he remembered suddenly the obsolete word, this *ditch*—was here because nobody thought to channel and save all the water for use before returning it to the oceans. Despite all his study of simulations and holos of Alvea, Skallon had never thought that ditches had to be here.

6

Alvea's star threw shadows along the rail route, its light now a mustard tint. Skallon tried to relax in the ample railcar seat. He was feeling more confident now. When he'd asked for a cart the woman had murmured a sour reply and simply led him to a crude wooden two-wheeler, gesturing that she wanted it returned when he was through. He had started to give assurances and then remembered that pilgrims were bound by strong moral constraints; she had no doubt that when his pilgrimage was done, he would return the cart. Skallon had read about this, but it still seemed incredible. In the dormitories where Skallon had lived, you had to nail down anything you wanted to keep.

Skallon sat so he could see the baggage compartment that trundled along behind this one passenger car. The cart was back there, and Scorpio inside it. A few of the red-caped passengers had helped Skallon heave the cart up the ramp onto the baggage carrier, but none of them gave a second glance at his robes or his face. Skallon was fairly sure he would pass even easier in the city. But Scorpio was a giveaway; he was now sorry he had agreed to smuggle the dog into their contact point.

He leaned back and watched his fellow passengers. They were all workers, each sitting in the sprawl a fat man adopts in a broad chair. Were their slabs of muscle an indirect effect of gene tampering? Skallon could not be sure. Their wrists, sticking out of their robes, seemed thicker and more wrinkled than his. He was still studying them, making comparisons, when one of the men stood up abruptly, waddled a few paces, and collapsed.

"Carrier! Carrier!" someone cried.

"Press the emergency signal! Stop the train. We must get off."

Skallon sat quietly as the others lurched out of their seats and twisted away from the crumpled figure. They crowded into the other end of the car. Some whimpered with fear. Suddenly the train squealed and began to slow. Skallon debated whether he should get up and make a show of cowering as far away from the fallen man as possible. But if someone happened to tug at his robes, the padding might be revealed. And he stood no real risk sitting here; he wasn't prey to Alvean diseases. He looked at the man and then noticed something odd.

The train thumped to a stop. The crowd bolted for the doors and swarmed out, jabbering. Skallon stood up and went over to the fallen man. There didn't seem to be anything wrong with him. Skallon glanced up, but no one was going to venture into this car until the collectors of the dead arrived, he was sure.

He rolled the Alvean over. The man's complexion was dark, typical of the natives. Skallon tested the man's arterial rate and flipped back the rough eyelids. The man stirred and croaked to himself in dry whispers. Skallon slipped a small plate from his cowl and held it in front of the Alvean's lips. It clouded a rosy pink.

"Vertil," he murmured to himself. "Damn."

A chill tightening ran through him. Fain couldn't have doped an Alvean with Vertil and had time to get the native onto this train. So wherever the Alvean came from, it wasn't Fain. But there were no sources of Vertil on Alvea, Skallon knew that. Earth had never let the drug get free; it would be socially destabilizing.

That meant someone from Earth was using it.

There wasn't another possibility. It had to be the Changeling.

Skallon felt a momentary panic. Now they had no advantage whatever over the Changeling. None. The Changeling could change identities and use the Vertil to expand his powers.

Now the whole idea of sending a two-man team seemed stupid. Sure, they wouldn't be noticeable, wouldn't make a ripple in Alvean–Earth relations—but they couldn't find the Changeling, either, not with this disadvantage.

This Alvean had been near the Changeling. And he was on the way into Kalic. Which meant the Changeling was moving, was probably ahead of Skallon already. That bothered him. Fain was supposed to deal with the Changeling, he had the experience, that was Fain's job. Skallon was a guide. Sure, he had field training in addition to a specialist rating in Alvean sociometrics. But he was on his first offworld assignment.

Now Fain wasn't here and this babbling Alvean was as clear as a calling card: the Changeling was moving fast. Skallon was alone, stuck with the damned dog. He had to get to shelter.

Skallon stood up. Some railway officials—he could

tell, they wore magenta robes with gold lacings—were standing outside the transparent doors, gesturing toward him. Contorted faces, lined with anxiety.

Skallon made a holy sign over the Alvean and stood up quickly. It was best to move with assurance and avoid questions. He jerked open the sliding door and shouldered the officials aside.

"I tried to render aid," he said quickly. "But I can stay no longer, brothers."

"You do great good by the attempt," one of the men said, obviously impressed. "Many of these are contagious."

Skallon nodded, bowed, and slipped away. He had to get the cart down and mingle with the crowd. He had to move. He had to get away.

7 ═══════════════════════════════════════

Skallon's feet were burning by the time he reached the jumbled outskirts of Kalic. Padding down the farm lanes was entirely different from skimming over them in a rail car. The native jungle thinned into the grasses and trees men had adapted to Alvea, and broad fields furrowed for fresh crops stretched to the horizon. He recognized the tall plants like mushrooms that flamed red at their crests: qantimakas, the primary Alvean staple. Large chunks of the domed crests were broken off along the ripened edges daily. Boiled, they reddened further and tasted like chewy potatoes. Blossoming, they gave a hearty, mealy fruit. The entire plant was programmed for use: the stems, dried and beaten, were woven into a coarse red fabric worn during the winter cycle by industrial workers. Skallon tugged his cart alongside others that carried racks of the drying leaves, which were used for wrapping. By the time he reached Kalic he knew far more than he cared to about the pungent reek of the shiny leaves. It seemed unlikely that facing the Changeling could have been worse than qantimakas.

Maraban Lane was a ravine of tall, ramshackle houses lurching toward each other at odd angles, as though they had been frozen in the balls across the pitted organiform street. The Battachran Hotel opened a black maw of an entranceway into Maraban Lane. A sour reek drifted out of this cobbled throat and into Skallon's face as he let the cart bang down on the organiform. The lights from within looked as though one were seeing them through bowls of blood. As evening fell the colors of Alvea seemed to get stronger, instead of dimming as they did on Earth.

Skallon rang the bell. Presently a fat man slowly made his way down the entranceway, shoes clattering on stone. The man eyed the cart warily. "You are how many?" he said in a surprisingly light tenor voice.

"Two. And this." He held up a signat.

"From where?" A show of uninterest.

"You will learn."

The man stroked the deep folds of fat that made his robes bulge. He sighed and with a show of casualness slipped the signat into a ring on his right hand. The ring glowed, first green and then a pearly white.

"Damn and—" The man stopped. "I never thought—"

"Anyone would show up? That's what you're paid for."

"Well, no, not precisely, I mean—I did not imply

that. You must understand that I am not accustomed to such, ah . . ."

"Procedures."

"Ah. Yes." With sudden energy the man stepped forward, as though he had made up his mind, and shook Skallon's hand. "I am Kish." He placed a massive arm on the cart. "I will help you."

Together they pulled the cart into the coach yard of the hotel. Skallon took a blanket from Kish and, reaching deep into the cart, brought out Scorpio wrapped in it. Kish looked at the lump under the blanket and wrinkled his brow. Skallon gestured and Kish led the way through a dark corridor. Skallon saw no one else. "How is business?" he said, trying to find a conversational opening.

"Oh, terrible. Quite terrible. These new plagues—" He kicked open a thick wood door. "—Even in the Fest times, the sickness strikes. It drives people into the countryside."

Skallon trudged in and dropped Scorpio on the cobbled floor. The dog tumbled out of the blanket and yelped. Kish stepped backwards, moving with surprising speed for so heavy a man. "What, what—?"

"A dog. A lower form. Bred for service," Skallon said mildly. "A very ancient animal." He stroked the bloodhound's sleek fur. Beneath the smooth sheen were lean, tough muscles.

"Native to Earth?"

"Of course. You must have seen them in holos."

"But I did not know they were so large."

"Where. We."

Kish stepped back two paces and butted into a stone wall, nearly knocking over a flickering oil lamp. "You said a *lower* form."

"Well, relatively. This one's been augmented."

"It *speaks*." Kish had a small mouth. He twisted it

upward in concern and a row of neat white teeth appeared to bite at the dark upper lip. His eyes swiveled from Skallon to the dog. "Does it understand us?"

"Yes. I. Have. Vocab."

Kish shot a questioning glance at Skallon. "Vocabulary," Skallon explained. "They can't say words that are too long." He knelt down. "Scorpio, we're in Kalic. In a hotel. Fain will be along soon. I will find you a place to rest."

"Food. And. Must. Learn . . . Smells."

"Of course." He stood up after stroking the dog a moment more. He felt a bit ashamed that he had taken out his feelings about Fain on Scorpio. The dog probably sensed his hostility.

Kish beckoned and Skallon led the dog out a small wooden door and into another gloomy passageway. Kish pulled at a handle and a yellow rectangle appeared; a small closet, just big enough for a bed. Did this pass for a hotel room? For peasants, maybe—but there weren't any truly deprived classes in Alvean society, he reminded himself. Ritualized, yes, and constrained by codes—but not poorer than the broad average. Or at least, that's what his text material had said.

"You must hide here for a while," he murmured to the dog. Scorpio whimpered a bit, probably with fatigue, and curled up on the bed. Kish stepped aside and a woman entered the cramped room. She carried a bowl of ground meat that reeked of decay.

"Is that food?" Skallon said sharply.

"Yes. Good meat. Have him try it." Kish poked a finger in the woman's back. She had stopped short in the doorway when she saw Scorpio.

"It is all right," Kish said softly to her. She wrinkled her brow and put the bowl on the bed beside Scorpio.

"It stinks," Skallon said. If the dog got itself poi-

soned here because of his neglect . . . and with Fain
gone . . .

"It is fresh." the woman said softly.

"The animal was slaughtered only this morning,"
Kish said reassuringly.

"Slaughtered?" Skallon realized that this meat was
from a living thing that had walked around, foraged
for its own food. The reddish mass wasn't a slice from
a protein gob. Incredible. Would it make Scorpio sick?

The dog sniffed, licked, tasted. "Smell." It ate a bit.
"Good. Though." Soon it was placidly eating.

When they returned to Kish's narrow "office,"
which had no desk or writing slate visible, the big
man nodded toward the slender woman. "I am rude.
My wife. She knows of your, ah, work. We shall en-
deavor to make you comfortable while you are here
on your important mission. We can assure you of every
help in finding information for—"

"Yes, yes, a *nullaha* thanks." Skallon turned to the
woman. "You are?"

"Joane." Her voice came from deep in her throat,
husky and yet soft. She was not pretty. Her nose
hooked down at the tip and the shadow from the
overhead lamp made it seem longer still. Her mouth
was not wide, but the lips flared out at the middle to
give an impression of sensuality. Their red fullness ta-
pered down to a slight upward curl at the ends, a per-
petual half-smile that was framed by small wrinkles at
the corners. Something about the woman caught Skallon's attention, even though Kish was gesturing him to
a seat, and to cover his hesitation he said, "You, you
know I am . . ."

"From Earth," she murmured. "Of course. My husband has expected someone. We were told to be prepared. The Earth Consul sent word the day he de-
parted."

"You will find we are steadfast," Kish said earnestly. He flicked a small insect from a chair and gestured for Skallon to sit.

"Your file says you were a trader," he said, easing himself into the broad Alvean chair.

"I found it unsuited to my tastes." Kish smiled. "Joane, please bring wooded ale. Our friend seems pale."

"My makeup probably isn't quite right," Skallon said, watching her leave. "Your 'tastes,' eh? Meaning you failed at it?"

"In a manner of speaking. You understand, I am sure. What was I to do?" He spread his hands. "Your Consul required information in those last days, yet he could not convey money to me without causing suspicion to fall upon us. No Earthman could venture into the streets in those dark days." He glanced at Skallon. "Nor can one now."

"Things are that bad."

"Yes. But the Consul must have told his superiors."

"He did. His reports were discounted somewhat."

"Why?"

"Isolated officials play up their troubles. It makes them look good."

"An odd practice. You place men here to observe. Then you do not believe what they tell you."

Skallon smiled. "It's the way they play the game. Don't ask me to justify it."

"But it is not a game."

"Played at more than ten parsecs distance? It's hard to treat it otherwise."

"But the overlight cruisers can reach us in weeks of ship time. That must be how you came."

"Yes. They can send a few men like us, sure. Or an equivalent mass. But the important stuff—military hardware, raw materials, exports—even Earth can't afford to boost those at faster than light."

"I see. I had hoped . . ."

Skallon leaned forward, elbows on knees, and peered intently at the fat man. It was hard to read the expression on a face wreathed in rolls of fat. Maybe the best idea was to watch the eyes, which seemed quick and glittering in a sea of brown. "You thought we'd come storming in here and sew things up?"

"Well, I had thought idly . . ." Kish made a small gesture with his fingers, spreading them to indicate that what he said was of no moment.

"Send a huge bioadaptant team? Stop the plagues? Tailor some cures? I'd like to," Skallon said with sudden intentness. "Believe me, I would. But there isn't the justification, not in Earthside's opinion."

"And by the time ramscoops could reach us . . ."

"Yes. Decades. And no crew would sign on for such a long voyage—they'd go crazy."

"Then why *are* you here?"

"To maintain order."

"Things here *are* orderly."

"They won't be for long."

And so Skallon told Kish about the Changeling. Word had filtered through the interstellar radio links, but Kish had no concept of how adroitly a Changeling could imitate any human being, of either sex. Kish could not possibly have known—because Earth kept the fact concealed—that the Changeling planet had begun a shift to the offensive. They were slipping into selected colony worlds, acting as apparently random saboteurs, stirring up chaos for its own sake. Five years ago, Changelings were caught on Revolium, a waterworld, and shipped directly Earthside by overlight cruiser. They cracked one, eventually, into frag-

ments of a personality. At the core was a psychotic
desire for disruption. A religion of sorts, lusting for
the fiery fruits of chaos. The Changeling culture believed that only by bringing down all man's orderings
could the human race begin to see the universe as it
truly was.

The sociometricians had a theory for the Changelings, of course. They always did. Simply put, the
Changelings' mobile features made them acolytes of
change. Their bodies ruled their minds.

The analysis ignored, of course, that this was precisely the Changeling argument against rigid normal
mankind. It didn't matter. To earth, this threat of an-
archy was even more dangerous than simple conquest.
The Cooperative Empire was a precarious, fragile link-
age; it could not bend far without breaking.

"So he comes here to purge us of order?" Kish
scoffed.

"He or she, yes. And don't laugh. Bar us, he'll do it."

"Do what?" Joane appeared in the slightly skewed
doorway, carrying a tray. Skallon gave her a con-
densed version of his tale while she thumped down
heavy mugs of brown stuff and clattered out dry-
baked vegetable shavings into bowls. Skallon tasted
the bits of curling green and liked them. He ate a
handful, noticed his throat drying from the salt, and
pulled a draught of ale.

"Awk!"—and he spattered it on the opposite wall,
hawking and blowing to clear his mouth of the sting-
ing stuff.

"What . . . what's *that?*"

Kish nodded sagely. "None of the Consul's staff
could brook the real ale, either. Lore-strong, this stuff
is."

"I'll thank you to give me no more of it," Skallon
said stiffly.

"Oh, of course not," Kish said blandly.

Skallon looked up from wiping his smarting mouth. Did he see a flicker of malice on that face? A tremor of a smile at this smug Earthman and his starships, who couldn't swallow a man's brew?

Skallon grimaced and sat down again.

8

An hour later Skallon lay on his bed and watched the last blue fingers of light seep out of the night sky. He had begged off further talk with Kish and Joane, at least for the moment, because he was not sure exactly how much he should give away. Fain would not like it if a native found out too much of their operations.

But now that he was here in a room, alone, he was bored. His meditation had taken twenty minutes and left him refreshed. He knew he could not sleep this early. Should he go upstairs and try Kish's real ale again? Not that he could truly blame Kish for a small gesture of self-assertion. Skallon was, after all, just another damned Earthman. He could certainly see the logic of an Alvean's dislike of Earth. Alvean art and culture were saturated with it; elementary psychosocial analysis showed that.

And as far as Skallon was concerned, the Alveans had a case. Alvea wasn't a colony, no. Times were more subtle than that. What began as an effort to conform humans to Alvea had now become a handy eco-

nomic tool. Military dominance by the Consortium
across the stars was impossible, of course, unless you
were willing to erase your opponent and ruin a planet.
But why use ham-fisted weaponry when subtle forms
of obligation were available? Alvea needed Earth-
based bioengineering to correct genetic drift and
ward off the worst effects of the native Alvean biochemistry. Only Earth had the techniques and vast
technology to keep the Alveans adapting to this
planet. Genetic stabilization was a necessity for each
new generation, a cellular consummation devoutly to
be wished. In return, Earth got rare minerals by robot
ramscoop ships that flew below light speed. A cozy—

Something rattled in the wall next to his ear.

Skallon jerked upright and switched on the dim gas
light. The wall was moving. More precisely, the wallpaper was bulging and pulsing with life.

A flap of wallpaper had parted from the thin wall
several centimeters higher up. Skallon pulled it back.
Small black bugs showered down and scattered across
his bed. There was a seething mass of them farther
down; their frantic scrabblings were what he had
heard.

Skallon pulled away in disgust. But in a way the
sight fascinated him. Insects had been strictly controlled on Earth long ago. None appeared in the bar-
racks or dormitories. He took a small flashlight out of
his pack and pointed it down the inside of the wallpaper. Wherever the beam struck, the six-legged creatures scrambled to get away.

Well, that was some relief. All he had to do was
sleep with the gas light on.

Skallon snorted. He would have to get a better
room. But for the moment a restless urge filled him,
and he didn't want to talk to Kish again. He had stud-

ied Alvea for years, and here he was lying around in
a rotten, fetid hotel room when he could be out,
seeing Kalic.

Madness, or at least stupidity. Fain would be here
soon and then Skallon's time would be controlled.
Even worse, Fain might well have killed the Changeling by now. A pickup drone could be on its way down
from orbit.

Skallon hesitated a moment. Then he tucked away
the flashlight and began to put on his Doubluth
robes.

Four hours later, Skallon drifted back toward Maraban Lane and the Battachran Hotel, shuffling along
on tired feet, itchy and aching from the Doubluth
robes and the Alvean disguise, yet still reluctant to let
go of the city and retire for the night. He had seen a
lot. The delicate pinnacles of the holy centers probed
the cloud-speckled sky behind him, signifying the city
center; he had climbed all the way to the top, for the
sprawling, smoke-shrouded nighttime view. Now the
pinnacles seemed dignified and remote, as though
made of something more than the rough-cut rock of a
laser worker.

He had spent a strange, haunting hour in a ceremonial field, watching a cremation. They placed the old,
withered man securely on the pyre, and bound the
arms. Skallon soon learned why. As the wood popped
and smoked, the heat made muscles contract and the
man's legs began kicking. The body wriggled as songs
spun upward around it. Then the belly exploded. The
bang was startling even fifty meters away, where
Skallon stood. It came at the exact peak of the song
cycle, though he could not understand how the mourners could possibly have timed the effect.

Death was a common theme in Kalic's streets. Frail women nodded in their wicker chairs, slipping into the long unconsciousness. Men tottered along sidewalks, one hand braced for support against the buildings, loose ropes of flesh hanging from them when their robes brushed aside; they were losing body weight rapidly. An automatic defense against some diseases. The sicknesses were so new they had no names. The older ones—Rattling, Watereyes, Clenching Rot, Breathstealer—Earthmen had cured, Skallon had read about. For these strange plagues he could do nothing.

But the people clearly thought Earth could help. A man in a cramped alehouse told him in rasping whispers of a special Earthside hospital, reportedly operating outside the city, where the diseases were being cured. Another cursed and pulled a gleaming knife, spitting out a tale of what he would do to any Earthers who showed themselves in Kalic again. His words met assent around the room. For the first time Skallon felt genuine fear that someone would notice a small wrong inflection in his speech or an error in his Doubluth robes, and find him out. He muttered an excuse and left, nearly tripping on his robes, and stumbled into the welcoming darkness of the city streets.

In fact, he very nearly gave himself away on the street outside by tripping over his own feet. All his life he had walked over the reassuring flat surfaces of Earth, where everything was floored. Even the farms, where he spent some vacations, were beaten into planes and flats by centuries of rolling farm machinery. But here in Kalic no street lacked potholes, few had well-defined curbs. An intersection of two streets would allow a little space for a grassy patch. In the muted shadows these caught at Skallon's feet; he had to learn to look down and navigate. Walking tired him.

A block from the Battachran Hotel he decided to stop
and rest a moment in a temple.

A ruined gate, its hinges squeaking in a brush of
wind, gave onto a courtyard. A round ablution tank
swirled with stream water and hissed as bubbles rose
in it. The shadowed courtyard of broken slabs caught
light from an alehouse farther down the street. He sat
and stared up at three ribbed arches that seemed tired
themselves, one sagging a bit more than the others. A
hanging lamp glowed blue and Alvea's smaller moon,
pocked and ruddy, rose over the temple's creamy
frieze. The moon's iron oxides contrasted well, to Skallon's eye, with the yellowing ninety-nine Names of the
One inscribed on the frieze. He read off a few of the
Names to himself, unconsciously falling into the
rhythm of the hollow drumming that came from a
street away, disturbed at times by shouts of dancing.
As he did so one of the ivory-white pillars of the temple moved. Then another rippled in the wan light.
Joane stepped out of the temple and into the wan
pink moonlight. She was looking to the left and did
not see him.

"Joane."

"Oh! You startled me. You are the . . ."

"Yes. Don't say the word. Is there anyone else
here?"

"No. No, I do not think so. But *you* should not be
here."

"Why?"

"I . . . well, one must remove shoes and all jewelry
before entering a temple."

"I did. See?"

"Oh. I am sorry. I thought you would not know
this."

"I know more than that small fact."

"Yes, you must, to have such a fine accent. Most

Earthers did not trouble themselves. Still, it is unusual for an Earther to bother with a ceremony, even if he knows it."

"Why not?"

"Consider. You thought there was no one in the temple. So did I. If you had kept your shoes and ornaments no one would have been here to see, in any case."

"The God of the ninety-nine Names would be here."

She looked at him closely, surprised. "So It would. A nice phrase, that. I shall remember it."

"Isn't the Naming the whole purpose of this shrine?"

Joane laughed, a liquid tinkling sound. "For me the purpose is rest."

"Why not relax at home?"

"I wish to be alone at times."

"I am sorrowed that I disturbed you." He stepped back into a well of shadow, as if to go.

"No no. Stay. I am quite finished here in any case. And if you accompany me to the hotel it will please my husband."

Skallon sat upon a marbled banister. "How?"

"He does not wish me to go out in darkness alone. He says the streets are becoming dangerous. Of course he is right. My sister was attacked some days ago, at sunset. They took her market basket and two days' food."

"Plague victims?"

"Most probable. But if I return with a reliable escort such as yourself, my husband will not mind. Indeed, he would be honored."

"I see." Skallon nodded. Neither of them made a move to rise and go back to the hotel. Joane crossed her palms. "Though I am not sure how reliable I might be," he said to fill the silence.

"But you are a special man. Someone worthy of sending across the stars."

"I'm not sure street fighting was what I was selected for."

"I do not doubt you could do so."

"Oh, probably." He shifted his weight and looked up at the pink moon, now high above the frieze. "They increased my military training several months back. Somebody clearly had something like this in mind, I could tell that. My special asset is my academic work."

"Aca—?"

"Is that the right pronunciation? Scholarly. Well, not exactly that. I studied Alvea."

"Out of concern for us?"

"Ah, not precisely. Earth selects a certain fraction of the population to study in certain fields. So they'll have someone always on hand who knows background. Several people for each planet."

"For diplomacy?"

"Partially." Skallon wondered how he was going to get this across. "As a reserve, I suppose. Here, for instance, all the Consul's staff is now barred from Alvea."

"I heard they were accused of dishonesty."

"Um. Yes." He decided to sidestep the point. "So Earth looked into its reserve pool, for this job. They needed someone fast."

"And you were most qualified."

"Well, the psycher noted that I wasn't the most aggressive in the field training. Lacked confidence, they said. But when they discussed it with me, they called it 'cautious judgment.' Meaning they didn't mind if I was that way."

"I see," Joane said. "your superiors required discretion."

"Ha! They want me to keep out of the way and let Fain transact his business."

"Fain?"

"The other man with me. I sort of wonder how reliable those psychers were. I don't *feel* reliable."

"I am certain you are." Something simple and direct in the way she said it made Skallon believe it, too. Maybe she understood him better than he did himself.

"The hotel," he murmured, changing the subject for reasons he did not quite understand. "I'll walk you back."

They made their way along a graveled track that intersected Maraban Lane, making a crunching noise that seemed to fill the darkness. Skallon took her arm as they negotiated the uncertain steps at the hotel courtyard. A single yellow lamp hung over the entrance portal. In a shadowed corner nearby Skallon saw a flicker of movement. The events in the railway car came flooding back into his mind. He fumbled beneath his Doubluth robes for a weapon. His hand found it but the butt snagged in the cloth. The shadows moved again. Skallon stepped away from Joane to clear his field of fire.

"I *asked* you not to go out alone," came a high-pitched voice.

"Stand there!" Skallon blurted.

"What?" A boy stepped out of the shadows. "Mother, I've been waiting for you. I really wish—"

"Sir, this is our boy, Danon." Joane draped an arm around the boy, who appeared to be about fourteen Earth years of age. Skallon nodded and made some conversation by way of introduction. He was momentarily taken aback. Joane did not look old enough to have a boy this age. Perhaps the shadows had hidden her wrinkles—lighting here was always dim, a significant change from the bleached-white corridors of Earth.

The boy seemed protective of his mother and somewhat wary of Skallon. For his age that seemed to fit the standard psychological profile, Skallon thought to himself as they went into the hotel. In the foyer they parted, Joane giving him her hand in a cool, distant way. Danon nodded crisply. Skallon made the traditional parting phrases and picked his way down the cramped hallways, thinking about Joane.

He pushed open the door to his room and was halfway inside before he noticed the figure sitting on the bed. He froze. The first thing that registered was not the man's face, but the muddy boots smearing the white sheets.

"About time," Fain said.

Part
Two

1

Down only a few hours now, and Fain already hated this planet. It stank.

He slipped through the thickening jungle. Twice now he had seen the darting blue bolts in the distance. Mother was eliminating some aircraft. Fain wished he was still in his suit, but there was nothing to be done about that. He would have taken Skallon's, but the Alveans at the air base were probably watching for a suit, ready to zap it. So Fain would come in under cover, looking as harmless as possible. He slid his right hand under his Alvean robes and checked to be sure he could get his weapons out quickly, free of snags. Then he moved on.

He wrinkled his nose in disgust. Everything smelled here. The forest had become more like a jungle. There were grotesque ferns, chunky things like mushrooms. The air was thick with pollen, seeds, and spores. His eyes watered constantly and his nose dripped mucus. A wet, warm mist blanketed the ground, and a heavy wind blew hard against his face. No, thought Fain, there was no place like Earth. A cliché, sure, but a damned accurate one. Fain had spent time on more than two dozen backworlds, and he hadn't liked any of them. Revolium, for example, the scene of his grandest success, a waterworld where the inhabitants, more like fish than real men, smelled of weeds and brine. The planet wasn't important. Fain had gone to

Revolium to perform a service and he had come to Alvea to do the same. Jungle or giant ocean, endless desert or evergreen forest, cities, mountains, plains— only the job really mattered. Until it was done, he thought of nothing else.

Still, he couldn't help missing the Earth, wishing he were home. It was an emotion he didn't like finding in himself. A good agent couldn't afford strings. The truth was that he worried about himself. What if the execs were right? What if he had indeed lost something? The incident back there with the Vertil—five years ago that would never have happened. Changelings never grew soft. Maybe that was why Fain hated them the way he did. It was a form of hatred tinged with envy and admiration. When Fain killed this Changeling, he would learn something about himself. If he failed again, he would learn something, too.

He remembered when it had started. Right after Revolium. He had met with Bateman, Vice President of the Consortium, up in the towers of Houston. Bateman puffed away at the butt of a natural cigarette. The habit was available only to men powerful enough to demand and receive the costly carcinoma treatments. "Congratulations, Fain," said Bateman, rising from his desk and offering a gloved hand. "I knew if we had a man capable of bringing one back alive, it was you."

Fain didn't like Bateman. The chances were good that fifteen years before Bateman had personally ordered the murder of a man named Dickson Fain. "I do my job." Fain ignored the extended hand.

Grinning thinly, Bateman sat. Past his left shoulder, a broad window revealed the glittering midnight skyline of the city. Fain knew it was a cozy distortion. Outside, the time was closer to noon.

"You'll want your reward," Bateman said.

Fain nodded. "You promised. In writing. I've got a copy. Anything I want costing less than three million list."

"A fair price." Bateman smiled broadly. "Well, Fain, what is it? Have you made up your mind yet?"

Fain knew exactly what he wanted. He'd known ever since he'd first maneuvered Bateman into making his open offer. "You have two daughters. I want five-year leases on both."

Bateman showed nothing. He had obviously never expected Fain to succeed on Revolium, but Fain had fooled him there. Fain was fooling him again now. Coolly, Bateman said, "I won't do that, Fain."

He didn't raise his voice. "You killed my father—"

"—a clear traitor to the Consortium—"

"—and now I'm demanding payment in kind. One daughter for one father."

"You said two."

"The other is for my services. My future services."

"You could be killed."

"Not when I'm worth more to the Consortium alive than dead. No other man knows the Changelings as I do. No other man could ever catch one."

Fain thought of the two women. Had it really started with them? Had loving them made him soft, or was it just coincidence? Neither were ringers. He had expected Bateman to try a trick, but the women's prints had matched. Fain had contacts in the Consortium Data Bank that allowed him to be sure of that. At first he had just hurt them. He'd had few women before and not enjoyed them much. In time he decided that these two were different. It wasn't their V-P status. Fain, through his idealistic, scientific monk of a father, had once held that. It was their attitude toward him: their fear and their admiration. When the lease had expired last month, the three of them had

promised to see each other again. Fain didn't know
how much truth was involved in those shared vows.
He did know that he wanted them again—them or
some other women just like them.

That was what disturbed him—that was the real
change. Before the women, he had never entered a job
with any thought for the future. Live or die, succeed
or fail, the job itself had occupied the totality of his
senses. Now, even with his eyes open, he kept seeing
the women. Flashes of them: eyes, breasts, knees. He
smelled them, too. Remembered their tastes. It had
been this way for five years—five years of failure. He
knew he had to clear his mind. The lease—his revenge—was over. He had to get back to the way it had
been before. If he didn't, he knew he might well be
dead. His usefulness to the Consortium was a thin
thread. Bateman would love having him killed. Fain
knew he had to prove himself here—and survive.

Alvea didn't much help. The dense undergrowth.
The ludicrous ferns and stinking mushrooms. He
moved swiftly, with instinctive ease. Ahead, with each
step, things stirred and scampered in the high grass.
Rodents and insects. Bugs and pests. Live things. And
the Changeling? Somewhere there ahead, too. Fain
drove the women out of his mind. He forced his senses to flow outward, merging with the exterior world.
This was his protection, his gift. He wouldn't fail this
time.

He heard the bubbling stream before tall grasses
parted to show the flashing green water. He paused
briefly for a drink, then waded forward. The rocks
were slippery. Overhead, a piercing cry ruptured the
stillness of afternoon. Fain didn't glance up. The bird
was a smackwing; he knew it from quicktreatment.
Ugly, but good meat, good food. Suddenly, he
stopped, thumbed his pistol to silent mode, threw up

his arm, fired. The bird cried out, banked to the left, disappeared over the jungle. A miss. A near miss, but a miss. Fain holstered his heatgun beneath his gown. He stood in the middle of the stream, water sweeping past his knees, and stared at his hands. He had never missed before—never.

He found the body on the opposite bank.

At first he thought the Alvean was dead. But no, the breathing was strong, if uncertain. The pulse was steady, if too quick. There was no indication of any sort of wound. An Alvean soldier, fatter—if possible—than the other two. Unconscious.

Fain sat back on his haunches, listening intently now to every distant sound. A lone man in the middle of the jungle, unconscious but neither dead nor wounded. Something to do with the Changeling, but—

The idea chilled him. He slipped a plate from his robes and held it in front of the man's lips. In a moment the plate clouded a rosy pink.

Fain stood up. Someone had drugged this Alvean with Vertil, apparently made use of him, and then left him here to recover.

But only he and Skallon had Vertil on this planet. It was outlawed here. So, impossible as it seemed, this sleeping Alvean meant that the Changeling, too, had a Vertil supply.

So the odds were different now, vastly different. And suddenly the fear blew through him like a cold wind.

Oh my God no no, he had screamed, running into the room. The hollow roar of the flame gun filled the house. The flames were already halfway around his father, burning through his clothes. Swarming toward the face. His father covered his face with both

hands and rocked backward. One of the assassins
fired again.

Licking flames. A ball of light that struck his father
in the chest and exploded over him.

Then the scream. Shrill, high. Agony and despair.

Fain took three steps into the room and someone
smashed him in the chest with the butt of a weapon.
Oh please God no what are you, why— Then he saw
the chevrons, the bits of cloth that meant this was all
legal, there was no mistake, that his father had to die
here today.

His father, awash in fire.

The hands came down as though the burning man
knew there was no escape, no point in trying. The
face was contorted, clenched. The mouth gaped in a
silent scream. The figure stiffened. The flames spread
over him, chewing. Then his eyes opened slowly, as if
he were forcing them, struggling for one last look at
the world. Fain's father looked out at his son and
swayed. His hair burst into orange flame. Acrid
smoke. The crisp burning sound. Licking, snapping
flames. His father's lungs filling again to scream. In
the burning man's eyes there was something ageless.
He looked at Fain, gazing out through his agony, and
between the two of them there passed the recognition,
the knowledge. Then his father toppled backward,
arms jerking, and the final scream came.

Fain stood rigid, bathed in sweat.

Whenever the fear came he fled from it, ran away
into the past. Back to the burning, falling man. Back
to the three assassins, making sure their job was done
and his father couldn't be revived in a healant unit.
Doing their grisly work on the living room rug. Brushing aside the babbling boy.

It was in the dark hours that followed, as the house

filled with police and officials and relatives, that the
glacial calm descended on him, never to leave. A cold,
serene knowledge. He had seen death and in that final haunted look from his father he had seen the answer to death. His father had given Fain something
that would carry him through life and make him unlike the others.

It was to that secret center, where the cold clear
truth dwelled, that Fain returned. The fear had seized
him for a moment there, but now it was gone. The
Changeling held a huge edge over them. It had neu-
tralized the only concrete advantage he and Skallon
had brought to Alvea. Very well: the problem was
different now. But inside Fain knew that he had nothing to lose here, truly. The best the Changeling could
do was kill him. That was all. And knowing that gave
Fain the key edge he had always had over everyone—
over man, over Changelings, everything.

Fain cradled his heatgun and went on. The moment
had passed. He had moments like it before, especially
during the past five years, but they had never really
mattered. This one would fade and disappear, too. He
was sure of that.

He had gone three kilometers when he heard the
first gunshots booming in the damp air.

Crouching among pungent leaves, breathing through
his lips to keep from gagging, Fain studied the landscape ahead. It was the Alvean air base. In one corner, piled at the edge of a cracked concrete runway,
there were nine reconnaissance airships. Two were
burning. Of the seven wooden buildings, three were
on fire. As he watched, a huge, round, squat Alvean
staggered out of one of the burning buildings. The
man held a primitive pistol high in his hand. He ran,
waddling, and fired twice into the air. Then he fell on
his face.

Vertil. Fain knew already what had happened. The
Changeling, in his guise of General Nokavo, had infiltrated the base. He had sent two uninfected soldiers
away to kill Fain and Skallon and had then gone
about his usual task. He had created chaos. The Vertil
must have made it very easy. Apparently, the effects
of the Vertil were now wearing off. Fain could see
sprawled bodies everywhere he looked. When the Alveans awoke, if they ever did, they would remember
little of what had occurred.

He ran forward. One building so far spared from
the fire stood bedecked with a half-dozen colorful
flags. Fain assumed this must make it local headquarters and he aimed his trajectory that way. A bullet
whizzed past his ear, Fain zigzagged and thought he

spied a flash of motion high in a wooden tower opposite the headquarters building. The Changeling? Not likely. Probably an Alvean sniper, crazed with Vertil. He didn't alter his course. He didn't use his own heatgun. A second bullet cut into the ground far to his left. Fain knew he had guessed correctly. No Changeling would ever miss twice.

Fain, not missing a step, hurled his shoulder against the bolted door of the headquarters building. The wood split like plaster and he tumbled inside. Losing his balance, tumbling, Fain bounced off a shoulder, rolled to his knees, and aimed his heatgun. "Make a move—any move—and I will kill you."

"Aye, sir." The Alvean grinned widely. Spittle washed his lips, and he bowed from his broad waist. "The General has intimated your immediate arrival."

Fain stood. "Place your hands on your head, turn three times, flap your arms, and make a sound like a bird—a smackwing."

The Alvean unquestioningly performed as directed.

Fain nodded, not relaxing. If he needed any confirmation of his expectations, here it stood—in the flesh—at least one hundred kilos' worth.

"Now stand still." Fain searched the Alvean, turning him easily from left to right. He seemed to be unarmed. The room itself, apparently some sort of foyer, was a mess of scattered paper and broken furniture. There was one door in the opposite wall and Fain never took his eyes off it.

He backed away from the Alvean and said, "Tell me precisely what has occurred here." Despite the open door, he couldn't hear a thing from outside. The shooting had stopped and only a faint odor of smoke remained. "How did this trouble begin?"

The Alvean shook his head defensively and showed one pale palm, a gesture of some sort. "There is no trouble here, good sir. Only our Supreme Commander, General Nokavo, has ordered a search for traitors."

"Then why are you shooting at each other? Burning your own buildings?"

"Why, to find the traitors, of course." The Alvean spoke with the wide-eyed sincerity that Vertil most often produced. Once under the influence, no Alvean could possibly understand why his distorted worldview did not make perfect sense to everyone.

"Who told you who the traitors were? Was that General Nokavo, too?"

"Oh, no." The Alvean shook his head vigorously, jowls quivering. "General Nokavo merely pointed out that each man's best friend must be suspected of treachery. He named no names at all."

"That was fair of him," Fain said drily. "And where might he be now? General Nokavo? Once he'd told you his secret, did he just happen to leave?"

"Oh, no. General Nokavo has remained in his office throughout, supervising the search for traitors."

"His office?"

The Alvean swiveled and pointed to the opposite door. "Through there."

Fain nodded. It wasn't what he had expected. If anything, it was too easy—the Changeling just sitting here waiting for him to arrive. Fain knew there had to be a catch, but he also knew he had no choice but to go straight ahead. If the Changeling was waiting, it wouldn't wait for long.

"Show me to him," said Fain.

The Alvean bowed. Turning obediently, he first stumbled a step, then wavered, then finally got a grip on the door. Fain could tell that the effects of the Vertil were wearing off. Any moment now and this man would collapse in a stupor. That was only one more reason for haste.

The Alvean opened the door—it was unlocked—and stepped through.

His heatgun ready, Fain followed.

This room was neat and clean. There were local books, bound pamphlets, and a wide plush couch and chair.

"There's no one here."

"General Nokavo's office is there." The Alvean pointed toward the ceiling.

Fain ducked back for cover. He cursed himself for failing to see the open square of the trapdoor the moment he'd entered the room. If the Changeling was up there, if it wasn't deliberately taunting him, he knew he ought to be dead now.

"How do you get up there?" he asked the Alvean, speaking from the shelter of the doorway.

The Alvean, who had not moved from his place in the center of the room, bustled with sudden energy. "I will bring the ladder." It was made of wood and hidden beneath the couch. In a few moments the Alvean had placed the ladder so that it poked through the hole in the ceiling.

Fain knew he'd be live bait perched on the open rungs of the ladder. "Start climbing," he told the Alvean.

"But, good sir, I cannot, without permission, enter the private offices of the Supreme Commander. To do so would—"

"I want you to climb the ladder ahead of me," Fain said slowly. "That's an order. You must obey."

"I must obey," the Alvean said. He shrugged, stepped up to the ladder, and began to climb.

Fain never took his eye off the opening in the ceil-

ing as he entered the room. He waited at the foot of
the ladder until the bulk of the Alvean nearly blocked
his view, then began to climb. He had risen two steps
when the Alvean, reaching the top, spread his arms
through the opening. If something was going to happen, it ought to come now, Fain thought. He raised
his heatgun.

The Alvean fell.

It caught him totally by surprise.

A hundred kilos of Alvean flesh fell three meters
down from the ceiling and landed upon Fain. The
wooden rung upon which he stood cracked. He fell.
He hit the floor, the Alvean on him. For a moment he
saw nothing. All he felt was pain. The heatgun fell
from his hand.

Joseph Fain lay pressed beneath the bulk of the unconscious Alvean, unarmed and in full view of the
hole in the ceiling.

He knew he ought to be dead. He stood up.

His ribs ached and his left wrist felt sprained. The
Alvean slept in a Vertil stupor. Fain kicked once, then
again. He heard a snap as the Alvean's ribs, concealed beneath the fat, broke. He raised his leg, then
stopped.

Fain felt soiled and foolish. He felt like—to use an
antique expression, however meaningless—like a man
caught with his pants down. He breathed heavily. His
hands were shaking.

Slowly, calmly, he crossed the room and retrieved
his heatgun.

He climbed the ladder alone, carefully avoiding the
broken rung.

The room at the top was empty. He had known by
now that it had to be but his anger was barely tem-
pered. He searched the room. It was dark and narrow
and filled with smoke. He tore open drawers and scat-

tered files. He ripped at the furniture and splintered a
chair. There was no meaning to his search, only a certain order. He started at one end of the room and
worked toward the other.

Halfway down the length of the room, in a wide
wall cupboard, he found the body of an Alvean. There
could be no doubt this time. A hole the size of a fist
had been burned in the Alvean's chest and his gar-
ment, a flowing white silk gown, was a mass of dried
blood.

Fain didn't have to think for more than half a second before identifying the dead Alvean. From his
clothes, from where he had been found, the solution
was simple.

Fain shut the cupboard and allowed General Nokavo to rest undisturbed.

He wasn't surprised. He had seen similar deaths before, on Revolium and elsewhere. Assuming another
man's identity presented the Changeling with only
one crucial problem: what to do with the original arti-
cle. In this instance the Changeling had undoubtedly
acted instinctively. It had killed General Nokavo, assumed his person and identity for a few critical moments, and then gone on.

Or had it?

Fain tensed suddenly. His gun was in his hand and
raised. He spun, pointed toward the hole in the floor,
and fired.

From below there was no response.

Fain dropped to his knees, crawled across the floor,
and looked down.

The room below was empty.

Fain remembered lying down there with the broad,
foul, huge bulk of the Alvean soldier sprawled upon
him.

That Alvean soldier had been the Changeling.

He knew it now as certainly as he should have known it at the beginning.

The Changeling had tricked him, taunted him, ridiculed him. The Changeling had made him look like a fool, an amateur.

And, what was worse, Fain realized the Changeling had not acted entirely on its own. Fain himself had helped the Changeling all the way.

He should have suspected something: one lone Alvean still awake while dozens of others slept. One lone Alvean who just happened to know exactly where General Nokavo was hiding. One lone Alvean who was the Changeling.

Cautiously, controlling the anger that rose like a wave in him, Fain descended the ladder. As he reached the bottom he heard, deep in the distance the murmur of an aircraft engine. The sound deepened as Fain stood poised. He tried to follow its direction and compare with his own quicktreatment knowledge of Alvean geography. South by southwest. Yes, of course: Kalic. The city. The Changeling was headed there, toward Skallon.

Fain holstered his gun and began to run. When he reached the street a sea of smoke shrouded the base. The padding he wore made running awkward; in the Alvean heat he was panting after only a few hundred meters. But he did not stop. He did not slow down. Five years of failure boiled up within him. Inside he knew there was his cold and certain center, the gyroscope that guided him. He would run now, and sweat out the years of lassitude. He would drive himself until the softness left his body and his mind. He would work from his center, his sureness. When the rest had burned away he would be able to think clearly again and he would track down this Changeling and he would kill it."

3 ══════════════════════════════════════

To be on a world again is good. The ponderous will of
gravity forms the air, tells each particle to step in the
Dance. The Changeling moves forward in the clattering machine of the air, carving the wind, staying only
slightly above the froth of vegetation below. Speed it
must have. And lightness. It sees below a spot, and,
learning from the awkward clanking machine as the
thing tries to do what it should, what the instant requires, the fleshy cargo comes fluttering to rest
among the packed wealth of life. Here are animals.
They seek the gas plants, making prayer and seizing
the plants with little sharp claws. The herd rejoices.
They separate the respiratory bulb from the photon-
eating pads. The plants, in anguish, release gusts of
rich gas. The Changeling plucks a few, eats, takes
knowledge of this world. Its cool snout nuzzles the
herdbeasts. It sees and licks. It feels the moment coming and rises up. The hand forms into blade and down
it falls, slicing red and wide. Guts spill on the dry
ground. Wet richness slops and steams. Globes of offal
sour the air. The Changeling sucks in this vast cargo,
brought to it on hooves. It cuts and chews and slurps
in quivering full life, the aroma of flesh, the juices of
gasping finish. And is renewed. It must add mass for
what is to come. Its ribbed flesh absorbs the moist

feast. Cells swell in thanks, sacs fill with seeping liquid, joints pop and creak as the body absorbs through pores and blood the richness of the welcoming world.

4 ═══════════════════════════════════

With his muddy boots casually tossed upon the crumpled white sheets, Fain sat with his hands behind his neck and glared at the wooden rectangle of the door. Skallon. Where was Skallon? Even an idiot should know better than to go out alone at night on a planet he barely knew.

Fain could have smoked a tobacco cigarette. The habit was one he had only lately acquired, but it was a strong one. The drug was apparently unknown on Alvea. Fat people rarely smoked anyway.

The doorknob turned. Catching the hint of motion, Fain reached easily for his heatgun. He gripped the butt but did not draw the weapon. A foot appeared through an open crack in the door. A hinge creaked, then an arm joined the foot. Fain relaxed but did not release his grip. When all of William Skallon finally showed in the dim light of the outer corridor, Fain let his anger and impatience take control. "About time," he said.

Skallon stopped dead. His mouth hung open and his eyes went wide. He stared at the spot where Fain's muddy boots stained the clean white sheets. "What?" he said. "What are you doing here?"

"Get in here," said Fain.

"Yes," said Skallon. "Yes, of course." He complied passively. The room was lit by the single flickering gas lamp. Skallon made no effort to sit. There was only the bed.

"Where have you been?" Fain said.

"I—I could ask you the same thing."

Fain smiled thinly. "And I'd tell you. But, right now, I asked first."

"Out," Skallon said. His surprise over, he spoke casually, no attempt at bluster. "I attended a funeral ceremony and saw—observed—other native practices. That is supposed to be my job here, isn't it? I am supposed to be the expert on Alvean culture. I thought that was why we—"

"Your job," Fain said, "is to do what you're told. By me."

"I don't think the situation is quite as simple as that."

Fain shrugged. The thrust of Skallon's thought did not interest him, and he never argued. Argument implied equality, and Fain seldom granted that quality to any man. "Where's the dog? You didn't take him with you?"

"No, of course not. I was alone. Completely alone. Scorpio has his own room. The innkeeper, Kish—"

"We'll move him in with me for tonight. It was stupid leaving him alone. Scorpio is a lot more valuable to this mission than either of us. Remember that."

"I'll keep it in mind." Skallon glowered, slipping toward the brink of real anger.

Fain decided to be soothing. He sat up—the native beds, stuffed with some cheap, lumpy stuff, were not made for comfort. "I don't mean to be completely negative, Skallon, but you've got to remember certain definite facts. You and I are strangers on this world. I don't care how many books you've read or tapes you've screened, these people are aliens. They don't look or act or think like us. They're bug-eyed monsters and we're real people. Don't trust the innkeeper. Don't trust his wife or her son. Don't—"

"But I didn't mean—"

"Shut up," Fain said. "I heard you talking in the courtyard and it wasn't smart. We have a job to do. It's an important one and we could both get killed. Understand? Now, from now on, when we go out, we go out together. No more wandering around looking for easy thrills. That goes for me same as it does you. We don't have to like each other but we do have to protect each other. Nobody else is going to do the job. Is that clear?"

"I suppose it is, Fain." He was angry, but he was also listening, and it was the last part that was crucial.

"Okay," said Fain. "Now, one other thing. In the course of all your wanderings, did you happen to bump into the Changeling?"

"How did you know he's in Kalic?"

"I've been chasing its trail all day. At the air base I almost caught up with it, but it gave me the slip and stole a skimmer. It must have downed that somewhere outside the city. The trail wasn't hard to follow. The Changeling has a supply of Vertil and it's not hesitant about using it. The last definite sign I found wasn't a kilometer from here. Two of your Alveans knocked cold from the drug."

Skallon said, "What I don't understand is how it could get—"

"The Vertil?" Fain shrugged. "Only one way— infiltration."

"On Earth?"

"Why not? They've infiltrated the backworlds. What makes Earth so special? It wasn't luck that got it this far. By now it probably knows who we are. These disguises aren't going to fool it."

"No," said Skallon, softly. "No, I suppose not." He sat down on the edge of the bed. Fain climbed to his feet. Skallon seemed to be taking this awfully hard. What was it? he wondered. The idea of a Changeling intelligence net on Earth? Had that disturbed Skallon's precarious sense of order? Utter chaos so close to home? Fain was amused.

"Get up," he said. "Get up and take me to Scorpio. I want to see him and I want to eat. Wake up the innkeeper."

"But it's the middle of the night, Fain."

"So? Don't worry. He won't argue. I'm loaded with Vertil." Fain pointed to his mouth.

Skallon stood up, showing a sudden and unexpected flash of anger. "What are you doing like that?"

"I had to get here, didn't I? I had to hurry. I couldn't afford to play around with my accent and my clothes. The Changeling was way ahead of me all the way. I didn't have time to be polite and ask for everything I wanted."

"But wasn't that rather—rather—" Skallon seemed flustered, upset. "Fain, wasn't that stupid?"

"Stupid?" Fain let his anger take over. "Who the hell are you to—"

But Skallon seemed sure of himself now. "Fain, these are people we're dealing with, not animals. Look at you." Skallon did so now himself, as if seeing Fain for the first time. "Your robes are a mess, your makeup is running. You wouldn't fool anybody into thinking you're a Doubluth."

"I said there wasn't time for the niceties. "

"Are you sure of that? Vertil ought to be a luxury. The way you're using it, you don't care about these people. I thought we were supposed to be different from the Changelings. I thought we were supposed to be saving the Alveans from them."

"That's what some people say." It was a point Fain could have argued. He knew full well—even if Skallon did not—that they were here to protect the best interests of the Earth Consortium. Alvea entered the picture only where her interests and those of the Earth happened to coincide. Fain could have argued all this with Skallon, but he remembered in time that he never argued. "Let's go get something to eat."

"Then you stay back. You stay out of the way. No Vertil."

Fain grinned. He already had a hand on the door. "It's a deal."

But, as the two men moved uncertainly down the dim corridor, Fain couldn't help wondering. What if Skallon was right? Had his decision to use Vertil really been the wisest means of reaching Kalic quickly, or only the most obvious, the easiest?

Have I made another mistake? Fain wondered. *If so, how many more can I afford?*

It was not a question he enjoyed contemplating; the answer was again too obvious.

Licking the empty plate set on the floor, Scorpio murmured in guttural satisfaction. Lifting his big head, the neodog said, "Skallon. Feed. Scorpio. One. Time."

Fain glared at Skallon seated across the table from him. "Scorpio eats three meals a day. You should have known that."

"I did. I forgot. Sorry." Skallon yawned. It was plain his late night walk through the city was catching up with him.

"Warm. Here," said Scorpio, moving over to where a wood fire burned in a broad brick fireplace. "I.

Sleep." The room smelled of smoke, but the odor was not wholly unpleasant. Even Fain had never before seen anybody burning real wood merely for heat.

"Bring me another helping, please," Fain said, holding up his plate. As Kish, the Alvean innkeeper, approached, Fain turned his head deliberately away. The Vertil had almost certainly worn off by now, but he was trying to please Skallon. At first Kish had flatly refused to provide a late meal. Skallon had been forced to beg and plead and entreat, while Fain, smiling to himself, waited patiently in the corridor. When Kish, muttering, finally appeared with Skallon, Fain said nothing.

"Additional meat?" asked Kish.

"It's not something we get on Earth."

"Dead animal flesh," said Skallon, coming awake long enough to frown in disgust.

"No worse than dead vegetable flesh," said Fain.

As Kish waddled away and disappeared into the adjoining room—the kitchen—Skallon started in again. "Look, Fain, I happen to be tired and if all you want from me is someone to look on while you eat—"

"Shut up," said Fain. He had just heard something— a sound like a cough—coming from behind the kitchen door. And the sound—the cough—was too high-pitched to have been made by Kish. There was someone else in that room. Fain motioned Skallon to keep silent, then stood, reaching for his heatgun. He could have kicked himself. How could he have neglected to check the other rooms? It was yet another mistake—and so soon.

Softly, on the balls of his feet, Fain crossed the room. Scorpio, beside the fire, came awake in an instant. He eyed the scene carefully through hooded eyes. Reaching swiftly out, Fain gripped the knob and jerked open the door. At the same moment, he drew his heatgun and pressed the trigger lightly.

He saw three figures. Kish was close to a burning stove. The second, a woman. The third, a young boy, yelped as soon as he saw Fain. The cry might have been one of surprise or even delight.

"Shut up," Fain said, moving slowly into the room. He jerked his weapon toward Kish. "Who are these people?"

"I can tell you that, Fain." It was Skallon standing in the doorway behind. "The lady is Joane, who happens to be Kish's wife, and the boy is Danon, their son."

"They're not fat." Fain turned the heatgun on the woman now. She seemed to realize its function and backed away. The far wall stopped her.

"Only adult male Alveans eat to excess. Don't tell me you haven't noticed that yet."

"I haven't had time to notice anything." But Fain did notice, to his own surprise, that this woman was surprisingly pretty. Not beautiful—not like Bateman's daughters—but oddly sensual, more corporeal, a firm and powerful presence rather than something formed from bits of silk, fluff, and finery. "The Changeling would have noticed, though."

"Joane isn't the Changeling."

"How do you know?"

"I don't, but Scorpio does. And he's gone back to sleep again."

Fain glanced back to be sure Skallon was correct and, when he saw the slumbering dog, holstered the heatgun. "I'm sorry," he told Kish, "but we can't be too careful. Skallon has told you why we're here. The enemy might be anywhere—or anyone."

"I know, I know, but—" Kish was staring at the floor, where Fain's second helping of meat lay in a moist heap covered by bits of broken dish. "There is more. I will bring—"

"No," said Fain. "Forget it. We've kept you up late enough. Go to bed. You, too." He meant the boy, who had said nothing the whole time, content to stare in wide-eyed wonder. "Your wife can bring us anything we need."

"Yes, of course. My wife. Yes, of course. Joane, more meat for our guests."

Fain turned back into the dining room. As he sat down, Skallon murmured in his ear, "You've just violated an important bit of etiquette. An Alvean woman serves no man except her husband."

Fain shrugged "They already know I'm a savage."

The woman appeared with a plate of cooked meat, which she placed in front of Fain. She was alone, so Kish and Danon had apparently gone away by means of some back passage. As he ate, Fain found that he couldn't take his eyes off Joane. She returned his stare from her place beside the kitchen door with what seemed to be a slight smile. Fain wondered, *She looks at me like she knows all about me, but how could that be?* The woman was an Alvean. Despite her broad hips, loose breasts, and thick pouting lips, she was a construct, a pseudo-human, a creature designed for life on this alien world.

And Fain knew that he loathed all people like that.

With an act of will, he drew his eyes away from the woman and focused on Skallon, who appeared to be half-asleep again. "Look," he said, "I didn't ask you down here just to introduce me to the natives. There are certain things I think we ought to discuss even before morning. We have to get our basic strategy clear. Changelings don't sleep, you know, and they seldom bother to eat. It's ahead of us already. We can't afford to fall farther behind."

"So what do you suggest?" Skallon tried to appear interested through the obvious barrier of exhaustion.

Fain glanced at the woman. Was this smart, talking in front of her? Well, she wasn't the Changeling itself, and they never worked through spies. He had a feeling, even if he sent her away, she would find a means of listening. If the conversation interested her. From her slack demeanor and blank-eyed stare, he guessed that so far it did not.

"To begin with," Fain said, compromising only by lowering his voice somewhat, "We've got to think like a Changeling. Its job here—its only job—is disruption. What it's going to do is set about that mission in the quickest, simplest, and most direct manner possible. Now you're the expert on the local situation, but it seems to me that these plagues are by far the best thing it's got working for it. All the time I was out today, I saw the signs everywhere—Alveans dying, dead, or scared to death of being dead."

"And they blame the Earth for it."

"Exactly," Fain said. "So what I'm saying is that the Changeling is going to notice that, too. It's not like it's faced here with a hard concrete, permanent state of affairs. Alvea is like a brick wall, with a hollow place hidden somewhere in the middle. Push on all the wrong places and nothing will happen. Find the hollow place and you've got a broken wall."

"And the plagues are the hollow place?"

"Sure. Don't you agree?"

Skallon nodded. "All of this was discussed back on Earth, but I've seen nothing here to make me disagree."

"Then I think we ought to follow our original line of attack. We know all the leaders of the planet will soon be gathering here."

"I've already seen a number of the high castes

traveling through the streets. They sometimes use motor vehicles. No one else is permitted to occupy one."

"Then that's where we'll find the Changeling. In one of those meetings," Fain said decisively. "He'll be disguised as high caste."

Skallon nodded. "What we have to keep in mind is that he can tap anti-Earth sentiment if he can expose us. In fact, what we have to be careful about is . . ."

But Fain wasn't listening. The woman was leaning against the wall and as he watched she stretched, turning her neck with a slow, lazy grace. A languid, sensuous movement; it reminded him of the two Bateman daughters. The memory of them, and the warm, drifting time he spent, kept returning. He knew this could be a weakness, could disturb his concentration at a crucial time. But another fraction of him knew quite well this hunger for contact, for the exquisite supple sliding of skin next to his; it was a necessary counterbalance to the professional Fain he had made of himself.

Through the long years of growing up and then of training, Fain had kept his private center, the gift his father had given him. That had enabled him to be the cold, level-headed Fain, a calculating machine with a rock-hard body. When the pressure mounted, Fain could always retreat to the place where the cold, clear truth dwelled. Fain could risk himself in deadly moments precisely because he held death in contempt. His father had given him that: a certainty beyond faith, a simple fact. Over the years he had learned by watching the men around him: ultimately, they would flinch from doing what was smart, because each had a limit, a boundary beyond which he would not put life on the line.

Fain had no limit. Certainty cleared the vision,

made him a fraction better than the others. Death was
nothing. Fain knew that the essential core of himself
would not die, *could* not. He would live on.

Precisely how he knew this was, to Fain, an endur-
ing riddle. His father had told him something, showed
him things . . . the images blurred, ran together,
were lost. The doctors said it was the trauma of his
father's death that brought it on. Fain was not so sure.
He dimly recalled wandering the streets on the night
of his father's death, walking endlessly through concrete canyons slick and dark with rain. Someone
found him as dawn broke above the tall buildings.

Of that night and the weeks which followed he now
carried only tattered memories. He knew he had spent
weeks in a psychomatrix center, and that the doctors
had worked on him. When he awoke one morning the
world seemed different, less fuzzy and disordered; later that day, they told him his recovery was complete.
Somehow they had erased the clenching fear and
dread he felt whenever he thought of his father. But
in its place was the clear certainty, something beyond
faith.

He knew he would not die. Irrational, he knew—or
thought he knew. But there it was: absolute faith in
his own destiny, his infinite life. Somehow this cold
sureness masked whatever his father had done for
him. Somehow it connected with the burning man's
eyes, locked in that last hail between father and son, a
signal across the abyss. Somehow. But Fain could not
unknot the knowledge. In curing him they had sealed
in something that, in a strange way, made it possible
for him to live. To work.

He could never discuss this with others. They
would not understand that his abiding inner certainty
made him what he was. He had tried a few times to
explain it, to get it out in halting, awkward sentences.

But the tangle inside tripped his tongue, sent him stumbling away from the subject, his face suddenly reddening, his eyes averted, his throat rasping as the words choked him. So he had learned to carry it inside, a relentless burden. And once Fain had acquired a reputation for being tough, sure, unflinchingly professional, it became even harder. Others began to lean on him. They depended on his lead. *What do you think of . . . ?* they would say. *That's the tricky part of the operation, give it to Fain. We haven't got anybody else who can handle it.* So in the end, when he saw his safety was threatened by always having to be the pivot point, he quit working in teams. He became a loner. Somehow, then, the balance of things shifted in him. Working alone had its own pleasures and its own costs. It was to escape that burden, not to flee the pall of death that hung over his profession, that Fain wanted the release of women. Their openness. Their acceptance. The warm enclosing musk of them.

Joane yawned and turned delicately, rising for a moment on her toes the way he had seen Alvean women do. With animal grace she padded softly into the kitchen. Fain watched her go. Skallon talked on, but Fain heard nothing.

Just before Joane disappeared through the doorway, she turned with a deft movement and met his gaze directly. Her eyes glittered. Then she winked. It came so quickly, and then was gone, that Fain was not perfectly sure it had happened.

5

Supple, it moves in lonely splendid isolation through streamers of dank jungle. A shadow, flickering. Soft padding of hooves, a slide of scaly flesh. Reek of salty trickling sweat as it slips through tangled vines, rippling their stalks in the breathless heat of this new, sticky air. Alien, yes. But nothing was truly strange to it. All forms were a mold. All could be played with. It could ease into the world of the darting greyrat, sample its muzzy universe, echo its thin squeak. It could make its hand into a leaping image of the greyrat. And an instant later, be the warped man who sighted down a long tube at the rat, pinning it with a firebolt, forever. Sing the rasping laugh of temporary victory, of an instant's vision. Sip of it and breathe it in and then gone, gone, slipping away into new plastic muses. Tasting the lives around, always tasting probing, knowing with zest . . .

Two Norms follow. It saw the falling awkward capsule and knows there must be two. Norms from Earth, the worst of all Norms. Weak, fearful, cautious creatures—else why did they love their machines so? Machines were crutches. Men who used them quake at the life of the One.

Norms breathe out a falsely ordered pattern of lies— and all patterns are lies—and say it is reality. Only the One can know the truly real. Only the One can stand away and say, dancing on the moment, *That is firm and true; this is false and elusive. Witness!* The Norms, in their fear, never guess at this. Norms lunge in terror away from the uncertain, the beautifully unknowable, the universe of loving flux, where for each embodied eye at each fresh second nothing is ever again the same. By their refusal, Norms fail. Uncertainty is strength, was strength, will be strength all times flowing into One. Change is the constant, words slip free of meaning and the One, who sees this, must emerge the dancing victor. The Norms may follow. But they will never move ahead.

It loves this jungle. The vaulting plants, the towering crusted grasses. Life runs and darts everywhere. Fountains of buzzing airflowings, scurrying black-ribbed beetles, bounding hoppers, softly pattering rodents. Strange snouts and beaks and clickings of tiny teeth. In the solid sky winds rake at clouds and a huge thin bird wheels past, shattering the serene moment with a shrill barking cry. In the canyon of ferns, the manform pauses to stare, raises a fist in sudden greeting exultation at this raw lovely changing moment. The dancing singing moment, yes. *Hail!* Fist wriggles, makes four fingers, then six, thumbs knotting into a hard wedge. That is life; life is that—change, divine chaos. Only death itself, the rude redness hovering behind all, is stable and certain, never different, though of course death, too, is illusion.

It brings death but blesses life. In the face of change, the changeless must perish, for that is their heritage. The Norms must die. The Norms do not know.

Knowing everything, it plans nothing. The Alvean air base, glimpsed from the air in flight, is a suitable destination. The Vertil, gift from another, is a probable weapon. There are possible maneuvers but no certain tactics. With chaos as a goal, the paths to take are infinite. Through the jungle, it walks sometimes on four legs, sometimes on three, occasionally on two. It slithers, crawls, hops and, when a flowing stream is reached, swims with the swiftness of a fish.

"I wish to see General Nokavo," it says, assuming the bright robes and gross fat of the highest bureaucratic caste. The soldier at the gate blinks in the face of such grandeur.

"Your name, blessed sir?"

"I am—" it thinks, though it does not consider "—Fain."

"You will follow me please, blessed Fain."

"Aye, you are a faithful fellow." A name—it has none. No, rather it has born hundreds and will, before the unspoken moment of extinction, bear many more. Fain is a name it has heard. The killer of change. The one who acts in the name of stasis. A contradiction, yes, but so perhaps is the Norm Fain. He is one of those who follow. It knows this again without the need for consideration.

"Stand still, place your hands upon your head, shut your eyes, do not speak."

Alone with General Nokavo, it probes the squat man's mind. Questions dissolve into the air. It learns of the powers of this puny base, its antique weapons, its lazy rhythms. But these limitations are unimportant. The armed Alveans can provide some help, still.

It orders the General, and he in turn orders his men. Into the copters, and off. Seek the Earthers. They will be here, within this radius. Vector on them. Be clever, be swift. Kill them.

They will fail, of course. These Alveans are as children compared with Fain.

The Vertil is working well. The General, however, is growing weak, confused. He blunders while speaking to an underling. Then he weaves groggily. A bad sign.

Regretfully, but swiftly—justice requires it—the Changeling plucks the weapon from the General's tight belt. Levels it. Fires.

The body is simple to hide. The Changeling eats more of the General's foods, which it finds tucked into a small antechamber. The Alveans have their starchy gruel everywhere, if hunger should strike. Or perhaps it has religious significance. Little matter. It sucks in the mealy repast, happy to add mass and strength to itself.

It assumes the robes and identity of the dead General. It summons the troops. One battalion it orders to attack. The enemy? The redoubt at the end of the landing strip. They are traitors.

Yes: The world explodes into gunfire and brassy explosions. Men run and die. Confusion lives.

High in the tower, it watches the fire and smoke, the flowing blood and changeless death. A gaudy, colorful play. Useful, but not enough. This will work once, perhaps twice, but no more.

It creaks, and shifts its willing bones. Born in a certain shape, it no longer recalls that form. It is not Fain, Nokavo, anyone. In the forest seen below, the lone figure of a man stealthily approaches. Squat, dark, Alvean. Master of disguise, it laughs. So the true Fain has come at last to observe the work of the masters. (But Fain comes alone. It is disturbed by this show of strength.)

"Make a move—any move—and I will kill you," says Fain.

"Aye, sir." It grins broadly, spittle washing lips, and bows from a broad waist. "The General has intimated your immediate arrival."

Fain stands. "Place your hands on your head, turn

three times, flap your arms, and make a sound like a
bird—a smackwing."

Doing as ordered, it feels a flash of hate and thinks,
Fain must die. But—no—a second thought: *Fain
knows death too well—he does not fear it. Fain fears
only himself. He must be destroyed, not killed.*

"I want you to climb the ladder ahead of me," says
Fain. "That's an order. You must obey."

"I must obey." Planning nothing, it climbs the ladder. The body of General Nokavo lies above. If Fain
finds that, then Fain will know—he will guess the nature of the changing identities that swirl around him.
Fain hates that which is different. It senses his strong
disgust.

And, sensing that, knowing what will wound Fain
the deepest, it falls, a hundred reeking kilos of brown,
transient, unreal flesh.

Part
Three

Skallon drifted up from fuzzy, hollow sleep. He heard the familiar murmur of people around him, his fellow bunk mates in the Institute dormitories. He knew if he concentrated he could pick out the angry mutterings of the gambling circle, where fools lost their weeklies in an hour. Or eavesdrop on the daily grunting coupling in the bunk next to his, where a pale girl wrapped thin calves around the latest sullen, groggy man as he ploughed dumbly into her, out again, in with a fresh thrust, a rhythm she seemed to accept without effort, working, sighing, in and out, eyes dim and glazed, not hearing the rattle of cups on metal piping nearby, the shallow rasping laugh from the line of three men, naked, who waited in line beside her bunk for their turn. She was always ready in the morning, before getting up for a job where she would be narrow-eyed and encased in a shimmer of steely efficiency. The girl gasped occasionally in a quick, fervid, clenching way. Skallon thought vaguely that he might roll onto her himself when the rest were done, ease himself of a pressing tension—but then, swimming higher into consciousness, he recoiled from the idea as he always had before, knowing the impulse was part of him but not wanting to acknowledge it now, clutching at the rumpled sheets and rolling over, burying himself away from the sounds as the stiffness between his legs seeped away. To silence the thought he concentrated on the dulled murmur of the long room, hauling himself up to wakefulness, opened an eye . . .

The peeling wallpaper, tawny sunlight, spiced air of Alvea flooded in upon him.

He sucked in air. The dormitory slipped away and he was *here*, on Alvea at last. The thin girl who serviced all comers each morning was only a sour memory—and yes, he had done her once, he recalled, when he was fuzzed from sleep; she hadn't said a word. Instead of her there was Joane, and rather than another day in the tape plexes, he could step outside this grimy room and find Alvea itself.

He heaved himself up and gasped. A chorus of aches sang at each motion he made. Incredible, considering that Alvea had slightly less gravity than Earth. But, Skallon remembered, he had to acquire a new gait and habits of movement. New muscles creaked as he got dressed. That, plus the clumsy padding to make him appear fat, and the bulky Doubluth robes themselves. Still, the aches surprised him. He was in excellent physical condition, he knew. He prided himself on that. Skallon felt an odd twinge of vulnerability. Maybe this was what it was like when you got old.

He shook off the mood and left the cramped room. The hotel did not seem so mysterious and dirty as it had at night. Perhaps someone had swept up or something. He followed his nose to the kitchen. He came to a thick wooden door and pushed it open. A babble of voices washed over him. A dozen people sat on stools around an immense fire, gingerly holding cups that steamed in the morning cool beneath the oil lamps. A few eyes found him, studied him for a moment, and returned to their business. The room was nearly

round, high-ceilinged, and musty. No windows let in
the day.

Skallon nodded and let the door bang closed without entering. This must be the Communal, the social
center of every home and hostel. It was an archaic institution, a holdover from the ancient times when men
were slowly adapting to the high ultraviolet flux from
Alvea's sun. In the very beginning it had sometimes
been necessary for the entire population of a city to
repair underground for considerable lengths of time,
and more than likely Kalic contained, beneath its
streets and houses, a complex system of caverns and
tunnels for that purpose. The communal dated from a
somewhat later time when, during the midday hours,
the early colonists took shelter in a windowless room,
usually, for convenience, in the basement. There was
no need to eliminate windows, of course; ordinary
glass topped the ultraviolet. But the psychological effect of being completely inside, buried and safe in a
man-created cranny, had been important. So the long
noontimes, the immense rich lunches and sleeping it
off afterward became an Alvean custom, even long
after genetic adaptation made Alveans invulnerable to
their spitting sun.

Skallon found his way through remembered pas-
sages. He nudged open a door and found it was a
kitchen. Joane's profile frowned at a pile of sweet-
meats and then turned as he came in.

"Why, morning greetings," she said softly.

"You are quite lovely in the sunlight there," Skallon
said, feeling a bit awkward. She did seem better-
looking in sunlight, somehow.

"Why, thank you. I enjoyed our speaking of last evening."

"Ah. Yes, I did, too. Is my, ah, partner . . . ?"

"He is eating. There." She pointed at a portal. Skal-

lon looked through and saw Fain methodically spooning in a dish of gray mush. Scorpio was chewing at
something underneath the table. It was the same room
they'd eaten in last night, though it appeared now a
bit more orderly. Probably Joane had been up early to
put things in better order. Skallon nodded to himself
in satisfaction. These were good people, reliable.

Fain looked up and studied him evenly, as though
deciding something.

"Get some food," Fain said.

"Good. Food," Scorpio added. Skallon wondered if
the dog was trying to make conversation. Was that
possible? The dog didn't seem smart enough to do it.
But then, it was hard to tell.

Joane gave him a plate of bubbling stuff, chunks of
meat wallowing in a brownish paste, with anonymous
vegetables afloat in it. He sat opposite Fain. After a
few mouthfuls Fain slammed down a spoon, spatter-
ing the table top, and said, "Enough of that. I'm not
eating this slop anymore."

"It's what there is."

"I'm carrying emergency rations. With that and the
local water—that's awful stuff, too—I'll make do."

"Alvean food is quite sophisticated, really. I don't
think this *complannet* is so bad, either."

"You'll get sick from it."

"I doubt that. We took internal bacteriophase treatments before lifting Earthside. There is really—"

"That meat last night tasted all right. But an hour
ago I shat it all, undigested."

"Metaphase adjustment. In a day or two—"

"*Frang that.* I'm going to crack open a protein stato.
Where's some water?"

Fain banged his fist on the table and, when no one
appeared, stamped out. In a moment Joane peered
through the open portal and raised an inquiring eye-

brow. Skallon shrugged, pantomined rage, slammed his fist silently on the rough wood table, bared his teeth. She tittered. He shrugged and waved her back as Fain stormed back in through a side door, one hand clutching a canteen and the other thumbing open a protein bar.

Skallon ate silently while Fain crunched his way through the bar. He was acutely conscious of Joane clattering dishes and pots in the kitchen. There was something about her that intrigued him. A certain way she lifted her head and turned it when she spoke. Now that he thought about it, her nose wasn't really too long at all. It suited her face. Gave it balance, somehow.

He probably shouldn't have handed her that half-truth about being selected for this mission, out of the blue. Munching at the sour meat of the *complannet*, he remembered the last week of field training, when the idea had come to him and, without thinking about it very much at all, put it into practice.

First he had rigged a smeller grenade, just a bit more salt-sensitive than necessary. When he dropped it on patrol, it activated, of course. Slocum was two hundred meters behind. Quick-witted Slocum, grim Slocum, the obvious prime candidate for Alvea. When the sniffer homed on him, Slocum's screen came up fast, but a frag got through. A neat rip through the upper thigh. Slocum bled like an open faucet and whimpered in a strange little boy's voice while they were waiting for the airborne medics to arrive.

Then Ising, who was easier. A creature of habit was Ising.

Every morning before a field exercise began, Ising cleaned the bore of his megaJoule torchgun. One morning there happened to be a whiff of Butyl vapor in it. The barrel blew open and a gout of flame gushed out. It set fire to a whole wall of the armory and caught Ising on the right arm, burning two deep holes through his insulation and leaving first-degree patches here and there. Ising took several weeks to regrow the tissue.

Which left Skallon. A reasonably good candidate for the secondary slot on an Alvean team, when and if such a team was needed. But of course everyone had known for weeks that a crisis of some kind was brewing. Alvea was slipping out of control. The news that the Changeling had escaped put a different cast on things, of course. Skallon had thought the Institute would be asked for a team of Alvean specialists, to go there on superlight drop trajectories and firm up support for the usual Earth-export policy. He hadn't really counted on the Changeling.

"Does that stuff taste any better than *complannet?*" he asked Fain.

"Um. P'robly not."

"You'll have to eat some of the local food, you know."

Guarded interest from Fain. "Why?"

"As a disguise. You've noticed Alveans have a pungent smell about them?" Fain nodded. "*Balajan* weed. It's in their diet. Not bad, really. A mild herb. But if you don't smell of it, somebody is bound to notice and wonder why."

"We won't be here long enough for that to matter."

"Oh?"

"I want to wrap this up right away. Finish eating and let's get going."

"Where?"

"I want you to nose around the streets. Find out what important meetings are going on."

"Important in what way?"

"For the Changeling. Whatever route would take

him to the top of the power structure as fast as possible. That's where we'll find him."

"I see. All right. I'll find out, but I want to take Danon with me. He knows this city. He can tell me where I'm likely to pick up gossip, as distinct from news."

"Why not the older one?"

"Kish?" Skallon thought a moment. "No, he's not right. There's some reason he's a failure. I think he probably doesn't have good judgment."

Fain nodded. "I figure the same. Then give the kid a wrist communicator. You can make better use of him that way and he can nose around on his own. Tell him to keep it hidden under his sleeve. We don't want anyone to get the idea there are Earthers lurking around the city."

They went on eating. Skallon felt oddly pleased at Fain's agreement with him. When he had finished breakfast he asked Joane, who had first suggested the idea, to call Danon. The boy agreed to lead him into Kalic's markets and bazaars, to ferret out information. He gave Danon a spare wrist communicator and showed him how to operate it.

Skallon lingered in the kitchen a moment afterward, exchanging an occasional word with Joane. She was cleaning up the greasy dishes, using cold water and a gray soap. It wasn't until he and Danon were about to leave that Skallon remembered that Alvean women waited on no one other than their husbands. Yet she had served food to him and Fain. He wondered what it meant.

It draws oxygen from the Alvean air. Exhaling, shedding gases, it breathes out something more: control. The drug Vertil, stolen from the constricted, fearful laboratories of Earth.

It imagines Fain's expression at the moment of his discovery. It laughs, a rare gesture, tinkling sounds rippling out of its flexing throat. Inside itself, mixed with the surging red and white motes in its blood, is the power. How simple the Earthers are, to think control and power meant order. False, false. Power is a rare quantity, a scarce vintage. Power is life, is death, is in the moment. Control, it has long since learned, exists only in secluded, random nooks of the universe; elsewhere, cosmically, chaos dances and sings beside the fires of the ruby stars. The Norms' greatest sin lies in their absurd concentration upon the nooks, their ignorance of the greater reality.

The fat, gross, pig-snouted Alvean stands before it. Mind skimming over the instants as they tick by, it squints at the Alvean and ponders. It exhales: control. The Alvean will do as it says. Here, outside Kalic, it must take a disguise from this dim, impermanent creature. And it must ponder.

The image of Fain ripples before it, shimmering in the air. The Alvean cannot see Fain because the Alvean is a Norm, too, dumb and fuzzy and its blunted perception of the All. But Fain is there and floats before it, beckoning.

The moment passes, another dawns. Here is the new: all three of them are strangers here, careless skaters on the smooth glass of simple Alvea. They will all err. They will fumble. How can this be the key?

A moment passes, seconds die.

It must be Fain. He is the strongest, the Changeling-killer. So Fain must finally be weak, Fain must crumble, Fain's soft core must be found and stabbed by the One. He is serious, solemn. His image, flickering in the warm air between it and the groggy Alvean, is hard and unflinching.

Laughter, then, will kill Fain. A thousand pinpricks of jibes and taunts will vex and rub him, stretching thin his vaulted calm, his sharp judgment.

Seeing this, knowing it of and in the moment as the seconds die and are born before its eyes, the Changeling scuffs its feet in fevered desire. Yes, here it is. The eternal Way.

Fain and Skallon blunder ahead. Already they are in Kalic. They do not suspect that they are allies of the One, that they will in the end of the Dance help the Changeling to cut Alvea from the Earther fold. It will use ·these Earthers against themselves. All, through a singing skipping taunting that will echo in Fain's clotted mind. The Changeling cannot free Alvea by itself; this secret the Earthers do not know. It needs them for this final work of the One, and joy and mirth will be the end of them.

The Changeling snorts and mutters, glee building inside. Fain and Skallon will not see the weight as it falls toward them, for they are blind. They cannot dance. For them all is order and plan. They sense not the One which lies below the simple toys of reason, they ken not the lilting song of intuition. The Earthers have long ago separated the left hemispheres of their brains from the right hemisphere, achieving a frail control of the world, casting it into words and forms. An illusion. A furious fiction. It is *reason* which is the dream, a lazy dream of the One. Order is false. In the Changeling the left and right hemispheres are united again, as men once were. There is no analytical dominance, no tyranny of the word over the All. Their *reason* is the mind divided against itself, held in the once-convenient chains of old Earth, the false dreams of subject/object; she/it; us/they; person/world; right/wrong: cutting the world into pieces when it so yearns to be healed, to be the One. To percieve is to separate and to separate is to die. The law of life is to merge, to know, to enfold, to sum.

The Changeling feels the new sum coursing through him, flowing power. The pig-snouted Alvean shivers as the drug wrestles with his mind, wins, brings a temporary peace to his house of false order.

Exhaling, the Changeling grins again. "Undress," it commands. It feels a need for the dull purple robes of this caste. A Doubluth. It knows this world and the absurd beliefs of its people. The Changeling has slept under the quicktreatments, studied the illusions these Alveans are infested with. That the escaping soul of the dying man passes into the waiting shell of the as yet unborn. Of course, souls do not exist. There is no birth; there is no death. All is the One, and the One Itself is mere illusion, the fine flecks of illusion from which the world rises, in triumph. These Norms, these Alveans, will learn. With Earthers gone forever—and the Changeling senses this ahead, coming, coming, a fruition—there will be time and place to reveal the true underpinning of Nothing that is the World. Time—itself a falsity—will bring the One to them. The illusion of the plagues now kills these Alveans daily.

Death is a leveler. It brings truth nearer. Like sex, it is a lie which, swiveling, reveals the true illusion.

The air hums around the Changeling. Singing, singing. Dancing. Yes.

It kills the naked Alvean.

3 ═══════════════════════════════════════

From inside the sculpted *Ganjanaten* Hall came a thumping boom, a chorus of voices equally high and low, a *plink plink* of thin-stringed instruments. The procession wound past the stall where Skallon and Fain squatted. A gust of wind stirred dust from the feet of the marchers, sending it skyward like tan smoke, and then into the eyes of Skallon as he studied the swaying lines.

"Anything?" Fain whispered. He put a hand on Scorpio's head. Skallon could not tell whether the gesture was one of affection or a reminder to the dog to keep its head down, out of view of the Alveans.

"No. Sign." Scorpio sniffed. "Dust. Makes. Smell. Hard. To. Tell."

"I know, I know," Fain said sharply. "You said yourself you couldn't get a reliable fix unless you could pick up the scent."

"Correct. But."

"Never mind," Fain cut in. "How sure are you you're really picking up each scent? There's the dust, and that incense stuff."

"Very. Sure. We. Are. Aug—Aug . . ."

"Augmented," Skallon put in.

"Yes. For. That."

Skallon was sure Fain knew the dog's capabilities better than Scorpio did; it was interesting to see events get under Fain's skin.

"We're not getting anywhere here," Fain muttered.

"We've eliminated the Lutyen Communing," Skallon pointed out. "And now the Mahindras. That's something."

"Not enough."

The final knots of paraphernalia passed: brass bells and hollow sounding gongs; chiming metalworks; Camjen-burners like grotesque lamps; a giant, slender-handled spoon for the doling out of the consecrated nectar of browned sweets, shreds of tulsu leaf, milky *ganjan* stalks. The swarthy Mahindras—mostly carpenters, as their caste and rolelives decreed—passed by solemnly, swaying to the singsong rhythms that boomed out from the *Ganjanaten* Hall.

"Anything?" Fain said again.

"Nothing. No. Sign."

"Damn." Fain slammed a fist into the dirt beside him.

Danon's idea had seemed a good one at first: set up a simple beggar's or worshiper's stall (they served both purposes, usually) near the entrances of the great gathering halls, and observe the processions as they wound in for the meetings. But they'd seen nothing. Scorpio picked up no sign of the Changeling. Skallon began to regret taking Danon's advice. He and the boy had set out from the hotel to sift through gossip from the marketplaces. They'd found nothing remarkable, and then Danon thought of this device. Skallon had returned to the hotel to help Fain carry the dog through busy streets in a concealing cart.

Danon had fetched a stall and set it up, leaving it at the appropriate spot for them to find while he patroled the area, looking for unusual persons.

"Where's that kid?" Fain said as the last member of the procession shuffled by. A straggling crowd of office-seekers and hangers-on followed until the vast metal doors of the Hall banged closed in their faces, sending up a wail of supplication.

"These are damned hard times," Skallon said. "It's forbidden to plead with the vernal equinox delegates that way. But people follow them right into the Hall."

"Yeah," Fain said. "Where's that kid? This idea of his isn't worth a damn."

"Over there." Skallon pointed across the vast square to a milling throng of peasants, a swirl of tattered rainbow robes. "Watching."

"Get him over here."

"I don't think it's a good idea."

"Why not?" Fain said with surprise.

"If we want to keep him a free agent, unidentified with us, we shouldn't all be seen together in public."

"Hell, the Changeling can't be everywhere at once."

"He has the Vertil. He can send out as many runners and spies as he likes."

Fain shrugged. Clearly he didn't think Skallon's opinion counted for very much. "Go find out what the kid's turned up, then."

Skallon walked across the immense square, trying to look as casual as he could. The sun reflected off the faceted high gables of the Hall and cast multiple shadows of the tower at the square's center. The noon sun had begun to raise a brittle dry smell from the flagstones. His thick-soled shoes slapped smartly and he noticed that the Alveans nearby made no such noise as they walked. He would have to learn the trick; maybe it had something to do with the low gravity and the curious rolling gait most of the obese natives acquired.

Danon was lounging in a shadowed portico, smiling at Skallon as he approached. The boy wore a formal robe, tailored well for his size, a pleasing array of webbed blue and green. The weave was appropriate for workers in service, which of course Danon would be when he came to maturity.

"The wind blows against us," Skallon said as he stepped into the bluish shadows beside Danon. He liked this particularly Alvean mode of expression, combining an obvious physical fact with an implication of their overall state.

"I wish I had a clearer idea of what we are seeking."

"So do we."

"In these bleak times the unusual is commonplace."

"It will pass," Skallon said, without for a moment believing it. Danon seemed an overly serious boy, his face lined more deeply than other children his age. Skallon felt he ought to lift the boy's spirits somehow.

"I heard a whisper in the market stalls just now. It may be false, of course," Danon said hesitantly.

"Fain's kind of sour on this approach. Anything new . . ."

"The time for the Central Assembly has been advanced, they say."

"It's not due for five days."

"It comes this afternoon."

"Oh." Skallon nodded rapidly. "Any reason why?"

"Unease, they whisper in the markets. Disruption. The plagues whittle away at our congruence."

"Um. Maybe so."

"What else?"

"The Changeling," Skallon said slowly. "The more

centralized power and decision-making becomes, the easier it is to disrupt."

"By disguising himself as . . . ?"

"Anyone he likes."

Skallon crossed the square again. Ahead of him a woman whimpered, cried out, staggered, fell. A knot of men nearby looked at her sprawled body for a long moment and then began edging away. Skallon knelt and studied her glassy face. He tested for Vertil; the plate clouded pink.

When he told Fain the older man grimaced. "So he's using Vertil still. Must have a lot of it. While we've been eating dust he's been scooting up through the Alvean hierarchy."

Skallon hesitated to tell him about the Central Assembly, and then hit upon the right approach.

"This meeting is different. It's more important, all castes are present. So *we* can get in. Doubluths send delegates."

"And they all know each other. We'll stick out," Fain said sourly.

"Not for a while. Doubluths are scattered. Representatives come from several outlying districts. We can squeeze in."

"Um. Late afternoon?" Skallon nodded. "All right. We'll do it. There doesn't seem much else we can try." Fain petted Scorpio and said, "Help me get him into that damned cart. We'll have to wheel him back to that stinkhole of a hotel."

"Good, good." Skallon draped a cloak over Scorpio and managed to block the dog from view as they made him jump up into the crude wooden cart. "I don't think I can go back with you, though."

"Why the hell not?"

"Danon and I are going to filter through the central

section near the Great Hall. We need to know more about the timing of the Assembly."

"Um. I'm not hauling Scorpio back by myself."

"Well, all right, I'll—"

"Forget it." Fain smiled. "Come here!" he called to a passing man. The man was a hot brownnut seller and, thinking he had made a sale, scurried over on his good leg. "Nuts. Two," Fain murmured, breathing directly in the man's wrinkled face.

"You're—" Skallon began.

"Quiet." Fain waved him away. The man's eyes glazed over after a moment and his knees sagged. "Stand!" Fain ordered in his rough Alvean accent.

The man staggered, as though drowsy, but remained erect. No one in the busy square seemed to have noticed.

"That is an unjustifiable risk." Skallon whispered fiercely. "You shouldn't even be prepped on Vertil."

Fain smiled without humor and shrugged off Skallon's intent stare. "It's a reasonable solution, right? We've got to split up, you said that yourself. So I arrange a little extra help. To pull that damned cart."

Fain pushed the man toward the cart. "Pick up the braces." He turned back to Skallon, the wind billowing his tentlike Doubluth robes. "The Changeling isn't the only one who can use this stuff. It's a tool, Skallon. Remember that."

Darkness swarms on the horizon. The blue frosted
light of the fierce star seeps through clouds. It scatters
among the brown-crusted stones of the houses, finds
the Changeling scurrying like an Alvean through
throngs, crowds, packed streets. It loves the odd song
of these people, senses their slow rhythm of careworn
pain. It rounds a corner, keeping well away from
Fain. They flutter in the distance as it moves forward
and back, always beyond reach. This is the Dance, the
Art, this merciless murder of minutes, as time layers
forces against the Norms. There is time in these mass-
es of swollen faces, time to smell the aroma of the
thin Alvean life. To lick of it. To spin amid its grind-
ing logic. And yet always—as the Hotel looms—to focus on the men ahead, their thick reason, their brim-
ming brains filled with the Lie. It has been to the
Hotel before, has seeped in through cracks and half-
opened windows, rubbed the flaking walls, felt what
must happen here. The weave of Alvean and Earther
is complex and worthy of tasting. Shall the Changeling take one of them? Shall it make an entrance, slip
lightly into their small Dance? Yes. The idea rises and
at once is true: yes. They are bags of decaying meat,
teeth shiny, skin flecked with vast pores, a sheen of
grease coating them, food wedged between teeth,
worn with bruises and sores and calluses. They ooze.

They stink. It loves them, wants to be them, must
have what world they know and can share. But which?
The choice must extend the Dance, make it full and
rich and long. But which shall he take? It walks the
nearby streets, sucking in life, and thinking. Yes. But
which?

5

They moved through the scattered stalls and gaudy,
aged decorations of the Fest. The streets were laid out
in the usual utilitarian grid, imposing a monotony on
Kalic that the inhabitants seemed forever warring
against. At each rectilinear intersection a small patch
of flowering bushes formed the focus of streamers,
filmy and thick with script writing. Each streamer
anchored on a building, frequently in the mouths of
yawning animal statuettes, gargoyles sporting strange
wings, claws, human breasts, even ancient eye specta-
cles and crutches. Skallon could not puzzle out these
weird beasts and when he asked Danon, the boy
shrugged. "The ancients left them," he said simply, as
though that explained everything.

"The early laser craftsmen?"

"No." Beneath his hood Danon screwed up his eyes
toward the high pinnacles of an especially ornate
building, heavily crusted with the grinning animals.
Some looked very nearly like men. "The work is too

smooth for that. Only a master can carve a scalloped
curve with a laser. No, that is hand work."

"But surely laser buffers are common on Alvea."

"Oh. Uh, I don't *verstet* the term."

"A small rotating disc. On one face are fixed tiny
carbon dioxide lasers. Use it like a brush, just above
the working surface. The many beams blend together.
The more you press, the more stone ablates away."

"I see. Yes, I believe the carpenters . . ."

"The Jalantakii?"

"Yes, yes. I have heard them talk about such crafts."

"They do this work still?"

"They, they must. Perhaps you do not understand . . ."

"Oh, I do," Skallon hastened to reassure the boy. Beneath Danon's cowl his expression, half-shadowed,
was difficult to read. "I understand the unique roles
on Alvea."

"Earthers never seem to . . ."

"Well, they are ignorant. Even Earthers are often
stupid," Skallon said expansively, to show he regarded
the issue as a laughing matter.

"We have noticed."

"In our own ancient days—almost prehistoria—some
societies on Earth believed as you do. That individuals must live their lives in certain well-specified ways.
That a man born as a tailor should die as a tailor."

"Tey lore?"

"A maker of robes. *Bulindaharin*. There, that's a
robe shop on the corner."

Danon studied the cramped little store front, rich
with displayed fabrics, as though he had just realized
its function. "My father—Kish, I mean—has not told
me of these."

"No need to. You're not slaves to an immense mass
of cultural data, the way we are. That's your secret

strength." Skallon felt a certain satisfying pride at being able to tell a native Alvean something of his home world. But then, a mere boy would not be terribly sophisticated, particularly in an information-poor sociometric as this.

"All lives come to all men at some time," Danon said, with the tone of someone reciting chapter and verse.

"The Twelfth Assertive, right?" Skallon beckoned Danon toward an open-air cafe, half-deserted, where men and women lounged and sipped drinks beneath the noonday sun. "I think I know them pretty well. Let's have something."

Skallon plopped down awkwardly in a chair at the patio edge. Danon stopped, looked around, shuffled his feet to and fro.

"Come on, sit."

"I would rather not."

"Why?"

"Well, perhaps for you . . . But I am not of your caste."

"I don't *have* a caste. Oh, I see—Doubluth, you mean? What does that matter?"

"This is not the place appropriate for me, a server."

"Oh, oh, I see," Skallon said in a suddenly hushed voice. "Where should we be?"

"Over there." Danon gestured unobstrusively—so as not to appear to order about a Doubluth, Skallon realized—at a smaller area nearby. The tables and seats were noticeably different, smaller and made of old plankings. It was also nearer the banging kitchen doors.

Once seated, Skallon let Danon order for them—a correct gesture, he remembered from his faxes—and soon was sipping a greenish bowl of mild, frosted syrup. Banks of skeleton fronds clattered high over their heads. The street nearby was a steadily growing surge of people and small steam carts. The exodus homeward for the long afternoon had begun. Kalic would sort itself, for the intense hours of the day, into hearthside groups. After the midday they would return to a caste grouping, for laboring. To Earthers this always seemed an unnecessary luxury and a dreadful waste of time. Skallon understood the social reasons for it, but even to him the logic appeared a bit thin. Centuries ago, genetic alterations made Alveans immune to the high ultraviolet flux. So why keep the anachronism of the midday refuge-seeking?

"Is anything in this crowd—" he swept a hand toward the murmuring street traffic "—unusual?"

"If you mean, would the Changeling stand out . . . no." Danon drank his syrup eagerly, not looking up. "I think we will learn little in the streets now."

Skallon thought, *That's for me to decide,* and then realized the boy was merely trying to be helpful. "Why did you recommend we do this after leaving the square, then?"

Danon peered at him impassively. "It kept us away from that . . . creature. And from . . ."

Skallon laughed. "And Fain?" He sucked noisily and heartily at his syrup, and then, recalling that on Alvea this was a gesture of contempt for the cuisine, looked around guiltily. No one seemed to have noticed. Thick-necked Alveans continued their low mutter of conversation. "You don't like the dog or its master, eh?"

"It is a strange one."

"You mean Fain, or Scorpio?" Skallon asked merrily.

Danon smiled. "The croaking animal. Is it truly the only way to find this other kind of man?"

"No, not really. But the dog noses into things, can move around, and doesn't need repairs. We've got lots

of gear that will ferret out a Changeling. But it's
heavy. On an operation like this, carrying everything
on our backs, Scorpio is handy. You know, Scorpio
wouldn't seem so alien if you'd grown up with dogs.
The Alvean colonizers decided dogs were unholy, according to what I read. They're really quite nice,
though."

"Fain *likes* the . . . animal?"

"Sure. Who else can he afford to like?"

"I find that difficult to believe."

"It's true. Dogs are a great luxury item on Earth.
Fain gets one for free—it's walking, talking equipment. And they've been through a lot, killed a number
of Changelings together. If men and dogs had still
been working together when the Alvean settlers left
Earth—herding, hunting, things like that—maybe the
ancient working stocks of dogs would've come to Alvea."

"I am glad they did not."

"Um." Skallon mused for a moment, reflecting that
he had a lingering respect for Scorpio. Perhaps that
feeling alone marked him as, basically, an eternal
Earther. He could never shake free of his origins.

6

Fain was in a sour mood when Skallon returned to the
Battachran Hotel. Skallon had left Danon at a nearby
government office to eavesdrop on conversations. It

seemed a pointless exercise. The Changeling was subtle, and surely would not cause a great stir before revealing its plans. But Danon was enthusiastic and leaving the boy where something might conceivably happen gave Skallon something to report to Fain.

Not that it did any good. Fain looked at Skallon for a long moment, slitting his eyes slightly so that crow's feet showed far back into his temples. "The kid's useless, Skallon."

"Perhaps. But we need a guide. He's small. He won't be noticed. Until Alveans formally enter their caste-roles they are nothing."

"How about Kish?"

Skallon snorted. "I thought we agreed he's unreliable. No judgment. And as I was saying, he's in a formal caste-role. As a server, an innkeeper, he cannot even approach some other castes. Not now, in a holy time."

"Uh huh." Fain lost interest.

"Where's Scorpio?"

"Asleep."

"He's been sleeping most of the time since we got here."

Fain's head snapped up, rigid. He scowled at Skallon. "He's not a normal dog. Not one of those puffy little doll dogs for old ladies with money to waste."

"I know, but—"

"Scorpio's got to strain every sense he has to tell a Changeling. Changeling skin fluids smell nearly the same as humans. We—"

"I agree. Let him sleep. We'll need him at the Great Hall this afternoon. Look—" he tried to find another subject "—come on and have lunch."

"That glop? I'll eat protein packs."

"Okay."

Skallon walked around the hotel checking all the

entrances and exits. It was an elementary precaution, since he had become disoriented in the night before, arriving late and tired. The Battachran was an old, rambling assembly of stone and wood, some parts seemingly balanced precariously on crumbling foundations. The lighter gravity made architecture simpler, more airy and fluid. He skirted around an immense fetid trash heap at the back. Evidently garbage collection occurred infrequently, or maybe never.

Flies lifted as a swarm from the tangled waste and moved off like a buzzing dust cloud. The amber fog trailed behind a small party of mourners eating their ritual fruit, a kind of blue pomegranate. The bier was of oily wood, the corpse wrapped in a dusky rag. The party marched slowly across the broken ground behind the Battachran, taking their time. One occasionally banged a deep bass gong. On a distant hill loomed the Alvean burial markers, triangles tilted this way and that in hummocky fields.

"Come. Rest."

He turned. Joane stood beside him, holding a half-filled pail of slops.

"Here, let me—" Before he could move she pitched the contents onto the heap. She smiled and beckoned him inside.

The sudden change from Alvea's sunlight to the unlighted corridors blinded him momentarily. She took his hand—a silken feel, cool—and led him a few steps. Then a door opened and he blinked.

It was the round, high-ceilinged Communal he had seen that morning. Fully twenty people crowded around the small tables, eating and talking at once. Oil lamps flickered their light over swarthy, lined faces. Each man or woman seemed a study in character, so different were each of them. On Earth an unblemished, smooth face was the ideal. Thanks to cos-

metic treatments, most people attained it for nearly all
their lives. Women of twenty and sixty were often in-
distinguishable. Joane tugged at his hand and when
he looked at her, her beauty seemed all the more at-
tractive because he knew that in time it would erode
and wither and vanish.

It was the traditional Communal. For those who did
not purchase a meal from the hotel the room had an
array of cooking pots, toasting forks, clinker coal fires
in small black vessels. The work of tending fires,
sweeping and clearing was done by the hotel, but otherwise there was no supervision. In ancient times access to a Communal meant life itself, shelter from the
spitting star. Joane led him to a table and sat, saying,
"I must oversee the kitchen labor, but we can talk be-
tweentimes. Lunch, then?" Skallon nodded. "Your
preference?"

He described an Alvean meal, from memory. She
frowned at one or two dishes and remarked that they
were very old, but she would see. She left him for a
moment and Skallon eavesdropped on conversations
nearby. A knot of women brooded over a relative,
driven to distraction and poverty by the plagues, who
was reduced to eating damaged vegetables and wore
newspapers for underclothes and made trousers from
a grain sack, giving up his robes.

Skallon noticed a chirruping note and found its
source: a songbird in a tiny plastic cage, blind. He
remembered that Kalic had been extensively mined
some centuries ago until men discovered the region
was riddled with vast domes of poison gas. Even now
occasional seams buckled and split and the Communals, buried deep, were first affected. The bird was
sensitive and would die before the people lost consciousness.

Alvea seemed in some ways like Earth, and in others vastly different. There were no crust deposits left to gobble on Earth; Skallon was sure even a deadly gas would've been turned to some use on Earth by now.

Kish appeared, slapping patrons on the shoulder and making ritual hand gestures of welcome. Kish greeted Skallon without any extra show and then abruptly moved away as Joane approached. "The first ladling," she said and set a plate of ruddy, spiced meat before him.

"Why did Kish leave?"

"He leaves me to my life," she murmured simply, and sat.

"You don't feel constraint?"

"How?"

"Your role. Granted, you're married to an inn-keeper. But you're not pinned to that for life."

"That is my station."

"Until death?" Skallon looked up from cutting the meat, which was unexpectedly thick and heavy. "You believe you will . . ." he rummaged for the right phrase. ". . . Be everything, every*one*, eventually?"

"It is proven."

"Gommerset's Four Hundred."

"Yes, and research since then. Research conducted here on Alvea. But surely you know and understand this. Otherwise you would not sense Alvea as you do."

"Ah. Yes." Skallon didn't know how to tell her that he knew it all, but nobody on Earth any longer believed it. "You partake of the, ah, absolute monism."

"We prefer to call it, so Earthers will understand, a nondualism."

"Which implies something like, well, a cyclic universe."

"So it does. Perhaps." She smiled. "That will be understood later."

Skallon made a show of digging into his meat. A sauce arrived and he heaped it on; it tasted vaguely of grannet nuts. He didn't want to tell Joane that Gommerset's data had been invalidated over five hundred years ago.

The famous Four Hundred were apparently well-verified cases of hypnotic recall. Under ordinary hypnosis, they recalled details of past lives in uncanny detail. Wherever the details could be checked, they proved valid. There were ship builders for Ferdinand and Isabella, farmers in old East Anglia, midwives from the Rome of Claudius. And some subjects had not one recalled life, but many. Historians nailed down one case with twenty-seven checked identities.

When Gommerset published his studies, religious revivals of every shade swept Earth. Reincarnation seemed to be a simple, hard fact.

"The subtle body passes on," Joane said lightly, as though she were making simple social conversation. "We migrate to another transitory tenement."

"We call that—those ideas—the Nondualistic Phase," Skallon muttered, chewing. He felt he had to say something. But he couldn't lie to her.

"Oh?" Polite interest.

"Our intellectual historians call it that. It fits with the cyclic repeating model of Earth history. Gommerset—well, not him, but the response to his data—was a product of the collapse in the twenty-first century."

"Alvea is its flowering," she said smoothly.

"Um. So it is. The ramscoop ships spread Gommersetism before it was really checked. That was what really killed it, too—on Earth, I mean."

"No one believes there?"

Skallon shook his head. "Without the ramscoops—or the faster-than-light transports, later—the Nondualistic

Phase would've won out. Just the way it did in prehistoria—I mean, the really ancient societies of Earth.
Most of Asia, that area . . . it's a continent," he
added, realizing that she knew nothing of Earth's geography. "Those nations stopped expanding, lost mo-
mentum, turned inward. Nondualistic sociometric is
fine for that—it lacks the tension between two poles,
so nothing happens."

"Nothing *has* to happen, my friend." She put her
hand over his. Her fingers were cool.

"But things *do*. Events have their own dynamics.
Unless Earth had gotten the ramscoops, we would've
settled down to gradual poverty, no resources, the
whole mess," he said earnestly, jabbing the air with a
forefinger.

"You have no resources now."

"Yes, but we can *get* them. From you, from the
other worlds. The Cooperative Empire concept is a
whole new era in human history. A Nondualistic
Earth couldn't provide the advanced technology, the
transport, the communication, the sociometric calcula-
tions and theory."

"I wonder if we need them."

"Of course you do. Ramscoops are available to
everyone, you have two in orbit now for loading. But
they're too slow to knit together the Cooperative Empire. There would be no true cross-cultural contacts
without the faster than light ships. Alvea would be in
a cultural dead end." He didn't add that it seemed to
him Alvea was very nearly stagnant anyway. That was
probably a passing effect, due to the plagues.

"The ships destroyed your faith."

"No, the data did. Nobody could duplicate Gommerset's results."

"Even using his Four Hundred?"

"Well, those were obviously jigged-up. Somebody'd been tampering with their frontal lobes, for sure."

"Gommerset?"

"Don't know. He was dead by the time a complete analysis could be done."

"It is simpler to slander a dead man."

"Well, look. I don't want to make a big point about this."

"You do not want to believe. Earth does not want to believe."

"Ah . . ." This time it was Skallon who reached out and took her hand. "Believe, not believe—hell, I don't *care.*"

"I think you do."

"If I die and come back in some other job, as an agrimech or something, fine. Nothing I can do about it. Same if I just wink out, *pfffft.* So I don't worry."

"Everyone thinks of these things. Everyone yearns."

"I don't yearn to return in every station of life. But that's what you think, isn't it? Since you'll have an infinite number—all right, a large number—of lives, why bother to change your social role now?"

"Our way gives inner calm."

"I'd rather have the, the pleasure of new things." He gazed at her seriously. His head buzzed slightly from the kerrin wine in his food. The room rippled with many intertwined conversations; the air was heady and filled with scents.

"You need the calming, too. All do."

Skallon declined the mellow sweets that were provided for dessert, so they left the Communal early, before the crowd had swelled to its peak. From the muted noise of talking and eating, the crisp snap of the open fire, she led him into the back corridors of the hotel. They passed Fain's room and Skallon felt an impulse to knock, but suppressed it. He needed rest, and the search in the Great Hall later would require all his alertness.

Joane opened a rough-cut door for him, into what he at first thought was his room. But it was larger, the windows giving out upon the rear fields. The air in here was fresher than below and it cleared his head.

She came to him as the door clicked shut. Joane was much smaller than Skallon but she seemed to engulf him, a scent rising between them of a new warm animal heat. He felt all elbows and knees. She murmured words as she kissed his neck; he could not understand them, could not focus on what he was doing.

Gradually he relaxed. It was not like all the other times, when he had been conscious of each move, each gesture, the implications of what the woman wanted and expected of him. Now, with Joane, all flowed together. Clasps parted, limbs slid smoothly through and around each other. He tipped over, they both fell with dreamlike lightness (*the gravity?* he thought; but no, it wasn't that) and coiled each into different forms, figures, enfoldings.

In a drowsy slowness of time he watched her beneath him, the pink circle of her mouth enclosing him in a deep rhythm that sent waves up into a space between his mind and his heart. Something seemed to ache in him, distantly. A tremor of odd, displaced fear shot through him. He had been with women before, of course, done all these things . . . but now they seemed to have new resonances deep within him, they struck strange chords. He moved her, opened her, entered. *Ah.* A thudding rhythm. When he came it was as though a sound burst out of him. He expected to hear it echo in the close room. When he drove deep he felt a constricted explosion and wrenched into it, coming, driving, deep and shuddering. The scented spicy reek of Alvea opened to him, the wash of heaving sound, a silken sheen that spun him down into more recesses of Joane, farther into a measureless darkness that swallowed him up, gasping, and he clawed to a new shore of her, orgasm complete and panting, solidly full, murmuring in her ear, and she whispering in short rasping sibilant sounds to him, words that coaxed him further into a gentle soft rest where he lay, sucking air and eyes lidded, mumbling, dozing, falling into sleep with Joane wrapped in his arms, a blurred center for him to rest upon.

7

He awoke, nostrils filled with the heavy musty scent of Joane's hair. He rolled slightly away from her and sat up. He felt thoroughly rested, though a glance at his watch said they had left the Communal less than an Earth hour before. The motion of sitting up caused a skittering rustle in a corner. Skallon saw two small animals, four-legged, pause and return his inspection, thick meaty tails twitching. Their mean little ferret eyes blazed up at him. They were ratlike, but larger. He wondered if these creatures would attack. He decided not. Unless they were deranged from disease or hunger, advancing on a man would be suicidal. His logic was rewarded a moment later when the two twitched, glanced sidewise, and vanished in a blur of motion into a hole in the wall that looked impossibly small for them.

"Hmmmm?" Joane's eyes fluttered and she was awake.

"I've got to go."

"Ummm. Where?"

"Sniffing out the Changeling."

"Oh."

In the afternoon sun which streamed through the thick windows Joane seemed strangely light and airy, her skin a pearly luster. She was the same anonymous color as Skallon and Fain; indeed, the same as everyone on Earth now, after centuries of homogenizing cross-currents in human cultures. The Gommerset believers who had colonized Alvea were primarily from Africa. Skallon had seen a few darker people in the streets, but even in as relatively minor and isolated a corner of the Cooperative Empire as this, all the races had been blended by time. Joane's black hair was not the racial standard; it showed traces of brownish flecks as she stretched and groaned.

"It happened to us awfully fast, didn't it?" Skallon said.

"Next time we can take longer."

"No, I mean . . . we met only yesterday."

"Oh. Well, I gave a clear sign."

"At lunch?"

"This morning."

"Ah. When you served me breakfast."

"Yes. You know Alvea."

"So you knew I would take it the correct way."

"Of course." Her voice again had that calm certainty in him that Skallon had sensed the first evening, at the temple. She smiled.

"It was wonderful."

"It was." She leaned over and kissed him, her

breasts swaying. "You are a fine man. I knew that when first we spoke."

"I hope I have not . . . you see, I am not totally wise about your customs . . . I simply . . ."

"You worry about Kish."

"Yes."

"What he will say. If he should be told. How we do these things."

"Yes. All that."

"Do not worry about Kish."

Skallon thought that she was certainly right. He would be here a few days, maybe a little longer. No need to get knee deep in Alvean entanglements. No point in it at all.

"You are a lion in the barnyard." She kissed him again.

Skallon smiled. "Maybe. It for sure smells like a barnyard around here."

"I will tell you of Kish."

While he got dressed, she did.

Skallon found Fain on a side porch of the hotel, pacing.

"Where were you?"

"Resting."

"Not in your room."

"That's right." Skallon didn't volunteer anymore and Fain didn't ask. Danon came shuffling onto the porch, scuffing up a film of dust as he chewed on a stalk of some purplish plant. Skallon recognized it as a cooked qantimakas. "Okay, Danon's here. Let's go."

"You're on the bounce today, Skallon," Fain said with surprising bitterness.

Skallon ignored the tone of the words. "What's wrong?"

"We need Scorpio to pick out the Changeling in a

crowd. It'll be impossible, just using our instrument diagnostic packages."

"Sure."

"Scorpio's sick."

Fain kicked at a porch railing and the wood splintered, cracked, revealed a rotten seam like a brown thread running its entire length.

"Huh?" He glanced at Danon, who shrugged, a universal gesture. "How?"

"Eating this crap food. He liked that rotten meat, gobbled it down. Now he's shat a boxfull of the stuff all over himself."

"Oh. Try something from the kit? We've got lots of bioreactants. They're for humans, but some of them—"

"I gave him three. No results."

"Well, they take time. The system—"

"We haven't *got* time. The damned Changeling is out there and we sit here, pinned down to this fleabag hotel. Look—" He gestured sweepingly at the bumpy, jumbled street of houses on either side of the hotel. They seemed to crowd together, all odd corners and misaligned walls. Kilometers beyond jutted the pinnacles of Kalic center. They were straight and erect, solid chunks of rock. Clearly more important than this scruffy street. The tallest was the Great Hall. "He's out there. Probably running the whole damned halfbreed planet by now. And we—"

"Let's go on without the dog."

Fain looked at him blankly. "Impossible."

"We can at least identify some suspects. Then Scorpio can nail the right one. Or we can use the instruments."

"I don't like it," Fain said. He absent-mindedly kicked again at the porch railing, staggering slightly backwards in the bulky Doubluth disguise. "Too chancy." But clearly he was thinking it over.

"We must go soon," Danon put in. "The Assembly will be—"

"Look, I think it's too risky," Fain said abruptly, ignoring Danon. "The Changeling's got Vertil. You know what that means? We've lost every advantage we had, plus Scorpio."

"The instruments—"

"*Frange* the instruments. Take too long to set up. Can be thrown off by anything, even the smell of cooking food. A Changeling will be klicks away by the time you've got everything plugged in."

"Not if one of us is holding a gun to his head."

"If it lets you, you mean. It's got Vertil, remember? It can use Alveans against us. Hell, it's even worse than that. It can interrogate an Alvean under the Vertil, pick up all the information it needs—then take the Alvean's place. That's the only trouble Changelings had on Earth—they didn't know what their assumed identities were supposed to do, how they acted."

"Okay, it's tough. But we've got to do it."

"Yeah," Fain said sullenly. He turned and looked at Kalic.

Fain's outburst had shaken Skallon more than he wanted to show. Probably it was the dog's falling sick; anyway, something had gotten under Fain's skin. For the first time Skallon realized how hopelessly outclassed they were in this operation. Two men, obviously unsuited for working together, against a Changeling. Earth must have been stupid to try this maneuver. Skallon knew it was a desperation move, that they'd probably fail and be picked up again, but even so, things hadn't looked this bad when they'd landed.

. . . *Fail and be picked up* . . . It suddenly struck Skallon that, if they didn't get to the Changeling in time and Alvea disintegrated into weary disorder,

Earth might cut its losses and not bother to pick them
up. Why expend an expensive overlight cruise on two
failures?

But if he and Fain were stuck here, they'd die. They
weren't adapted for Alvea. There were delicate bio-
logical adjustments they lacked, and of course, the increased ultraviolet flux. A few years and they would
sicken. If they weren't knifed by anti-Earthers first.
And—

Fain spun around from the railing. "We go. Let's try
it." Something had been restored in his voice. It had
regained its edge of authority.

"Great." Skallon motioned to Danon. They went out
a side entrance of the hotel, moving swiftly.

Skallon looked back, hoping to wave good-bye to
Joane, but he sighted no familiar face at a window. He
had wanted to talk to her more. She was quite sensitive, with that business about serving him breakfast.
On Earth a girl would've simply given him a tap and
a feel, maybe a murmured invitation and her bunk
number. Then, next break, they'd meet and undress
without a word, and she'd rock herself to a grunting
completion, using him as a convenient fleshy ram.
Afterward they'd gossip impersonally, perhaps agree
to meet and hump again, but just as likely never give
each other another passing glance in a corridor. But
here on Alvea, a woman served a meal, and that was
nothing and everything. On Alvea, men and women
were not yet highly civilized, neurosis-free animals.
He thought again, wistfully, of Joane's delicate touch
as she caressed him. Incredible, that so much had
happened to him, that a whole new world lay open
before him, in just a matter of two days. He recalled
the artful way she had coaxed him on over lunch. It
did not occur to him that, when she had served that
first breakfast to him, she had also waited on Fain.

"But this is the best route, the only way of reaching the Great Hall quickly," said Danon, squirming in Fain's tight grasp. "To go another way would require entering those streets frequented by the beasts."

Fain understood the meaning of that—he had once accidentally stumbled upon such a street and its thick odor of manure—but still shook his head. Clutching the boy's arm, he turned to Skallon. "I don't think it's wise. There are too many people out today. Anyone could be the Changeling and we'd never know."

"So?" said Skallon calmly. "We're disguised—he won't recognize us."

Fain knew that wasn't true—after the air base, the Changeling would surely know him again—but that wasn't why he wanted to avoid these streets. No, the Changeling had nothing to do with it. The reason was simply the mass of people found here, hundreds of them, walking, strolling, standing, talking. In his life, Fain had never endured such a great clot of humanity—pseudo men or otherwise—in such a limited space. It made him uncomfortable, nervous, too easily spooked. He had never liked people coming close to him, and he especially didn't like Alveans touching him. "There's got to be another way."

Skallon shrugged. "Danon ought to know the city better than we do and—" Skallon peered at the dark yellow sun, dust-cloaked, hugging the horizon "—we're already late."

"All right." Seeing no alternative, Fain released the boy, who immediately danced ahead, slipping between the broad wobbling bellies of two approaching Alveans. More slowly, Fain and Skallon followed. The Alveans, nodding slightly, made way for them, but there were others—many, many others, Fain observed—beyond.

"The boy is bright," Skallon said. "You don't know what an immense help he's been to me during my observations of the city. He's really as quick-witted as most grown men on Earth."

"That's not saying much," Fain said. He knew, as well as Skallon did, that simple genetics explained that: space colonization had drawn only the brightest.

"Of course Kish isn't his real father."

"He's not?" Fain strove to appear interested, while keeping his eyes focused on the threatening crowd around them. They passed a series of street stalls, where food, clothing, and goods made from the skins of dead animals were sold amid shouts, screams, and howls. The mob was even thicker here. A fat thigh brushed against his. Fain sucked in his breath and bit his lip.

"Oh, no," said Skallon. "It's complicated, but if you understand the various local cultural patterns, it does make sense. Kish, when he was a member of the trader caste, was married to another woman, one much closer to his own age, but she died in one of the plagues without bearing him a son. Now, among the trader caste, the presence of a male heir is almost a necessity, because trading rights and franchises are always passed through the generations. Without a son and the guarantee that his business would survive after him, Kish found it very difficult to obtain new contracts. So what he had to do was marry again, but there was a problem there, too, because I gather the main fault for the lack of a son in the first place was Kish's own."

"He told you this," said Fain, who whispered, still unaccustomed to a world in which electronic listening devices were unknown. Skallon insisted that for an Alvean eavesdropping was a worse sin than murder.

"No, not him. Joane did. She's told me a lot about local customs and mores."

"I see."

"Well, the upshot of it is that Kish found a bride who was already pregnant with another man's child, and that was Joane. Her father was a very minor trader and he eagerly made a marriage contract with Kish, despite the great disparity in ages, which would normally have presented a major stumbling block. There was only one stipulation, and that was inserted at Joane's insistence. Apparently, she disliked Kish from the beginning and didn't want to be forced into having sexual relations with him."

"And he agreed?"

"Yes, of course. He needed the son."

"But he's not a trader now. He's an innkeeper."

"Yes, and that's what happened next. Joane's father, it seems, was so proud of the agreement with Kish that he couldn't keep quiet. When Kish's trading contacts heard the story, they laughed at him. Kish felt humiliated in the eyes of his peers and his business dwindled to nothing. He was fortunate to find the Battachran Hotel to keep."

"He was an idiot. Women aren't that hard to find."

"But now he hates Joane. He blames her and Danon for all his troubles."

"He should."

"Not that I blame him," Skallon said, with an odd

tremor in his voice. "Was it her fault she can't stand him?"

"She could pretend."

"Pretend what?"

"That she thinks he's the hottest item on this planet."

"But he disgusts her."

"So?"

"So it would be impossible to pretend about that."

Fain could have laughed, but he let the matter drop. Someday he'd tell Skallon the history of the art of female prostitution, but not now. Skallon obviously was sleeping with the woman. That was risky enough. Fain wasn't going to worsen the problem by making him defensive.

"Is that the place there?" asked Fain, pointing ahead to where the spiked roof of a wooden building rose above the ramshackle trading huts surrounding it. Danon had paused in the middle of a crowd and was waving at them to hurry.

"Yes," Skallon said. "That must be the Great Hall." All of a sudden he was nearly running, brushing past Danon and vaulting ahead. Fain had to waddle furiously to keep pace. "I haven't seen it this close before. This is wonderful—this is the greatest day in my life."

"Keep your damn voice down."

"You can't understand how I feel," Skallon said, clearly hurt that Fain did not share his enthusiasm.

But Fain was hurrying now, too. If nothing else, the fabled Central Assembly of the Great Hall would provide some relief from these crowded, stinking streets.

Once each Alvean year, Fain knew, the leaders of the various castes gathered in all the planet's major cities to decide in a series of open meetings the general patterns to be followed by the entire world during the time of the next year. Fain thought the whole idea was crazy: decisions had to be reached on the spot—they could never be planned that far in advance. But Skallon insisted that for the Alveans with their weak governmental structure, the meetings were a necessary and very sensible democratic institution. Fain just shrugged. He also knew what wondrous opportunities such a system offered a Changeling.

Danon had left them at the door. On their own, Fain and Skallon managed to squeeze into the interior of the Great Hall. Despite its size, the hall was already packed past the bursting point. Fain saw every conceivable shade of the rainbow represented by someone's billowing attire. Like every public place on the planet, the hall exuded a stale pungent odor. The babble of shrill, shouting voices stung his ears.

Spotting an empty chair off to his left, Fain started to move toward it, but Skallon grabbed his arm.

"No, not there."

"Why not?" Fain had to shout to be heard. "My feet are killing me." The extra padding he wore more than offset the weak Alvean gravity; Fain found that his legs ached constantly.

"Because we have to be seated with our own caste, with the other Doubluths." Skallon pointed to a distant splotch of dull purple. "There they are—over there."

Fain suppressed a groan. Skallon, as eager as ever, began clearing a path through the mob. Fain had said nothing to Skallon, but he seriously wondered whether their presence here was serving much good. Would the Changeling, fully aware that it was being pursued, be apt to make any sort of move in such an open and obvious place? Logic said that it wouldn't. Changelings knew their work well, and there were a hundred subtle ways of bringing down a planet without ever once attending a meeting like this. But Changelings also liked to do brazen things. They liked to taunt and sneer and take crazy risks. Changelings never thought at all, never planned, and that was what made them so dangerous.

At the edge of the purple section of seats—Fain noted sadly that every chair was already filled—Skallon glided to a stop, laid his hands neatly together under his chin, and murmured, "We have come to express a desire to join our brothers in consultation."

Fain, who had been thoroughly briefed on the necessity for this ritual, did likewise. For a long moment, however, none of the Doubluths seated near them gave the slightest hint of recognition. Most seemed busily engaged chatting with a neighbor. Their words came too quickly for Fain to overhear.

Then, somewhere near the middle of the group, a man stood up, smiled, waved, and began moving toward him. Fain, his hands still tightly clasped, watched the Alvean's progress with some interest. This was the first really old man he could recall seeing on the planet. He was as fat and grotesque as any of the others, but even the soft folds of flesh on his cheeks and chin failed to conceal the deep lines and wrinkles that creased his face. "The senior," whispered Skallon. "You know what to do."

Fain didn't need to nod. This was not a moment he had been anticipating. As far as he was concerned, it was only another reason why he should have stayed away today. Only Skallon's practical ignorance—and the possibility of some severe blunder—had convinced him finally of the need to attend.

The old Alvean, the senior, bowed deeply in front of Skallon. "I welcome my younger brothers to our congress with much pleasure and delight."

"The pleasure must lie with us," said Skallon. Bending slightly, he lowered his lips and kissed the old Alvean upon the forehead.

Fain, steeling himself with care, edged over until he stood beside the old man. Without a word, he dropped his head and performed the necessary kiss. Skallon had warned him that, because of his still inadequate accent, he should say as little as possible.

There was a taste on Fain's lips that reminded him oddly of old tea.

Skallon said, "I am Thomas and my companion is Joseph. We are both men of the South who journeyed here in order to greet the grandest masters of our craft." Skallon had explained that such pilgrimages, though not common, would create little surprise. The areas near Kalic were dominated by the financial and commercial castes. Doubluths from the agricultural southern continents would find the meetings held here closer to their own interests. Skallon had warned that they might expect to be questioned rather closely by the senior regarding mutual friends and acquaintances. It would be the quickest means possible for determining their own beliefs and concerns. Fain had memorized a few rote phrases regarding the Alvean economy. Otherwise, Skallon would have to lead in this deception.

But the senior, after a murmured "I am Jal," turned away from them and hurried back to his seat.

Fain now noticed that a disturbance had broken out there. One Alvean, surrounded by a crowd of purple-gowned listeners, was waving his fists and shouting. Even Fain could pick out certain repeated words. One was *Earth* and another was *plague*.

The senior, when he arrived, took the wildly gesticulating man by an arm and tried to guide him toward an empty chair away from his crowd of listeners.

The man resisted at first, but the senior appeared to whisper something, and the man, with an angry shrug, finally moved obediently away.

"What was that all about?" Fain said.

Skallon shook his head in apparent concern. "It's not good. The man was complaining that the Doubluth program is a failure because it doesn't call for an end to all interstellar trade."

"So?"

"Well, it's absolutely unheard of for anyone to criticize the program of his own caste. The idea is to come to these meetings and fight with the other castes for your own plan. Without a united front, each caste would be equally weak."

"Then what did the senior say that made him quiet?"

"Only some matter of ritual, I assume. I don't think the man was convinced he was wrong."

But Fain had spotted something that took his attention totally away from Skallon's explanation. It was an empty chair—two of them—at the rear of the Doubluth section.

"Hurry," said Fain, pulling at Skallon's robes.

They reached the empty chairs just before the two men who had temporarily deserted them to listen to the anti-Earth agitator returned.

Fain slid quickly into one chair and pulled Skallon down into the other.

The two Alveans glared but Fain pretended not to see.

After a few moments, the Alveans went away.

"You shouldn't have done that," Skallon said. "As pilgrims, we shouldn't intrude upon our hosts."

"Then stand up and go for a walk," Fain said. "I'm not holding you here."

Skallon grinned. "No, but my feet are. Fain, I'm beginning to understand there's some use for you, after all."

"Now tell that to the Changeling."

"I will. If you'll point him out to me."

"Not yet," Fain murmured. "But soon—damn soon."

The meeting, largely as Fain expected, proved to be a hopeless bore. Fain fought to keep alert, as caste succeeded caste upon a wooden platform in the center of the hall. Each speaker, as nearly as he could determine, rose to offer a detailed and, to Fain, indecipherable plan for running the planet over the course of the next local year. The Changeling, if it was present, gave no obvious sign. The speakers, according to Skallon, were uniformly bland in their words and presentation. Earth was attacked only in the softest and most general terms. The plagues, when they were mentioned at all, were described as a medical problem with possible solutions. The heat in the room, the constant hum of nearby voices, added to Fain's drowsiness. Afternoon stretched invisibly into evening. Night came. Skallon perched on the edge of his seat, swallowing each word. Fain let his eyes close. It was warm. It was cozy. The Changeling had gone far away.

He had no way of telling how long he'd slept before Skallon touched his arm. In an instant, Fain was alert.

"Look," said Skallon, whispering. "I think something's wrong with that man."

Fain looked to where Skallon was pointing. A purple-gowned Doubluth had at last gained the platform. By squinting, Fain thought he could identify the man as Jal, the senior who had greeted them. But Jal wasn't speaking. Instead, his hands held high above his head, his robes twisting with the movement of his body, he seemed to be dancing.

"It's the plague," Skallon whispered.

Fain needed no one to confirm that diagnosis. He sensed that every eye in the hall now watched the jerking, twisting dancer. So far no one had spoken, shouted, or cried out, but an atmosphere of suppressed terror, of panic on the verge of eruption, filled the room.

Then someone shouted. Fain turned to his right and saw the young Doubluth who had caused the earlier disturbance now standing on a chair. "Look," the man cried, pointing toward the platform. "See what they have done to us now."

No one needed to ask what he meant by *they*.

"It is our senior," the man went on. In the silence of the hall, punctuated by the pounding of the senior's dancing feet, his voice boomed like a cannon. "It is my senior and master. They have murdered him. Haven't you been warned? We hold our assembly and speak of wondrous plans, agricultural quotas, and trading rights. We speak, while all about us men die, murdered by the selfish greed of the Earth Consortium and its so-called Cooperative Empire. No, this is blasphemy. It is an obscenity in the eyes of the God with a Million Names."

Fain clutched his arm. "Fain, do something."

Along with everyone else, Fain watched the dancer. The senior moved more slowly now. His arms hung uselessly at his sides. His head jerked spasmodically back and forth. "What do you suggest?"

"Stop him. Stop that man from talking. Can't you see he's trying to blame the Earth for—for that?" He jerked his head toward the platform.

"Maybe he's got a point."

"Fain, that man may be the Changeling."

"And he may not be. Shut up and let me handle this." But Fain made no move to act. For the moment he was content to watch and listen. He did lower his hand and press the comforting bulk of his heatgun.

The speaker was saying, "Watch that man. Watch him dance. See him jerk his head and throw his hands to the sky. He is a puppet. He is a creature controlled by another. He is the Earth's puppet. They have made him dance and—as surely as I stand here now—they will make him die."

Just as the man said that, as if on cue, the dancer on the platform threw back his head, let loose a dreadful shriek of pain and despair, and collapsed in a motionless heap.

"Dead," said Fain, without feeling.

And then the panic—held in check until now both by the dancer and the speaker—broke loose. Men screamed. Men shouted. Chairs fell to the floor. In a mass, everyone seemed to be rushing toward the exits.

Fain held Skallon tightly. He had to shout to be heard over the sudden pandemonium. "Don't move. Stand where you are." Even Fain could feel himself drawn irresistibly toward the fresh air outdoors. But he did not intend to be trampled to death. Not here on Alvea.

Fain led Skallon in the opposite direction from the mob. He kicked a chair out of his way.

"Where are you going?" said Skallon.

Fain pointed to the platform ahead of them. "I want to take a close look at that man."

"But, Fain, he's dead."

"I know that."

"But—but—we—" Skallon kept swiveling his head. The rush of the mob had managed to knock a hole in the wall. Nearly everyone had made it outside by now. Everyone except those broken bodies that lay scattered behind, dropped by the crush of the crowd.

"Skallon, we're safe from any possible plague

strains. There's no reason for us to be afraid. You, of all people, ought to know that."

"Yes, yes, of course. You're right. But—"

Fain made himself pat the other man's arm. "You don't have to explain. Panic is a catching disease. I felt it myself back there."

"It's just hard to think clearly. With all this—all this chaos."

"Yes," Fain said dryly. "Exactly."

He mounted the platform. It was empty, the last place on this world most people would want to be. The sudden excess of empty space came as a welcome relief to Fain. He felt he could think more clearly now.

Taking the dead body of the senior, Fain turned the man over on his broad stomach. Gripping the thick flesh at the back of one arm, he pinched down hard. "There," he said, gesturing at Skallon to look. "I thought this was too good to be true."

Skallon looked but shook his head. "I don't see anything."

"The flesh. It's discolored. See where I'm pinching." He let go of the dead man and stood up. "This man has been hit with an injector—and recently."

"Vertil?"

Fain was already moving away from the platform. He walked quickly but did not run. From outside, he could still hear the loud rumble of the mob, but the interior of the hall was now deserted. "There's no need to inject Vertil. No, I'd guess it was the plague that killed him."

"But the Changeling couldn't have obtained that— not a local strain of plague."

"Then maybe it brought its own."

"But then—we—we—"

"Exactly," said Fain. "We might not be immune."

Skallon, like Fain, began to move quickly, but then a sudden thought seemed to strike him and he slowed. Skallon knew as well as Fain that haste would do them no good now. "Then the Changeling must have been that Alvean, after all. Remember, we saw them standing close together. He could have used the injector then."

"He could have, but so could nearly anyone else." Fain shook his head. "No, I'm not ready to make any definite guesses—not yet."

The way outside was easily enough reached. They picked a path through the broken wall and soon saw the blaze of stars overhead. The crowd had largely dispersed. A few scattered clots of people remained. Fain took a deep breath of clean night air and felt instantly better. He was too tired to stand around listening to a few idiots denouncing the Earth.

"What happened in there, good sirs?" It was the boy, Kish's son—no, Fain corrected himself, Joane's. Apparently he had waited outside the whole time. "Some say it is an outbreak of plague."

"Something like that," said Fain. He gave the boy a gentle push. "Show us the way home and I'll let Skallon here tell you all about it."

As they moved through the twisting streets of the city, as dead and empty now as they had been crowded and alive before, Fain couldn't help drawing Skallon close to him. "That Doubluth—the one who spoke against the Earth—remember him?"

"Yes, of course. And I still think he was the Changeling. Otherwise, the whole thing is just too coincidental."

"Did you notice him when he was speaking?"

"Notice him? What do you mean?"

"His eyes, his stance, the way he was talking."

"Yes. No. I mean, not that carefully. I was watching the senior, I suppose. What are you getting at?"

"Vertil," Fain said. "If anyone in my life was ever acting under the influence of Vertil, it was that man."

"Then—then he wasn't—he couldn't be the Changeling."

"No," said Fain, "but it was there. It was there, and it was very careful to let us know it was there."

Skallon moved in silence for a moment. Ahead in the darkness, Fain could hear the pounding of the boy's feet preceding them. "What does that mean, Fain?"

"I wish I knew." Fain shook his head from side to side. "I really wish I knew."

9

Drawing the comb gently through the soft fur of the dog's back, Fain said, "Now, isn't that better? Don't you feel cleaner?" He and Scorpio were alone in Fain's room. It was late at night, but Fain didn't feel tired. He had spent a good part of the day napping during the meeting at the Great Hall.

Scorpio made a wheezing noise, halfway between pleasure and pain. "Cleaner. But. Sick."

"You are better now," Fain said.

"Sick."

Fain understood. Despite augmentation, Scorpio remained an animal, incapable of drawing keen distinctions concerning the state of his own health. But Fain knew he was right. Scorpio was much improved. In a day or two, he could join the search for the Changeling. If only some way existed for smuggling him inside the Great Hall . . . "But you're going to live."

"I. Will. Not. Die." There was a genuine note of surprise in the dog's tone.

"No. I meant that you could have. You might have. You're all right now."

"Good," said Scorpio.

"I think so, too." But Fain doubted that the dog was capable of appreciating such a feeling, especially since what he'd really meant was, if the dog had died here, he would not have readily forgiven himself—nor Skallon. No, Scorpio was too much like Fain himself to care about friendship, compassion, or guilt. Scorpio, like Fain, lived in the present moment, and if that moment was proving sufficiently tedious for Fain—the endless ramblings of the Alvean Assembly—then it had to be that much worse for poor Scorpio, who could only lie in his room all day, surrounded by these grotesque half-humans, and wait. Scorpio, like Fain, wasn't made for waiting. He patted the dog. "It won't be long now. Soon enough, you'll be up and out of here. Then we'll catch that Changeling and go home."

"I. Am. Ready."

Fain laid the comb aside and tickled the dog's ears. "So am I."

But when? he wondered. *And how?*

She entered without knocking.

Fain, who had heard her bare feet approaching in the hall long before the door actually opened, turned casually. "Drop the bolt," he said. "We don't want to be disturbed."

She wore only a thin wisp of cloth. Her usual night

clothes? he had wondered before. Or something special? Something for him?

She hadn't moved, her spine pressed against the smooth wooden door. "I do not like that animal." She pointed to Scorpio. "He is a disturbance. An—an unreal thing."

Fain couldn't help smirking. She should talk. Unreal? What did she think she was—she and her sixty million fellow pseudos? "Scorpio stays," he said, on a sudden impulse. "He's sick. I don't want to leave him tonight."

"But hasn't he been sick before, the other times when I came?" Her words were spoken tentatively. Fain guessed that she knew what he was doing—perhaps even understood why. "Skallon says the animal is much improved and will soon be able to confront your enemy."

Fain shrugged, moved away from the dog, and came toward the woman. "Bolt the door, Joane," he said softly. "I don't want Skallon stumbling in here."

"Is it that you fear him? His wrath? His jealousy?"

"No, I don't fear him."

"Then why not leave it open?" Her voice rose shrilly, but she remained in control—complete control. "If the dog can watch, then why not Skallon, too? Or Kish? Or Danon? Why don't we let everyone watch us, Fain? On Earth you said that they do that."

"This isn't Earth." He started to move past her. He caught Scorpio's eye. The dog gave no warning move. Good; she was all right. "Bolt it," he said, stopping at once.

She moved immediately to comply. One hand flew to her mouth and she giggled in a high-pitched, tautly controlled way. In a ripple of filmy cloth, she showed him her round backside as she dropped the heavy wooden bolt across the door. Her buttocks were

broad but hard. Strong muscles showed in the backs
of her thighs. Joane's body testified to the many uses
it had served. There were wrinkles and calluses, firm-
nesses you never saw in women on Earth. Maybe that
helped explain why he had unresistingly violated his
own principles and had taken her veiled offer, that
first time. In her own way she faced the world square,
unflinching. She was stuck in this stupid Alvean
swamp, but she didn't whine. She didn't suck up to
him, like most Earthwomen.

Fain shook his head slightly. No point in getting
sloppy about her; there was a kind of contract between them, an agreement to have some sex and not
to lie to each other, and that was all there was.

"At least the thing is tired," she said, gesturing at
Scorpio. Fain saw the dog had tucked his muzzle into
his shoulder, curled up and gone to sleep. He smiled
slightly. Her little speech about his watching had
been enough.

"You have been so tense, since you returned. I
thought perhaps you disliked what you have seen of
Kalic."

"It's okay."

"Is it much different from—" Fain reached for her
to stop the flow of words. Small talk was pointless. It
helped you get along with some people, the kind who
liked to babble on about nothing, but he knew with
Joane he didn't need to keep up a pretense. They
could talk later, maybe, when it might really mean
something. For now, it would just get in the way. He
pressed her to him. She responded, and he could feel
a sudden quickening in her. At once her breath
shifted to ragged gasps. After a few minutes they tumbled onto the bed. He kissed her, stroked her, but she
set the pace, led him on, felt him, tugged at him,
licked him. Beneath her hands he abruptly felt the

stirring pressure of an orgasm. He shoved her back.
She shuddered and pulled him down. She bit his lips,
bringing the rich, dark taste of blood into his mouth.
Fain rose and descended. Scorpio, in his sleep, grum-
bled a word. Joane held Fain between pincerlike
thighs. Her strength amazed, delighted, defied, and
taunted him. On Earth, the women were never physically strong. There was little need for that, not with
the abundance of machinery. He came inside her silently. She had no way of knowing and continued to
tremble beneath him till, in a rush, he drew out, cal-
lously beading her thighs. On Earth, treating a
woman this way would have brought instant scorn
and certain shame. Here, light-years distant, he could
do as he wished. When he looked back at her, Joane
was smoothing her gown across her legs.

"Do you want me again?" she asked.

"Yes." He didn't know if that was true or not, but he
did know that he wanted her to stay. Why? Because,
he also knew, if she did leave, she'd go immediately to
Skallon. One night, he'd followed her and seen that
happen. Was it different with Skallon, better for her?
Fain assumed it was. Skallon would feel compunctions
about ensuring that Joane shared his orgasms. But she
came to Fain first. He noted that and noted also how
it filled him with pleasure.

"Now?" she asked, reaching for the hem of her
gown.

He shook his head with a wry smile probably invisible in the dark. *Jesus.* "I think I ought to wait." He
went to the door, removed the bolt, and glanced into
the corridor. A sweet, sharp odor assailed his nostrils.
Food. Meat. This late at night? The fat Alveans seldom rested from their prime means of entertainment.
It could be Kish below in the kitchen but it could as

easily be someone else in the Communal. Fain decided not to worry. Turning back into the room, he clicked his tongue. "Scorpio—here."

The dog came at once. He never had been asleep, Fain wasn't surprised. Scorpio, unlike many humans, knew the value of modesty.

"Fain. Called," said the dog, pretending sleepiness.

"I think you ought to go back to your room now. Rest. Sleep. In the morning, if you're still feeling better, maybe we can think of some way to use you."

"Good." Scorpio started to go out.

"And, Scorpio," said Fain, knowing there was no need for this but that it might help reassure Joane, "if you run into Skallon, say nothing. About Joane, I mean. About her being here with me."

"Skallon. Speaks. Not. To. Me."

Fain nodded and went back inside. After bolting the door, he faced the bed. Joane had ignited the lantern. Its hard light shadowed the planes and ridges of her face. He lay down at her side.

"Fain," she asked, "do you fear Skallon?"

"No." Her question struck him so oddly that he felt no anger. "What makes you ask that?"

"Because of what you told the animal."

"I said that for your sake. So you wouldn't have to worry."

"About Skallon?" She laughed. "But he is only a boy. Like Danon. He is not at all like you, Fain."

And who am I like? Fain wondered. *Kish?* But he said nothing. "If Skallon knew we were seeing each other, it would upset him. He'd be hurt and angry. I have to work with him. I want to keep him happy."

"But we are not betrothed. Not you and I. We are not wedded. It is Kish who should be angry, not Skallon."

"Skallon would be angry," he said patiently. "Not because of you—because of me. Skallon hates me. He may love you. He certainly thinks he does."

"But I love no one." She said it casually, like a child. Fain was remembering what Skallon had told him about Kish and Joane and, for the first time since hearing that story, he began to feel a certain real sympathy for Kish.

"Neither do I," he said.

"Then we are alike." She put her arms around his shoulders and brushed his neck with her lips. "We are from different worlds, but we are the same. Tell me, Fain. On Earth, are the women like Skallon? Do they fall in love?"

"The women on Earth aren't women anymore. I don't know what they are."

"You do not like them."

"I like very few people, Joane."

"But you like me."

It wasn't a question. She knew. "I like you."

"If you desire," she said, "I can stay away from Skallon. I went with him before only because he asked. I think you are probably better, Fain, than Skallon. He tries too hard to be like us, like an Alvean. You are only yourself."

Her offer did not displease him. Fain admitted this quickly to himself, but then said, "No, don't do that. If you have to stay away from either of us, make it me. I'm not the one who needs you. That's Skallon."

"But what if I am the one who needs you, Fain?"

He didn't believe that. Still, when she drew closer, he made no effort to resist. Her fingers probed skillfully. He responded. All the while, the lantern burned. When Joane mounted him, Fain opened his eyes and studied her face, the deep furrows that creased her brow, the squiggly lines that spread out from the corners of both eyes. Joane was pretty, he decided, but not beautiful. On the Earth, where all women were beautiful, none were pretty. Joane was pretty. He liked that. It was a difference, and Fain was not incapable of appreciating the beauty of something different.

The sound from the corridor brought him instantly alert. He jumped, reaching for his heatgun. Joane, spilled from her perch upon him, cried out. Fain rushed to the door and threw it open.

Had the Changeling at last drawn too close?

But all he saw was Kish. Poor, fat, foolish Kish. The innkeeper stood with his hands raised high above his head. His eyes bulged like those of some frightened animal. He licked his lips, trying to speak.

Fain lowered the heatgun. He felt embarrassed and ashamed and his awareness of those emotions made him angry. "What do you want here?"

"I—I was passing." Kish spoke quickly. His hands, still raised, were shaking. "I thought I heard—I heard a noise. A cry."

"That was me," Fain said. "'A bad dream. A nightmare."

"I thought it might be . . . your enemy. The one who makes himself over into other things. I thought he might have come here to—to attack you."

"There's no chance of that. Scorpio will keep him away from here." Fain guessed that Kish was lying. He glanced behind. From where they stood, only the foot of the bed was visible. Kish could not see Joane. But there had been that cry. He must have heard that, if nothing else. "Have you seen Skallon?" Fain asked. He wanted to change the subject.

Kish dropped his arms in a whoosh of expelled breath. "No. He must be sleeping, too."

"Then, if you don't mind, I'm going to try that. Skallon and I have a long day tomorrow. Another important meeting. Those things have a tendency to drag on for hours, you know." Why was he babbling like this? It was small talk—he hated small talk. Kish meant nothing to him. Why should he feel guilty?

"I would not know about the meetings. I am not of the high castes, to be sure." Kish spoke stiffly, showing real emotion for the first time. He was bitter. But at whom?

Fain stepped back into the room. "I have to go now. I don't want to detain you any longer."

Kish took a step forward, as if he intended to follow Fain into the room, then stopped suddenly with his tiny feet together and bowed past his broad waist. "A good night's rest to you, Mr. Fain."

"Yes, of course. Yes, thank you." Fain shut the door upon Kish's dark, smiling face and bolted it surely behind him. He waited a moment until the thump of footsteps moving down the corridor convinced him that it was safe to speak. "Go back to your room," he told Joane.

She had hardly moved upon the bed. Her nakedness showed boldly. Either she had been certain that Kish would not enter the room, or else she did not care. Whichever it was, Fain realized he had seen enough of her for one night.

"Why?" she asked. "Kish has gone away now. You need not fear him."

"I don't fear him." Fain found her gown bunched in a ball at the foot of the bed. He threw it across her breasts. "Go."

Then she started laughing. It was the last thing he had expected, and several moments passed before he understood that she wasn't entirely in control. "He—he—he heard us," she said, gasping to get out the words between frantic spurts of laughter. "He heard us and knew what we were doing and did nothing. It's funny, Fain. Can't you see that? He was afraid. Afraid of you. Of us. Kish was afraid . . . afraid . . . afraid—"

Fain slapped her. Not brutally. That wasn't necessary. He slapped her not because she was hysterical or loud but because, for a moment, he hated her. He hated her because she was laughing and because he knew that he was the cause of it. He remembered what Skallon had told him about Kish and Joane and the real nature of their marriage. Remembering, he wondered how much of that story, if any of it, was true. He also wondered why Joane had seen fit to tell Skallon and not him.

Holding her cheek gingerly, Joane stared at Fain. Her eyes showed nothing—not pain, not shock, not remorse. "I—I have wronged you, Fain."

"No, not especially." His hatred had ebbed as quickly as it flared. "But I think you ought to go. Kish is our contact here. Skallon and I have to depend upon him. I don't think we ought to betray his trust any more than necessary."

She dressed. "But it was so funny, Fain. I heard every word he said. He was so afraid."

"We're all afraid sometimes, Joane." He sat on the end of the bed with his back facing her.

She placed her arms upon his shoulders. "Then I cannot come back to see you ever again."

"I didn't say that." He turned around and looked at her. "Maybe another time. Maybe tomorrow. But not tonight. Tonight I want to think."

"I understand." She stood and went toward the door. "You Earthers are always doing that—always thinking." She didn't say it as an accusation. To her, it was true. One of the characteristics of the Earth-born human being: constant thought.

Fain waited until she had gone out. Where? he wondered. He guessed that she had gone to Skallon, but he deliberately refused to listen to the sound of her disappearing footsteps in order to learn their direction. No, he was thinking of something else. He was thinking of how odd it was.

In all the time he had spent at this inn, he couldn't once recall finding Kish here in the upper corridors late at night. What had brought him here this particular night? And—something else he had to think about—Kish's odd smile there at the end. What was the meaning behind that?

Fain realized with a start of surprise exactly where his thoughts were taking him: how could he be sure that Kish was Kish at all? How could he be sure that Kish wasn't the Changeling? There were few firm reasons for suspecting that, but there were even fewer for rejecting it.

Fain stood rigidly still. When you were tracking down Changelings these moments would come: the sudden fear that everyone around you was a Changeling, an ultimate form of paranoia. Joane had passed by Scorpio this evening, and the dog had checked Skallon earlier. But he couldn't keep checking everyone in the hotel. No—he had made the hotel a base and he would have to treat it as relatively safe, or else never rest easily.

Fain relaxed, letting his hands dangle, easing his muscles. He sat on the bed and meditated, drawing his breath soothingly through the nostrils and letting it out again in a long lazy rhythm. He let go and soon reached in. He found the calm center, where it always was. Serene, cool, opaque as a milky pearl. He would live, no matter what. There was no need to fret for life, since living in separate forms was an illusion. Let go of it. Concentrate instead on the moment. A warrior had to be firmly rooted in himself. From that strong mooring he could go out to confront the world; but the mooring was the essential. Without it, there was no judgment, no true seeing of the world as it was.

Fain let himself bask in the cool hardness he carried at the center of his mind, and again thought of his father. He knew there were rages burning inside himself, pains that would never escape. He used them for energy, to give him that certain fine edge in his dealings with the world. But at the center was the milky riddle, the sureness.

After a while he stood. In the morning he would use Scorpio and test Kish and Joane again. He would make a point of it whenever he had Scorpio available. And beyond that, he sensed something new in the odd contest he was in with this Changeling. Their prime flaw was their pride: they could not resist toying with mere men, whom they considered slow-witted and dense. So if this Changeling knew Fain was here, there was a chance it would seek him out, if it could. Fine. Let it. In fact, the balance of the pursuit might be shifting even now. The dull day in the Great Hall had probably bored the playful but deadly spirit of the Changeling. It, too, could get bored. Order, to it, was an insult, a perversion of the natural flow of things. So the Changeling might change from pursued to pursuer. It could happen, though it seemed unlikely.

Some tension still laced his muscles. Fain paced the room. To ease it away, he finally went out into the creaking hallways of the hotel and roved through them, listening to distant sounds. There was nothing suspicious.

When he passed Skallon's room, he heard the tinkle of Joane's laughter.

He paused at a grimy window and looked out. Wan
orange bulbs lit the street below. In the dim pools of
light a few Alveans talked, or gestured, or slumped
against a ruined wall, sleeping. Beyond them lay the
city, not bright and phosphorescent as the cities of
Earth were, but shrouded in night, the streets barely
lit. Somewhere in that darkness was the Changeling.
Fain felt the presence of it now, sensed the thing
watching them. And somehow, now, the calm center
inside him did not seem enough to protect him from
the brooding pressure of this alien darkness beyond
the pale lights. The Changeling was death, madness,
the final blackness; Fain felt this now as he never had
before. Was something in him slipping away? Was
there something about Alvea, its bleak and shadowed
streets, its old religion—something that was changing
him? The sense of the alien beyond the darkness . . .
Despite himself, Fain shivered.

10

"Did Joane come by your room last night?" Fain
asked Skallon. The two men waddled with accustomed ease through the heavily congested morning
streets of Kalic. Fain, barely conscious anymore of the
thick wads of padding circling his middle, spoke
loudly to be heard above the steady beat of a procession of chanting monks who happened to be preced-

ing them. Fain believed that after all these days he was at last beginning to feel at home on this world. Skallon would not have agreed. Skallon continued to find fault with his accent, his manners, his way of holding himself. But Fain knew that wasn't the point. The point was how he felt in his mind. And he felt comfortable. The Changeling would not, could not ever feel comfortable. No Changeling ever felt at home anywhere, not even, perhaps, on its own world. And that was an advantage. Fain intended to make use of it.

Skallon shook his head. "No, I haven't seen her since early yesterday. Was she looking for me?"

"Not her, no. Kish. He came by my room last night and asked if I'd seen her."

"What did you say?"

"I lied. I said I thought I'd seen her go out."

Skallon shrugged. "It was probably the truth. She often goes out at night—to one of the temples."

"Then maybe that was it."

"I'm just surprised that Kish even bothered to look for her."

"Maybe he wanted his socks washed."

"Alveans don't wear socks."

"Then his robes." Fain saw no reason to pursue the subject. The first thing this morning, exactly as he promised last night, he'd smuggled Scorpio unannounced into the kitchen and let him sniff the innkeeper at close range. The results proved negative: Kish was only Kish. Fain, realizing that he had allowed some sort of lingering guilt to arouse his suspicions the night before, had felt an odd mixture of disappointment and relief when Scorpio told him no. If Kish had proved, after all, to be the Changeling, it would have been so easy: a single quick blast of the heatgun and the job was over. Easy, yes, and perhaps too easy. Fain knew he needed more of a challenge if he wanted to renew the confidence he'd once felt in his own abilities. Now he had the challenge again. But was he ready to face it?

The passing of a silver-gowned procession of young, brightly painted women momentarily deflected his attention from his own thoughts. The women's gowns ended far short of their bare knees. Fain couldn't recall having seen a publicly displayed naked leg since his arrival on this world.

Skallon was smiling. "Imperial concubines," he explained. "They've never had anything like an emperor on Alvea, but the caste dates back to the Gommerset era on Earth, and the Alveans have never seen fit to change it."

Fain shook his head, staring after the women. "I think I can see why."

"And they're virgins, too, all of them. They live in small houses near the temples and exist on public charity. They're seen in public only once each year, at fest time. They can't have sex, because they're reserved for the emperor's use, and there isn't any emperor."

"Then where do the new ones come from? I thought the whole point of a caste system was father like son."

"Not these women. They're chosen. The prettiest girls from all the country."

"Isn't that a contradiction?"

Skallon shrugged. "I suppose it is. But don't tell an Alvean that. I'm sure he'd have an explanation."

"Then I guess the best idea is to be born ugly."

"Why?"

"Because I don't think the life of a virgin concubine can be much fun."

"What woman's life on this planet is?"

Fain was tempted to answer that question but decided to spare Skallon's feelings. Besides, who was he to criticize Joane's morals? On Earth what she was doing would have been the norm.

"We better get going," said Fain. The crowd, most of which had stopped to watch the procession, was flowing again. Fain led Skallon into the middle of it.

They had gone a few more blocks toward the Great Hall when Fain remembered something else. "Where is Danon today? Did he decide to stay home and do some work for a change?"

"No, he had to go out early this morning, just before you came down with Scorpio. He said he'd try to meet us at the Hall."

"Good." Despite his original hesitancy, Fain had come to admit that the boy's assistance was helpful. Danon's knowledge of local customs far exceeded any of Skallon's scholarly wisdom. Several times the boy had helped them out of tight spots caused by their own ignorance. Fain had a distinct feeling that if anyone could penetrate the Changeling's present disguise that person would be Danon.

The boy met them in the broad plaza that fronted the Hall. He seemed inordinately excited and came running to meet them.

"I have found him!" Danon cried. "It is your enemy! I have seen him with my eyes!"

Fain wasn't about to be taken in by yet another false alarm. He told the boy to keep his voice low, then asked, "What have you seen that makes you so sure?"

The boy screwed up his face in noncomprehension and looked toward Skallon, who repeated Fain's words in a more decipherable accent.

Danon replied quickly and excitedly. Fain had an

easier time understanding than in making himself understood. Danon said, "A man in black robes has entered the Hall."

Fain saw Skallon's surprise and knew this must be
important. "So what?" he asked.

"It is not done," said Danon. "It is impossible."

Fain looked at Skallon. "Maybe you better let me in
on the secret."

Skallon frowned, plainly thinking how fruitless
Fain's quicktreatment in Alvean affairs had been.
"Only one caste on Alvea wears black robes: the assassins. Danon is saying that one of them has actually
entered the Hall."

"So? Maybe he's supposed to kill somebody. That's
hardly our problem."

Skallon looked even more irritated than before.
"Don't you even understand that much, Fain? These
are people who believe in reincarnation, of souls that
pass on from body to body. For them, murder is a terrible deed. It's an interruption of life before it can be
properly completed. Killing a man isn't just killing a
man: it's making it so that he can't be born again."

"That's gibberish."

"Not to them."

"So? You still haven't reached the point."

"The point is," Skallon said, speaking slowly, controlling his anger, "the caste of assassins are really out-
casts. They cannot speak with other castes, eat with
them, socialize with them in any form. If an assassin
came into this street right now, it would be absolutely
deserted inside of two minutes. But one wouldn't.
That's the point. They never come out in public. They
ride in coaches, dark coaches, the blinds drawn, the—
there, look!"

He pointed. Fain looked and saw what Skallon had
described: a dark coach, the door hanging open.

"So now we know how he got here. So what?"

"So the only way an assassin would ever think of entering the Great Hall is if he wasn't an assassin after all, if he was—"

Fain finished the thought: "The Changeling." He gripped his heatgun and turned on Danon. "When? How long has he been in there?"

"Only a few moments," the boy said. "Only just before I observed your approach. I saw the coach and then it stopped and he—the black-robed man—came out. I ran but then I saw him enter the hall."

Fain glanced at the high doors ahead of them. Even as they spoke, high-caste individuals were passing inside. "If what you've told me is right, then why haven't they come out? There ought to be a riot."

"Maybe they're too frightened to riot," said Skallon.

Fain had to think for a moment. Was it possible? Could the Changeling make this bad a mistake?

The Changeling would know even less than Fain about this world. The Vertil could help him. But if it had grown careless, if it had simply assumed the identity of a high-caste Alvean without bothering to find out more, then it could be possible. He had known Changelings to make similar blunders before. They were smart, but they were also cocky.

"Danon," he said sharply, "you stay here. Climb up a post or a tree, find a nook where you can observe the Hall. If the assassin comes out while we're in there, you watch which way he goes."

"I—I'll follow him," said Danon.

"No, don't do that. Just watch him. And, Skallon—" Fain turned "—you'll go in with me. We'll split up once we're inside and come at him from either side. If you shoot, make sure you hit him cleanly. We can't go around killing the natives without blowing our cover sky high. If this is the end of it, it's got to be the final end. Understand?"

But Skallon was shaking his head. "Shoot?"

"Yes, shoot. Kill. You know, like an assassin."

"But what if we're wrong? What if this man isn't the Changeling?"

"I thought you just got through telling me he had to be."

"But . . . well, we could be wrong. I mean, there could be another explanation for the assassin's presence."

"What?"

"I—I don't know."

"Then just do as I say. Do as I say and, in another few months, you'll be home again safe and secure in your nice warm dormitory."

"But, Fain, I really do think we—"

He caught hold of Skallon and propelled him toward the Hall. "Be quiet and hurry. We can't let this chance slip by. If we do, don't think we'll get another."

They made their way into the Great Hall. Fain hadn't set both feet inside the assembly room when he spotted the assassin. It didn't take any keen powers of observation. The black-robed man sat all by himself, with his back facing the door. Around him on all sides stood a broad ring of frightened Alveans. Fain could see only the back of the head and shoulders of the assassin. But he was thin—thinner than any Alvean Fain had ever seen. He studied the frozen faces of the Alveans. The entire scene reminded him of a strange old painting he had once seen: "Death Comes to Visit." The black-robed assassin was certainly death, but whom had he come to see? The Alveans apparently could not decide, for not one of them had so far moved a muscle.

Fain found himself whispering. "I can't get a good shot from here. We'd better penetrate the crowd. You go that way and I'll go left."

"But, Fain, that can't be the Changeling. He wouldn't just sit there, not doing—"

"How do you know?" He gave Skallon a shove. "I said go—now go."

Fain moved himself. The Alveans gathered around the assassin refused to budge. Fain had to reach ahead and physically push each man aside before moving onward. He thought about Skallon's half-voiced objection and knew that what he'd been trying to say hadn't been entirely devoid of logic. Surely the assassin, Changeling or not, must be aware by now that he had erred seriously in deciding to enter the Hall. Shouldn't he be trying to get away as quickly as possible? Fain wondered. Which really did make more sense? For the Changeling to go running wildly off, affording Fain and Skallon every opportunity for finding him on their own, or for him to remain exactly where he was, alone and isolated, where it would be very difficult for anyone to catch him unawares? Fain began to move with additional caution. He removed his gun but kept it hidden against his upper leg. He kept his head bent low and tried to part the crowd ahead of him without unnecessarily disturbing its shape. On the opposite side, Skallon ought to be doing the same. If he wasn't—and Fain knew damn well Skallon would probably mess it up—then that ought to help deflect the Changeling's attention from where the real danger was approaching.

When Fain reached a spot just back of the first row of Alveans—but still a good ten meters from where the black-robed man sat alone—he paused. He tried to get a good look at the assassin, but there was nothing to be seen there. The man, as well as he could be seen, looked like any other dark-robed, pale Alvean.

The Changeling?

Fain saw no reason to think that he wasn't.

Well, he thought, *whoever and whatever you are, Changeling infiltrator or Alvean assassin, I'm going to kill you.*

He raised the heatgun, thrust it between the shoulders of two broad Alveans in front of him, aimed, squinted, sighted, squeezed the trigger gently.

Someone shouted. Startled, the Alvean jerked sideways.

The voice, coming from directly behind, startled Fain. The heatgun went off as he followed the Alvean, but he missed. It was as Fain had expected. The man was the Changeling and it had been waiting for Fain to show himself. Now the man ran. He rushed toward the crowd that stood nearest the door. The Alveans stepped fearfully back to let the black-robed figure pass. Fain could have fired again, but for an instant he hesitated.

A fist came down solidly on his arm. Fain caught the heatgun before it hit the floor and spun around.

Skallon stood beside him. "Fain, we can't—not yet. It's murder. It's plain, cold-blooded—"

Fain hit him. Not hard. Just hard enough to knock him back. Fain turned. But precious seconds had been lost.

All Fain saw was a sweep of black robes as the assassin raced safely through the open door.

He swiveled back, grabbed the stunned Skallon, and shook him. "You dumb, stupid, soft, simple bastard. If that thing gets away, I swear I'll kill you with my own hands."

Skallon held his jaw. "Fain, what if we're wrong?" he said softly.

"Then we're wrong, damn it. What else?" Fain raced toward the door. He heard Skallon pounding after him. There was still a chance, after all.

11

In the broad, fanning plaza outside, Skallon's heart thumped so solidly he could feel it imposing its own rhythm against the background chanting and clanging of the processions. Alveans milled around them. Skallon searched the crowds, tasted their sweaty, reeking euphoria.

"See him?"

"No," Fain replied. "Hell, he's had forever to get away."

"Where's Danon?"

"Can't spot him. Chances are—"

"There! Up there on the stone spike. That's Danon."

Fain squinted. "Right, that's the kid. He's waving."

"Smart. He climbed up there to see down into the crowds. Look he's pointing."

"That's the way. Come on." Fain started to jog through the milling Alveans.

"I'm with you."

The next ten minutes were frantic. They joined Danon at the base of the massive stonework buttresses. He led them down a cramped alley, one of the canonical passageways for the Elect of the high castes. Until the caste members returned for their deliberations, it was empty, a public concourse. They raced along as quickly as they could through surging knots of worshipers. Ahead they caught glimpses of the man they pursued, his robe flapping as he moved quickly and deliberately through the mobs. There was a fever in the air, and they all three caught the scent of a chase. When the three of them reached an intersection, each took a different fork and surged ahead. They kept in contact through their wrist communicators. At each separation, a moment's pursuit found the fleeing man again and the two who had followed a wrong path ran to catch up. It was effective. They never lost him. Danon, who knew the diagonal short cuts of the city, was often in front.

The man then cut through narrow alleys, obviously knowing he was being followed. The crowds thinned. The man ran faster. Skallon's breath rasped as he struggled along under the Doubluth robes.

Abruptly the man dodged into a massive, tiered building of gray stone and wood. Fain came pounding by Skallon at the same moment and yelled to Danon—"Around the back!"—before reaching the front entranceway, where the man had entered a moment before.

Fain motioned for Skallon to check the side. There the pursuit ended, because the man did not reappear and Fain did not want to leave an exit unguarded so one of the three could follow inside. Skallon waited in shelter a few paces from the small side entrance, muscles jumping with a will of their own.

In a few moments Fain appeared, leading an Alvean with a cart. Skallon frowned.

"Push it in front of the doorway," Fain ordered the Alvean in a terrible, almost unintelligible accent. The man did so. The cart completely blocked the exit. "Now we've got him."

"You want to go in?"

"In time." Fain seemed self-assured now. "We've got him boxed. Danon says there's no other way out of this place."

"Why wait?" Skallon stepped forward to talk to Fain, who was leaning behind an ornamented pillar.

"Get *back*," Fain cried. "He could blow you to pieces from that angle."

"Oh," Skallon skipped back to cover, feeling foolish. "But . . . why are we waiting?"

"The kid and I are waiting. He'll let me know if the Changeling comes out his way and I'll cover the street. I've decided we're going to do it your way, Skallon, no cold-blooded murder. You go back to the hotel, get Scorpio, and bring him here."

"That's what we should have done before," Skallon said.

But Fain was grinning. "No. Before it didn't make sense—now it does. I'm not a beast, Skallon, and I do like to use my head."

The hotel was no more than a kilometer from where they'd caught the Changeling. Skallon started to run, but then spotted a messenger and hired his bicycle away from him. Bursting into the hotel, Skallon hurried upstairs, where he found Scorpio well and apparently fully recovered from his bout of illness. He packed the dog inside a thin box, struggled to carry him downstairs, and then loaded his burden upon the carry platform of the bicycle. Within moments, he was pedaling through the streets again. The crowds had thinned considerably now. Darkness was rapidly falling. It had been a long day. With any luck, it might also be their last one on this planet. Skallon frowned at the thought. He would miss the zest and color of Alvea.

* * *

Despite himself, Fain grinned when Skallon wheeled up, eyes bright and robes askew, pedaling energetically out of a side alley without exposing himself to fire from the front entrance of the looming gray building. It took Fain a moment to remember that they were in this escapade because Skallon had screwed up the kill back at the Great Hall. Yet he had difficulty staying angry. Something inside him signaled a warning. He should keep his slow, burning rage; it would drive him forward, sharpen his wits. But, even as he thought the problem through, Fain saw that he no longer had control over his emotions that way. Something in him was slipping away.

"Check your charge," Fain muttered. He took Scorpio out of the box. The dog whimpered softly as he sank down into the shadows. The ride must not have been an easy one. "Okay, boy?"

"Think. I. Am."

Fain explained slowly, repeating himself often, that they were going to slip in through both front and rear entrances. And suddenly, in the middle of it, Fain remembered the looming warm presence of his father leaning over him, pointing to some numbers and a statistical graph, lips moving, calm still voice . . . the reassurance . . . explaining some fact . . . something . . . the place where the inner certainty came from . . . so much. So much, now all lost, the years dried up, the milky riddle inside Fain now a crutch instead of the blazing reality it had been when his father told him. Now the son was kneeling here on a distant dustbowl of a world. All the son had was a dog and some thin memories.

Fain shook his head irritably to clear it, and continued.

* * *

It seemed like a decent plan, Skallon thought. Danon would remain outside to check if the Changeling escaped in some unforeseen way. Skallon would take the rear, Scorpio and Fain would slip in the front.

Skallon maneuvered around to the back. Danon was a shrunken dot of shadow near a garbage bulwark. "Anything?" The boy shook his head. He was nervous, jittery, afraid and intrigued all at once. "Just stay here. Use the wrist communicator if you see anyone leave. Anyone at all. Remember, the Changeling can be completely different the next time you see him."

In a moment Skallon had melted from one shadow to the next and was inside the rear entrance, a heavy door of brass encrustings. He heard a slight scuffling noise from the front. Fain and Scorpio, perhaps. The door gave onto a narrow corridor lit by weak oil lamps. Every ten meters a door of greasy wood signified a room; it looked like a sleazy lodging house.

Skallon moved silently down the hallway. Another dim hall sliced diagonally across this one. At the far end of it a pool of light enclosed a desk and some chairs.

Probably, judging from the building, Fain would come down that way. Skallon moved gingerly toward the light. He was acutely conscious of how exposed he was here. If a door flew open and a gun came out, he was a dead man, by all the odds. That, plus the chance that he and Fain would shoot at each other in this dusky light.

The pool of light drew closer. He heard a soft wheezing noise. Breathing. A man whooshing out air as though slightly winded. Skallon eased forward.

Two things happened at once.

Somebody sat up in one of the chairs, robes flopping out onto the floor. At the corner of his eye he saw a shadow flit across the entry to another hallway, branching to the left. He swerved to cover it.

"Skallon!" The shadow had Fain's voice.

He swept his gun hand back around to cover the man who was now getting up from the chair. It was the same one they'd been chasing.

"Don't move," he said calmly.

The man, looking unconcerned, turned to regard him. He was young, with the face of a fuzz-cheeked boy. Maybe it was his thinness that made the difference. The assassin—the Changeling—looked more human than Alvean.

Fain came out of the shadows. Scorpio came with him. Skallon watched them, then turned back to regard his prisoner. His hand tightened upon the trigger of the heatgun. He suddenly knew just how easy it was to kill. Just squeeze the trigger. Easy.

"Not. Him." It was Scorpio's voice.

"You're sure?" said Fain. "You're damn sure about that?"

"Does. Not. Check." Scorpio sounded weary. "Not. Him."

Fain came over to the Alvean in short, choppy steps and slapped the man. The sharp crack was soaked up by the stillness of the building. "Why did you run?" His voice was calm.

"I enjoy running." A boy's voice. Shrill.

"No, talk," said Fain, and he slapped the man again.

"I . . . love the wind . . . it is so cool . . . I . . ."

Skallon lowered his gun. "I was right," he said. "You almost killed an innocent man—a boy."

"Vertil," said Fain. "We've been chasing a damned Vertil ringer. A plant. When the hell is it going to get down to business and quit playing games with us?" When Fain looked at Skallon, his face was dark with rage.

12

Dusk was long in ending here. Skallon moved through the cooling air amid late knots of celebrants, all on their way from the Kalic center after the day's assemblies. He walked easily, almost carelessly, trying to give the impression of not caring whether he was followed. At ease, yes. Oblivious.

Behind him, he knew, Fain kept in the shadows a block or two away. Scorpio was with him, glad to be free to prowl at last, safe in the insulating dark. If Kalic had been an Earth city the illuminants would have burst into life as any living thing moved by them, making tracers of light down the streets— expending only the necessary power, but providing full data on who lurked in the streets, easy information for the computer surveillance. In Kalic there were welcome pools of shadow, entire blocks without a lamp. Poor planets had their advantages.

Skallon stopped, idled, bought a roll of hot qanti-makas seeds with lacings of dollegen spices. He chewed it, welcoming the blossoming crisp taste. Was that someone stalling on a street corner half a block back? He couldn't quite tell. Fain wouldn't be that close.

So: maybe it was working after all. Fain proposed this old double-tailing snare before they left the lodging house. They sent Danon a message to stay put,

hide in the shadows for at least an hour. Then Skallon
left boldly, hoping the Changeling had stayed in the
vicinity to watch his ruse come to completion. Fain
would follow by a slightly different route, shadowing
Skallon to see if anyone followed him.

It wasn't until Skallon hit the street that he realized
what a risk he was taking. What was to stop the
Changeling from punching a neat heathole through his
chest when he stepped out the front? On the nearly
deserted street he was a simple, stupid target.

As he crunched into the qantimakas, irritation rose
in him. He'd walked seven long blocks now. Either
Fain had picked up somebody tailing him, or he
hadn't. Or maybe Fain was paying too much attention
to his precious dog to keep an eye on the drifting,
robed figures. That would be typical.

Ahead, light showered down over the sculpted mahogany face of an official building. The Planetary
Museum, tended by a saffron-robed Spatemper caste
guard of two at the arched doorway. Skallon stroked
the rubbed wood; not mahogany, of course—that ancient wood had vanished—but something like it, with
light eddies and whorls in it. He hesitated. Fain and
Scorpio certainly couldn't follow him inside here. The
Changeling could. But he doubted the Changeling
would attack him in a public place; it had ample opportunities to do so earlier in the day.

And it would be an unexpected move. Maybe that
was the reason he liked it. Fain would be frustrated—
but so what? Fain's silly fits of anger at that chase
fiasco were contemptible. Why couldn't the man think
coolly about these things? The Changeling was sending them off on dead ends, admittedly. So what?
Perhaps the Changeling thought he could do the job
without a lot of bloodletting. Or maybe Earth misun-

derstood completely what the Changeling was here
for.

Skallon finished the tangy qantimakas and turned
in, through the archway and into a vault with a high,
groined ceiling of fretted stone. Fain could stand outside and see if anyone followed. If not, Skallon got a
few minutes to enjoy himself.

Inside the grill-worked doorway was an ancient
burnished hull. Skallon studied it, hoping to catch reflected in it the image of someone loitering at the entrance, waiting for him to come out. A young woman
left the building, swaying, but no one came in.

Skallon read the descriptive plaque. It was a frag-
ment of the first orbiter-lander, unmanned, that sur-
veyed Alvea. Above it, shiny, were photos made even
earlier by the flyby probe, boosting at high ramscoop
accelerations. (*Where was it now?* Skallon thought.
Probably beyond the rim of the galaxy.) This prehu-
man Alvea was a mottled ocean world, its continents
brown smudges. The first colonists had taken the
trouble to hunt down the lander and some ancient
craftsman then laser-etched faceted scenes on it, de-
picting the first years of the colony, the rich decades
and first century, up to the time of the first plagues,
Breathstealer and Clenching Rot. Probably one of
those two took away the artist.

Skallon ambled away, eyeing the empty archway.
He found himself in an historical gallery. Social docu-
mentary work, mostly, of intriguing quality. Many
pastels, some oils. In each, the poor were slim and
their faces bleak, pale, drawn. All the obviously good
people—the ones contented in their ordained place—
were corpulent, thick necked, bulging with rich and
certain virtues. They beamed out at him. Happy folk,
sure that they were bound for each appointed slot in

the pyramid of Alvean society, knowing that Gommerset had shown the only true way, they were frozen here forever, the only traces of them now left.

Unless, Skallon thought, *Gommerset was right.* Joane's quiet sly objections had slid under the ribs of his own ceramic certainty and pricked him where he least needed it. It was *true* that Gommerset was discredited after his death, when he couldn't defend himself, and his followers were scattered. Earth's administration *was* hostile to Gommersetism, and always had been. Had they rigged the new data? Sweeping such a major fact under the rug wouldn't be beyond the administration.

Something stirred in Skallon. If Gommerset were correct, even partially . . .

He shook himself. To believe that implied an immensely larger universe than Skallon had ever conceived. He would take awhile to come to grips with it. But how could he decide, really? Research into Gommersetism had ceased centuries ago on Earth, outlawed by the Essential Activities Rules. No, the only place Gommersetism could be freely tested was Alvea. Maybe while he was here he could set something in motion. It was a funny problem: low probability that Gommerset was right, but a virtually infinite payoff in understanding if he was. Suddenly Skallon wanted to *know,* wanted to see if the rest of humanity could possibly be wrong about so vast a question. If only he could do something . . .

A Spatemper caste guard strode through the echoing galleries, summoning viewers to leave. The museum was closing, though it was only early evening. Alveans wished to be off, to gather again in their Communals and celebrate the Festing time.

Skallon made his way out cautiously, studying each person who emptied out of the connecting vaults. The ruddy stone slabwork reflected back the bubbling chatter of these people and Skallon relaxed, more comfortable here than he had been for hours.

When he reached the street he turned right, walked a block at a quick pace, and stopped in a shrouded ceremonial archway. In a moment he heard a panting in the darkness nearby and Fain appeared, followed by Scorpio.

"What in hell was that for?"

"To expose anybody tagging me."

"It didn't work."

"Well, you didn't see anybody earlier either, did you?"

Grudgingly: "No."

"Then that dodge of mine was worth a try. Right? Come on, let's go back to the hotel. Maybe Danon's seen something We've got to do some thinking."

13

Joane waited with Skallon, sitting on a ruined wall that framed part of the courtyard of the hotel. Fain had gone inside to feed Scorpio—who still wasn't feeling well—and think. Skallon cheerfully turned over that function to Fain; he was tired of this shadow boxing against a Changeling they never saw, whose purposes he was beginning to doubt.

Danon came trudging up the slope of Maraban Lane in the last glimmerings of early evening. Skallon felt slightly guilty at placing such demands on Danon, who was, after all, still a boy. "See anything?"

"No." Danon slouched against the mortared wall. "Nothing came or went in that back alley. How about you?" His voice rose with hope.

"We tried a trap. Nothing."

"The dog and Commander . . ."

"Fain? They're inside. I think we've run flat out of ideas."

"Mom? I'm hungry." Danon, so eager at the beginning, was clearly losing interest in this new game.

"Yes, little one." She stroked the back of Danon's head, watching him. Skallon, who had been studying her through a lover's eyes, found this gesture, denoting motherhood and family and other roles, slightly jarring.

"Let's go inside," he said. "The Changeling can wait until tomorrow." Joane took them to the main hotel kitchen, where cooks sweated and waiters clattered dishes. In the midst of a plague, Skallon was surprised to find great piles of food—yellow animals like pigs, glassy-eyed in death; great pale blocks of butter; strings of odd green sausages; cheese like grindstones. Joane sliced out Danon a meal and the boy took it away, nodding to Skallon like a fellow warrior as he left for his room. The boy was sunken-eyed with fatigue.

He and Joane talked, tentatively and with a certain ease now. Around them the kitchen reeked of food and sweat. She paused to give orders in a mild, clear voice that instantly caught attention from the cooks and assistants. Waiters, barking orders with half-moons of sweat at their armpits, were breaking tough roots into a salad, jamming thumbs into cream pots to flavor the mix. One washed his face in a sink where

clean crockery was rinsing; Joane caught him, up-
braided him, and set him to a menial task.

Skallon enjoyed watching this facet of her unfold.
She inspected the waiters and sent them out to open
the Communal. It was instructive to watch them enter. A sudden change came over them. Their shoulders
stiffened, their scruffy robes were gathered in and
tucked securely, the hurry and irritation of the kitchen
fell away and they glided out with a solemn air.

Joane beckoned and they went round to the Communal, entering through the public portal.

The brick-floored room was packed already with
people talking, eating, some singing in small clusters.
Kish dwarfed a small side bar. Skallon saw Fain
spooning some green liquid out of a bowl, perched on
a stool at a table next to the bar. Fain ate stolidly,
head down, ignoring everything around him. Kish was
plainly bothered by the Earthman sitting silently
nearby; his eyes shifted over at Fain every few moments. When Kish spotted Skallon and Joane he
brightened and beckoned them over to the bar.

"Your friend is not pleased with your work?" Kish
kept his voice low, though there was no need in the
babble of the Communal.

"He'll get over it," Skallon said dryly.

"I believe his mood has affected Danon," Joane
said. "He was very tired and depressed when he returned." Kish nodded, as though this confirmed his
conviction that Earthers had a bad effect when they
were thwarted.

"He is always in a rush," Kish said. "Can I not offer
him . . . ?"

Skallon nodded. "A drink."

He caught Fain's eye in a moment and beckoned
him over. Kish set two mugs before them. "Try it,"

Skallon said, raising his voice to be heard as a burst of song rippled through the crowd at the far end of the room.

Fain sipped, then drank. Skallon found it a thick, mealy ale with a curious iron aftertaste. "Um," Fain said impartially. "Not bad."

"A stout. Velvet stout." Kish poured more.

They talked about nothing in particular, Fain saying little and Kish rolling on, oblivious to Fain's silence, spinning out tales of larcenous merchants and affronts to his honor, all duly rectified by a few dashing commercial maneuvers. Joane listened dutifully though she had undoubtedly heard all this before. Skallon studied the crowd.

"Approve this." Kish slammed down full mugs again. A lighter brewing, this time. Bubbles beaded its amber surface.

"Ah . . ." Skallon began, after a sip.

"This is crap," Fain muttered.

"You are right. Quite right." Kish nodded assessingly, a critic of his own wares.

"An excretion better left in the horse," Skallon said, remembering an old Alvean satirical text.

"To the point!" Kish said merrily, beaming. "Approve *this*, then."

Mugs slapped down with a bang so that a fraction jumped out onto the table, as though to avoid the coming judgment. "Excellent," Skallon said evenly, meaning it. The dark mellow stuff went down without effort.

"Umm. Good," Fain agreed. "Good."

Kish beamed more. He went to a back niche and brought forward more tinkling brown bottles, uncorked them from their wire tresses, and poured further dollops into fresh mugs. "The evening sings!" he said, and bade them drink on.

Skallon spoke to Fain for a moment and they both took from their belts small pills and swallowed them to free their bloodstreams of alcohol. It was a good precaution. Kish waxed warm and expansive, thumping down samples of rare ales and bitters from distant provinces. Here, plainly, was the center of his gusto.

Danon came in, a bit rested and ready for some more supper. They gave him a sip of ale and the boy sat beside Skallon, watching as the crowd swelled and the air thickened with veils of smoke. The neighborhood gathered here, in the largest available Communal, particularly in Fest seasons. There were smiths, potters, butchers, fruitsellers and qantimakas strippers, porters and maids-of-all-work. Skallon loved the rich assortment of faces and ages. There were cadaverous and silent ale-soakers, steadily pouring brown bubbling liquid down themselves. Several women half-danced, half-staggered from table to table, mumbling songs and poetry, making it up as they went along, ready to rhyme anything. Everyone was happy, overwhelmingly certain that the world was a good place, the plagues would not wrap smoke fingers around this frothing circle so bright, and that the inhabitants of this room were a noble and notable set of folk. A girl danced, her knees tied together with rope, a man lumbering with her wielding a yellow-painted wooden phallus the size of a rolling pin. The room rocked with laughter. The girl rolled her eyes, licked pink lips in anticipation, submitted to a jerky thrusting mount. Then the man collapsed, slack-mouthed. She laughed and whirled away. Another man snagged her elbow and diverted her to his table. Laughter followed them, pealing in the close-packed room.

Fain was growing restless. He drained his mug. "Think I'll go out for a while."

"Why?" Skallon asked.

"To nose around. The Changeling's got to have some effect on this city."

"You won't find it at night."

"The Changeling's got to be nearby."

"Unlikely."

"It's thumbing its nose—if it has one—at *us*, Skallon. That dumb chase—it was a joke."

"That's why I'm wondering about the Changeling's motives. Maybe he's not trying to go to the top of Alvean society. Maybe he doesn't give a damn about the high castes."

"I don't know. That was the pattern before."

"On Revolium? When you caught him before?"

"Yeah. There and everywhere else. Where I've killed them."

"But that word—'pattern.' The whole thing about Changelings is that they don't follow patterns. They're pure intuition."

"That's why I think it's keeping close to us. We zig, it zags."

"He'll never get any power in Kalic that way."

"Why not? That's where *we're* hanging around, waiting for it to show up."

"True." Skallon sipped a thick, aromatic bitter Kish had poured.

"I think it's watching the hotel."

"Staying here, you mean? A guest."

"No. Too risky—Scorpio would spot it."

"That's why you want to go out at night. With Scorpio."

"Right. The Changeling knows us by sight. Okay, deprive it of that. Scorpio can pick out a Changeling in the dark."

"I . . ."

"See you later," Fain said abruptly and waded away through the crowd.

When he knew what to do, he acted. Skallon had a certain admiration for that. No second thoughts, no doubts, no alternate theories. Pure action.

"Approve this," Kish intruded on his thoughts. "An unusual brewing method. Here—" Kish handed the two mugs to Danon, who was clearly showing some effect from the drinking. The boy fumbled the mugs, spattered a brown film on the bar top, and steadied himself with a shaking hand. As he gave Skallon a mug he mumbled, "Believe . . . I need to clear . . . my head."

Kish laughed, his voice booming out over the Communal. "The boy must learn." He winked at Skallon. When Joane looked over at him his face went a decorous blank.

Smoke layered the dense air. Skallon was thinking muzzily of going off to bed, perhaps with a sign to Joane for her to follow after a discreet wait. The Communal was less boisterous now; some faces were slack, staring into space. The singers mumbled to each other. Others sniffed the smoky euphorics. Skallon had breathed some of the acrid stuff as it drifted in the room. It seemed to have some effect on him. The Communal seemed smaller, the walls pressing in, and he balanced woozily on his stool.

The faces caught in the flickering oil lamps had turned inward. They seemed to perceive that now, on the downward slope from the evening's opening hours, they were not splendid creatures in a fine world, but rough-handed workmen and women grown squalidly and dismally drunk. A graceless and mangy crew, indeed. But Skallon saw through this layer of remorse and revelation that had descended on them all. He perceived in these people a hard, tough core that the plagues could not defeat. But they were adrift, there was the smell of that. A stable society pays for its security through inflexibility.

Danon came back in, eyes bright.

"Something's happening a few blocks away. I can hear the noise. A crowd," he said breathlessly.

"Is Fain there?"

Danon shook his head, his cowl fluttering. "Don't know."

Skallon lurched to his feet, the fog of the Communal clearing slowly from his mind. "Let's go. Keep in the shadows, though." He nodded to Kish, to Joane, and they left, shouldering their way through the people.

Skallon heard the muffled sound of many people talking, shouting, when they reached the street. Maraban Lane was sunken in darkness, but down a connecting street reflected a glow. He and Danon hurried toward it.

Everything was very clear. They rushed along smooth empty streets, feet scuffling and clacking, air caressing Skallon's face. The diffuse light resolved into street lamps and hand torches. At least a thousand people were standing in a ragged crescent, listening to a fat Alvean on a raised platform. Skallon saw the man was standing on a vegetable cart, feet crushing qantimakas stems.

The crowd rustled and murmured, as if urging the speaker along. He was saying something about the vicious defilement of the Festing times by disease. By intrusion. By the Earthers, who snatched life itself from the bleeding lips of the starving poor.

Skallon listened intently to this, scanning the crowd for a sign of Fain. Nothing. Was there any indication that the Changeling was behind this? Skallon frowned. Hard to tell.

Meanwhile, the faces in the crowd occasionally turned toward him, inquiring eyes boring into his. Perhaps something was wrong with his robes. Skallon looked down, tottered, straightened a tuck here and there. Everything seemed all right.

The crowd's faces made up a fabric, crazed and weaving, fine as a speckled lace. Each knotted face, each intent set of eyes and mouth, was poised in a sharp and well-defined space. Framed, yes, unnaturally spaced to be fresh and clean, like in a well-designed painting. A painting, yes. Unsigned, of course. Yes.

The speaker bellowed out his simplistic truths. Devious. Faithless. Vermin ruthless Earthers. Alvea had cast them out but the plagues went on. Their stamp remained.

Skallon nodded, shook his head, nodded again. The Alvean didn't understand what was happening. Obviously the man had no knowledge of social dynamics, of genetics, of history. The fat man was spinning out a plausible but hollow argument, missing the real points. Skallon remembered crowds like this he had been in, assembled in yards and fields and dormitories. Instructors had told those crowds what was expected of them, what the penalties were if they didn't measure up, why it was all necessary. Nobody ever got to talk back; the crowd stood numbly, taking it in.

But this jam of Alveans was different. At each shouted invective they rustled like leaves in a wind, a fierce breeze blowing away from the gesturing, sweating speaker. Some shouted encouragement.

Skallon listened carefully, trying for a fresh grip on each moment, each word. He felt himself drifting through the edges of the mob. Danon whispered something, urging him back. Fingers plucked at him.

The boy fell away, behind. Words washed over Skallon. Jumbles of phrases. Faces turned toward him, fluttering in the gale.

The cart loomed, larger than he had estimated. A mouth, asking questions. A shove, arm out stiffly, and it went away. He moved on fragile knees. Hand on the cart, breath rasping, boosting up. Speaker turning. Another face, that's all, just another face like the others.

Skallon barked out a sentence, another. *I bring clarity.* Hands picking at him. He gave them an elbow, another shove. They fell away. A hush washed over the framed faces below. Eerie, the expectant silence. *A union of aims.* Danon in the distance, a clear definite tight little boy's face. Like the others, tilted up to hear the truth. *Listen to . . .* A fresh, enlightening breath. *Strength through knowledge. . .*

To show them, he slipped back his cowl. Loosened the tucks and folds and false fronts of the Doubluth robes. His Earthly features lifted clear in the dim light. *Yet I do know you . . .* A gasp. *And your planet, this rich world . . .* Movement. *. . . yet wracked with rot . . .* Hands. *. . . false history . . .* Grasping. A muted angry roar from below him. *You must see . . .* Speaking very slowly, clearly, so they can understand the subtle point he must make.

But the hands. Clutching. Wrenching. A blur of motion. The faces in wan orange light sliding by. Chill air. A cart wheel seen upside down. A wad of noise enveloped him. Somehow, something had gone wrong.

14

People, so many people. They pressed on all sides. Angry faces. Noise, shouting. No words, just sounds.

Then Fain. A tight face, mouthing something. Walk? Run?

His feet touched the firm, forgiving earth. Fain leading him. Frightened Alveans running away in the watery light. Fain. Shadows. Through narrow alleys. Fain glancing back, then surging ahead. Hurry. Run.

Maraban Lane. Into the hotel, quick clicking of feet behind them. Someone looming out of pooled light. Danon? No, Joane.

Through a corridor. The kitchen. Warm, spicy. Scented air. He felt himself tilt forward, head down, face to the table.

Time drifted by. Joane's quick words, darting. Fain, an edge in his voice, panting. Shallow breaths. Scorpio whimpering.

Kish, a muddled voice, cut off abruptly. Words, all jumbled together. Skallon gave up piecing together the puzzle and a warm dull buzzing came over him. He explored his teeth with a thick tongue.

Up. Up. Hands lifting him until gravity came again and he was on his feet. The kitchen began to weave around. Suck in moist air. One step. Two. Joane, whispering.

More walking. Shadows. Skallon? This way. Here. Scorpio's gruff voice: Safe. Inside.

Caverns. Moldy rock walls. Walking, squeezing, walking. Dim ruby lights dotting the walls. Fain stumbling, cursing. Thick stone pillars. Wooden beams. Chill damp air. Splashing steps as they waded through a trickling stream. Muttering. At last, a place to sit. To slump. Footsteps fading away into the lengthening shadows. Distant voices.

A dull humming in his head. Then sleep. Sleep.

15

Joseph Fain sat in the center of his rumpled bed and sipped a mug of Kish's dark ale. The cold bitterness of it hit his stomach like a clenched fist, but Fain knew he needed it to focus his thoughts. *The Changeling*, he thought, *always sly, always different*. After the dumb charade in the hotel, he had decided on a change of tactics. Fain had followed Skallon's advice too much on this job, and that made both of them look dumb. You always made mistakes operating in a strange culture, but this time it was laughable. Okay, fine. Admit that fact. At the hotel Fain had decided to use it against the Changeling. Continue looking stupid. Let Skallon keep tripping over his own feet. Look dumber and dumber and finally the Changeling would overreach itself. Fain had used that method before and he knew it could work. Wherever the Changeling was, it

was laughing at the moronic Earthers. Good. Let it
laugh. He had to admit the damned Changeling had
brought off a real coup last night, plastering Skallon
that way, using him to incite the crowd. If Fain had
been a little faster he would've nailed the Changeling
right there. Next time would be different. Fain lifted
his mug in a mock salute. "Till we meet again," he
rasped, and drank.

A soft tapping at the door.

"I'm here," said Fain.

Joane entered hesitantly, showing her awareness of
the changed situation and her uncertainty about her
own present status. Fain assumed she had never seen
a man in a quiet, calculating rage before. Her life had
been spent in controlling boys: Kish, Danon, even
Skallon. She couldn't control Fain and he knew that
was what disturbed her. He knew but right now he
didn't care. "Well?" he said gruffly, making no move
to ease her discomfort. "What did you find out?"

"We—we did as you said, Kish and I. We went out
and—" Unconsciously, she turned and started to bolt
the door.

Fain interrupted. "Get away from there."

She spun, her face tinged with embarrassment. "But
I only meant—"

"I know what you meant. Now get in here. Talk. I
want to know what's going on out there." He pointed
to the walls of his room. "Spill it."

"Trouble," she said hurriedly. "Great trouble. Kish
and I, we both hear the same things. The Earthers are
here—on Alvea. They are disguised and are creating
the plagues. One was discovered last night, but there
are many more. Three men were torn apart by mobs
near the Great Hall. A speaker said they were Earthers."

"And were they?" Fain asked mockingly.

"No, of course not. You know that—"

He held up a hand. "I was joking. But what about Skallon? Have you had time to drop down and visit him today?"

"Danon is with him, not I. I have been with Kish as . . . as you directed."

"I'm glad to hear that," he said dryly. "But what about me? Did you hear anything about a second Earther? I want to know if it's safe for me to go into the streets."

"That is difficult to say. No one is sure how the Earther got away. Some say he didn't—he was killed. Others say a group of Earthers took him. Some think he managed to run but is now hiding. But everyone is looking for Earthers now. If you went out, you would be discovered, surely. You must stay here and wait."

He shook his head, not because he didn't recognize that what she said was true, but because right now he didn't want to hear her advice. So the Vertil had indeed worked last night to cover his tracks. That, if nothing else, was a pleasant sign. He had taken an inject as soon as he'd spotted Skallon among the crowd and realized what he intended to do. The Vertil had allowed Fain to distract enough of the mob to get Skallon safely away. He thought he'd made it back to the hotel without being seen. Danon, who had been with Skallon, had suggested a hiding place: the caverns beneath the city, seldom used since the early years of the colony when it had been necessary to live at certain times underground to avoid being fried to a crisp by the sun. Skallon was there now.

"Skallon was drugged, you know," he said.

"Yes—yes, we thought that might be the case."

"It means you're going to have to watch his food. Cook each bite yourself. His food—and mine. Keep

Kish away, everyone. Tell them I said so and, if they
don't agree, then tell me."

"I did that this morning with Skallon's breakfast.
Only Danon was with me."

"Well, do it from now on, too."

"Then you trust me."

"No, not especially. But, this way, if either of us
does get poisoned, I'll know exactly who to blame."
She smiled, but he didn't want that, either. "When do
you expect Danon?"

"It is nearly noon now. He should be coming shortly
for Skallon's lunch."

"When he does, send him up here. I may want to
follow him back."

"You'll want some lunch yourself. On an empty
stomach the ale is like a bitter fire."

He glared at her. What was it she wanted? Sex,
love, control, or just kindness? Right now he had nothing to offer. He jerked a thumb at the door. "Get out
of here, Joane. Leave me alone."

Looking hurt, she nodded, bit her lip, went softly
out. Fain looked at the closed door and sighed.

Failure. That was what was eating him. Plain, simple, ordinary failure. Hell, it happened to people every
day of the week. They tried something, it didn't
work out, they gave up, and they failed. But Fain
wasn't ordinary. It shouldn't happen to him—ever.
This world was beginning to remind him too goddamn much of Jado. The Changeling was playing
with him again, taunting him. Should he keep on playing stupid, even without Skallon's assistance, hoping
to draw the Changeling in? That just didn't seem like
enough.

The Changeling not only had him stymied, it might
very well have him beaten.

Testimony to that effect reached him through the walls of his room. He could hear the noise of shrill, angry voices in the streets below. All along he and Skallon had discussed the precarious state of order on this world. One thing could tip the balance over into chaos. Last night that one thing had occurred: the discovery of a disguised Earther in the streets of the city. They had done it all themselves—the Changeling had only applied the last crucial push.

Another knock at the door—more forceful than before. Fain grunted, and Danon came in. The boy looked haggard, drawn. Fain realized that he had probably waited up all night with the drugged Skallon. Fain himself had gone immediately back to the room after depositing Skallon in his hiding place. But he hadn't slept. There would be time for that later. If nothing new happened, plenty of time. On Earth. As a failure.

"How is he?" said Fain.

Danon rubbed his eyes. "Skallon is fine. He is asking for you."

"Does he remember anything of last night?"

"Only a little. He was not aware of what he had done."

"Did you tell him?"

Danon nodded.

"What did he say?"

"He said he thought he had been drugged by the Changeling."

Fain stood up. He'd had enough inactivity. It was time to be doing something, even if as yet he had no idea of what. "I'm going to go with you into the caverns, talk to Skallon. Wait around for me. I'd bettter put my padding on."

"You will come alone?"

Fain looked puzzled. "Sure. Who else would I bring?"

"The dog. Scorpio. It was Skallon's suggestion, not mine. The caverns are dark and sometimes mysterious. Skallon fears the Changeling may also be hiding down there."

Fain thought about that for a moment, then nodded. "It's not such an impossible idea." And one, he knew, he ought to have realized himself.

"So Skallon thought—do you remember how the room where he is hidden is situated? It lies at the end of a narrow tunnel."

"I remember that, yes." He was trained to recollect that sort of tactical detail.

"Well, Skallon thought if you returned with me, you could leave Scorpio at that place. Then, while you and Skallon spoke, the dog could keep watch. That way, if the Changeling came near, Scorpio could catch him."

"It's worth trying," Fain said. He had just finished attaching the last of his bulky pads and now quickly slipped into his Doubluth robes. "I'll get Scorpio and meet you in the kitchen."

Danon bowed, grinning, his teeth like tiny lights against the darkness of his face. "I am happy that you are pleased."

As Fain waddled down the hall toward Scorpio's room, he idly wondered whose idea that really was: Skallon's or the boy's. There were times when Danon showed signs of being many years sharper than he had any right to be.

Scorpio's room stank from his many days' idleness. The air was thick with the odors of food and dung and musty animal. Fain wrinkled his nose. As quickly as he could, he explained to Scorpio what he wanted him for and why. Scorpio, once he understood, was more than agreeable. He, like Fain, seemed to welcome any relief from the constant tedium of waiting.

The two of them went out. Fain moved cautiously through the upper and lower corridors, but no one was about. He could almost sense the utter emptiness of the rooms he passed. Why? he wondered. Where was everyone? Outside? He thought he knew. The crowds had claimed them. Alvea was like a drum drawn too tight. Skallon's actions last night had burst the taut, fragile skin.

Joane was alone in the kitchen. Seeing Fain, she started to speak, then hesitated.

"Where's Kish?" asked Fain.

She hesitated again and he saw that was indeed the source of her anxiety.

He cocked his head toward the wall. "Outside?"

She nodded tightly.

"And the rest of them? Your cooks, your employees? Them, too?"

"Yes. It is like—like a Fest outside. There is excitement and—and anger. The men feel it is better to run about and rage, better than waiting to die."

"And you don't?"

She shrugged. "I believe that death is not an end."

Fain suppressed the impulse to agree. He realized she was exposing a part of herself to him that she had previously kept well hidden. This was how she must talk to Skallon, he thought, and for a brief moment he felt an emotion very like envy. "But can I trust him? Kish? Is he running around outside for fun, or is he going to end up leading his friends in here to tear me apart?"

She refused to reassure him. "I never know what Kish may do."

But Fain knew he didn't have any choice. If he left the inn, he could only run and that would mean leav-

ing the city—and the planet—firmly in the hands of
the Changeling.

"Where's Danon?" he asked. "He was supposed to
meet me here."

"He went on ahead with food for Skallon." She
seemed to appreciate the return to a subject that carried less emotion for her. "He said Skallon becomes
anxious when he's left alone. He left instructions with
me on how to reach the hiding place. Do you need
them?"

"No, I can find the place. If I can't, Scorpio can."

"You will be back?"

He nodded. "I will. Shortly. And you'll stay here?
You won't let anyone come through after me?"

"I will try, Fain."

"Thank you." He spoke sincerely, even though he
knew her gesture of help was largely useless: no
woman was apt to stop the Changeling. Still, Joane
was the one person on this world whom he trusted. If
nothing else, Scorpio's presence in the kitchen testified to her honest faith. At least Joane was who she
said she was.

Beyond the kitchen was a small room, in a corner of
which was a trap door leading directly into the underground caverns below. Kish often used the space underneath the inn as a storage facility. Fain threaded
his way past stacks of canned food and bottled liquor
and then, igniting the flash he carried, proceeded to
follow the intricate path that would eventually lead
him to Skallon. The tunnels were generally broad and
spacious, branching frequently into wide caverns big
enough to hold several hundred men. Fain experienced no difficulty recalling his steps from the previous night. That was his training again, and he felt
pleased. The air was surprisingly clean, almost crisp.
There was some water seepage through cracks in the

stone floor, but Fain easily avoided the few shallow pools.

They had covered perhaps half the distance to Skallon's hideaway when Scorpio began to sniff loudly and fall behind. Fain waited for him in a cavern. Scorpio stopped a few meters away and placed his nose against the floor. Then he lifted his head and told Fain, "It. May. Be. The. One."

"The Changeling? You're sure?"

"No. Not. Sure. Weak."

"Old?" Was it possible the Changeling had used these caverns and tunnels as a hiding place all along?

"Not. Sure. Steps through . . . water."

"Then it may be recent." The Changeling would not bother to disguise its tracks unless it feared pursuit—from Scorpio. "We'd better hurry then. But be careful. I don't want to bump into it around the next corner."

"I. Will. Sniff. Fain."

"Good." Fain set out again, moving this time with a mixture of caution and haste. After a few hundred meters, Scorpio reported that the scent had grown weaker. It was definitely an old trail now, at least by a few hours. Fain felt relieved. He couldn't conceive of a worse place to confront the Changeling. The darkness and limited space down here would destroy nearly every advantage he possessed. He would be at the Changeling's mercy.

Reaching the entrance to the narrow tunnel that led directly to Skallon's room, Fain had Scorpio make a quick reconnaissance of the area. When Scorpio reported the same weak scent as before, Fain decided to go ahead with Skallon's plan and let the dog stand guard. He told him to be careful. "If the Changeling does come—if anyone comes—don't attack unless you're sure it's safe. Let it enter the tunnel, then let up

a howl. I'll come running and that way we'll have it
trapped between us."

"A. Good. Plan. Fain."

He nodded, not so sure as the dog. "I hope so. But
if not—if nothing happens—I should be out in an hour
or so."

"Good. Bye. Fain."

"Good-bye, Scorpio."

The place where he had secured Skallon after the
riot last night lay two hundred meters farther on. He
had to stoop to enter the tunnel and, before he
reached its end, move on all fours. A great place for
a sudden ambush, he thought, and a lousy place for
moving quickly. He began to think less and less of
Skallon's plan. He worried about Scorpio; the risk to
the dog seemed too great. But he didn't turn back.
If he'd had a better plan of his own—even a better
idea—he might have considered it. But he didn't. His
mind was a disturbing blank. For the moment, he
had no choice but to let Skallon—or Danon—take the
lead. As he moved, he turned his flashlight forward
and back. But there was nothing. Just himself. Some
water. The dark tunnel.

He came to the door of the cell and knocked. That
was what the room had been centuries before—a cell.
The door was thicker than both his legs and the one
small window barred. Danon had stumbled upon the
cell as a very young child and had never forgotten its
location.

Skallon said, "Come in, Fain."

There was a single dull lantern struggling to illumi-
nate the entire room. A cot, a desk, and a chair made
up the only furniture. Danon had secreted these here
long ago when he'd used the cell as a lonely hiding
place. There was a door in the opposite wall, but it

led into a shallow closet. The way in was the only way
out and Scorpio was guarding that. Fain left the door
open so that he could hear the dog. Skallon lay on his
back on the bed. He was alone.

"I wondered if you'd bother to come." Skallon sat
up, but slowly.

Fain shrugged, keeping one ear cocked for Scorpio.
"Why shouldn't I?"

"Because of the stupid thing I did last night."

"That wasn't you. That was the Changeling. You
were drugged. Just like an Alvean on Vertil. You
couldn't help yourself."

"You're sure of that? You know I was drugged?"

Skallon seemed badly in need of some reassurance.
Fain saw no reason to withhold it. "I'm sure. As sure,
at least, as I ever am of anything. It could have been
me as easily as you. It just happened that you drank
the wrong mug of ale."

"I'm glad to hear that, Fain, but it's still over, isn't
it? Danon told me it's really a mess up there. The people are rioting, hunting everywhere for disguised
Earthers. It's only a matter of time before they catch
us, Fain. We can't get away, and we can't stay here."

Skallon's analysis wasn't far from Fain's own, but he
saw no need to go into that now. Instead, he concentrated on something else Skallon had said: Danon.
Where was the boy? "Didn't Danon bring you your
lunch? He was supposed to have left before I did."

"No, I haven't seen him," said Skallon.

"That's odd."

"What isn't on this world?" Skallon came off the
bed, suddenly animated. "I tell you we never should
have come here in the first place, Fain. That was our
first mistake—our only real mistake. We should have
let the Changeling come in and do as it wished. This
isn't our world. These people are pseudo-men, closer

to the Changeling than they are to us. What makes
them our responsibility, our worry?"

Fain shook his head. Skallon was blowing off, letting his anger run. "I thought you were the one who
admired them so much."

"That was before they tried to kill me. Think, Fain.
Look at how we've employed our best minds trying to
conquer their plagues. And how have they repaid us?
Fain, they'd kill us in a second if they caught us, tear
us apart. It's not just the Changeling, either. The
Changeling follows chaos the way Scorpio does a
scent. It doesn't create. It reinforces what's already
there. These Alveans aren't people. They're nothing—
absolutely frapping *nothing*."

Fain came close, trying to calm Skallon, but Skallon
pulled out of his grasp and headed for the door. "I'm
going to piss. I'll be back in a second."

"Sure," said Fain. He still didn't fully understand
Skallon's outburst. He had sounded more like Fain
than himself. Was he serious? Was there some real reason for all that fury?

Then he heard it. More than likely the sound had
been present in the room for some time but muffled
by Skallon's angry words. It came from the closet. It
sounded like a man's choked voice.

Fain went over to the closet. The sound was coming
from here. Tentatively, he opened the door.

Inside, he saw a man bound and gagged in torn
sheets. The man's eyes rolled with strain and he struggled to speak past the mass of the gag.

The man was Skallon.

Fain swore. He spun and drew his heatgun in a single flash of motion. He sprinted for the door, ducked
down, and ran as fast as the tunnel allowed.

He slammed a shoulder into the stone and winced.

Ahead was darkness, waiting darkness, and he lunged senselessly forward, his face rigid, after the Changeling.

Part
Four

Sliding, stepping, singing, the Changeling skates clean and smooth through the streets of Kalic. Doubluth robes flutter about its legs. Its face ripples in sympathy, taking on echoes of the features of the strangers it meets. Here a man, heavy and jowly. There, a woman, face drawn and tight, lips puckered. Echoes. Its face is in and of the Dance. Echoes.

It nears the place of the Earthers. The world watches, murmurs, sings in anticipation. Here, the yellow lights. A worn building, smooth with years.

It has let the city seep into itself, bathed itself in the many wilting moments of the Alveans. Now it knows, the answer floats up from nothingness into its mind: the time to enter the nest of the Earthers, the crucial time, is now.

The doors of the Battachran Hotel lie open. Within lurks Fain but—worse—his dog. Carefully, cautiously, it penetrates this sanctum. The purple robes of its new caste reek with the stench of the apparently dead man. There are voices—human. It shies back. One—Fain?—speaks like an Earther. If Fain is present in that back room, the dog must also be near.

"Honored, sir, may I be—?"

It spins, huge body awkwardly tilting. A heatgun hidden in its belt. But, no. It relaxes. A boy, small child, Alvean, growing now toward first plumpness. "I seek," it begins, in the gentle, musical tones of a native Doubluth—

"Fellow pilgrims," says the boy, edging toward a flight of stairs. "If you'll take a room, I can—"

It grabs his arm, pulls. Face against face. It breathes harshly, waits, whispers, "Those men in the back—who are they?"

". . . Men of Earth," says the boy, in the flat tones of the Vertil-drugged. "Fain and Skallon."

"An animal is with them?"

"A dog. It speaks."

"And you? Your name? Who are you?"

"I am Danon. My mother—Joane—is wedded to the innkeeper, Kish."

"You live here?"

"Yes."

It is made too easy—giggling gift from a chaotic universe. "Outside." There are deep shadows here—vacant streets. It questions the boy in considerable depth, knowing from long practice the exact areas to penetrate. In time, the drug runs thin. The boy nods, sleeps, wakes. It grasps his hands. "Not yet—no. A further question—please."

The eyes of the boy flicker with thin awareness. "Yes—I—yes—"

"Your life," it asks, uncertain of what will come. "Tell me if you have enjoyed it."

The boy stammers, hesitates. In spite of the Vertil, he cannot formulate an adequate response.

It shakes the boy brutally, snapping his neck back and forth. In his stupor, the boy does not resist. "Answer me—yes or no. I must have an answer to my question."

"I—no. No, I have not enjoyed my . . . my life. I think that . . ." He sleeps. That quickly. Gently, approaching tenderness, it lowers the boy to the pavement and arranges his limbs in a comfortable posture. Then, crouching, dropping to its knees, it leans heavily across the boy, clutches his throat in its fat hands, squeezes.

No! It is not easy. The boy awakens, groans, thrashes. This is not a fat Doubluth who is dying but a boy, mere child. Squeeze. There is no meaning to the act of murder. No birth—no death. All is nothingness, cosmic illusion, part of the One. *I curse you*, it thinks savagely. *I curse you, oh One, for creating this universe in which boys must die without living. You are All but All is chaos—it is evil.*

Something snaps. The boy's head bobs weakly.

No, not easy. Breathing heavily, it rises to its knees in a posture mocking prayer. The slide into death is a beautiful thing, a sad thing, worthy of tears and mad laughter. The mere Earthers and Alveans sense it not. The loss and the replenished joy.

The body must be disposed of. A shallow grave. It finds soft earth in a hidden alley and claws with its fingers. On a world where death comes quickly for many, one more grave will attract little attention.

It screams as the willed transformation begins. Fat, gross Alvean body torn asunder. The Doubluth robes are too big. It undresses, slips into the child's gown. Stumbling, ending its tears, it enters the hotel again. Silence. The Earthers—Fain and Skallon—have gone.

"Danon, where have you been? I've been looking all over for you."

An Alvean woman approaches him with her hands outstretched. From the dead boy's description, he recognizes her. "Mother," he says, letting her hug him. "I went out. Those—those men. I am afraid of them."

"No," she says, touching his hair. "They are good men—they have come to help us." She radiates a warmth he can almost feel. A strange sensation. Love, he supposes. On other worlds he has visited, it exists as well. "And you should never go out. Especially not at night. There is sickness and disease, bad people. You must promise me never to go out again. Please. Promise."

"I promise, Mother." A simple act. It is Danon now—it is he. The dead boy in the shallow grave is mere rotting flesh.

She stands, smiling, still touching his hair. "And now to bed with you. Kish believes in rising early—you know that."

"Kish believes in making me work because he's lazy."

She starts to protest, then laughs. "How true." She guides him softly toward the stairs. "But I have another idea, one where you won't have to work for Kish."

He pauses. "What, Mother?"

"It will necessitate helping the Earthers. Are you sure you're not too afraid of them?"

"I'm not afraid of them at all. You told me not to be."

"Good." She smiles. "It is Skallon, the softer of the two Earthers. He wants someone to guide him through the city. I cannot do it and Kish will not. You could. It'll be easy work and, with the Earther, you can protect each other."

He pretends to concentrate. "I'll do it, Mother. It is the other Earther I hate—that one and his animal."

"Then I'll wake you in the morning, dear."

The room he occupies is small. There are many toys. Soft dolls. There is an aircraft which, when thrown, glides smoothly through the air. A colorful metal box with a handle. He turns the handle. Music. A catchy tune. Turning farther, there is pressure. Suddenly—*whang*—the top pops off the box and a puppet

on a spring vaults through. He falls back, laughing in
boyish wonder at the trick and his own resultant fear.
On the floor, he curls up and attempts to sleep. Creatures such as he rarely require actual slumber, but he
is more tired than usual, spent from so many identity
changes. Dreams dance in him, spinning in fog. Yellow, green. Ugly visions predominate. Pain. Suffering.
Death from plague. Murder. Shivering, he awakens
within a few hours. One tiny window affords an angled view of the empty, dark street beneath. Awaiting
dawn, he stands and watches. The red sun arrives in a
burst of fire. From the door behind, a gentle knocking
sound. "Danon, are you awake?" says Mother.

"But this is the best route, the only way of reaching
the Great Hall quickly," he says, squirming weakly in
Fain's tight grasp. "To go another way would require
entering those streets frequented by the beast."

Days have now passed, and his most difficult task
has been avoiding the dog. Fortunately, a mild illness
engendered by the beast's more savage impulses has
lain the animal low. Guiding Skallon through the city,
he has come to know the man more intimately than
any Earther before. With Fain, great killer of Changelings, he proceeds more cautiously. All of this is part
of the plan which cannot be a plan. To taunt Fain.
Frustrate and anger him. To force him to doubt himself. To worry him with inactivity. Then to strike.
The key to chaos on Alvea lies with Fain himself.
Only he can hold it back.

To the Great Hall. Where the highcastes of the
planet convene to devise intricate plans. A joke. The
One must laugh. A deception. He decides nothing
now himself. For example, as Fain and Skallon, disguised, enter the Great Hall, he could easily expose
their true natures. And yet, what would occur? Fain,

using his supply of Vertil, would beat back the angry mob and easily escape. No, Fain must be broken first. He must be shown the truth of chaos. Alvea is less crucial than Fain. The planet can be easily shattered, but not the man.

Outside, he waits, but not passively. The supply of drugs hidden under his gown can again be used. Some Vertil remains but he chooses a plague strain. Dancing, rotting sickness, not native to Alvea but certainly fatal. Murder means nothing this morning. A cleansing wind whips through the city. In past days, he has injected the strain into a local water supply. Now, as an old Doubluth staggers past, plainly a senior of the caste from his bent back and wrinkled hands, he acts. The old man cries, "*Ow*," and touches his arm. He shrugs. Insect bite. Enters the Hall. Will die.

Some hours pass. He remembers moments of play on the homeworld. The Dance of Death. Children in a circle. Round and round as music plays. The song stops. The children fall. The last to touch ground can be killed by the others. Usually, he is not. Mercy may be granted instantly or after a savage beating. Sometimes, death results. Popular children die but the hated as well. His first lover, a bright blond boy, fell late, had his head torn from his torso. Rivers of blood. The Dance of Death. No patterns could develop. A game that children play.

Once boredom holds sway over the Great Hall, slipping inside is a simple matter. He sees Fain nodding, Skallon entranced, but avoids them. A young man in purple Doubluth robes. Self-injection. Vertil. He leans close, breathing harshly in and out, and whispers, "Kind sir, a man will soon die in this Hall. When he does, you must stand and denounce the Earth for killing him." Then back outside. The wind has fallen and a warming sun washes his back with gentle heat.

Beauty lies within the universal pauses. He admires the dead black suns. The airless satellites. The changeless glory of a neutron star. He nods briefly but a terrible nightmare spins him awake, screaming. From within the Hall, harsh voices now rise. Soon there is panic. Escape. He takes shelter behind a post and observes the fleeing crowd. In time, Fain and Skallon appear. He rushes to them. "What happened in there, good sirs? Some say it is an outbreak of the plague."

But Fain knows better. Fain knows what has been done to him and why. Suddenly, he—the boy and the Changeling—fears this cold shell of a human being. Fain is the antithesis of all true disorder. Fain is all-knowing, all-seeing. Fain is the living remnant of the long dead God.

He screams in fear of Joseph Fain.

But only inwardly.

Fear is mere part of the changing disorder of the cosmos.

He observes while Fain has sex with the woman Joane. A dangerous, risky whim. A peephole in the wall of an adjoining room. The dog is present with Fain. Though ill, it may possibly scent the presence of an intruder. Flesh within flesh. Fain and Joane. Her heavy legs flap spasmodically about his plunging thighs. He moans; she shakes. On the homeworld, lots are chosen at random moments. A green marble for male, a blue for female. Twice he has drawn the green and on four occasions the blue. Most recently, holding the blue marble, he grew swollen with child. The process of birth proved an endless pain, a searing fire oblivious to soothing waters. He laughed at the final moment. The newborn child wept. His son. Or daughter. Whisked away by the medical ones. Never seen again. Nor forgotten.

In order to continue the species, birth is a necessity. But the One, jokingly, has made pain a prerequisite for birth. And—a further, greater joke—made pleasurable sex a prerequisite for pregnancy. Pleasure, then Pain, then simple necessity—an odd, chaotic, senseless pattern. Which does Fain feel now? He moves brutally, passionlessly in and out of the woman. Not pleasure. Joane, who has born a previous child (now deceased), seems to the observer to be ripe for another. Not pain. Her hips are wide, her buttocks, turned up, like slabs of dark meat. Necessity? No, not that. The act is barely a moderate joke. It is evidence. Fain suffers a weakness of the flesh. (Skallon, as well, but that is not important in the dancing singing moment.) As he watches, a burning truth blooms, skimming lightly.

Fain is doomed. He must fall. The climax draws exhilaratingly near. He draws away from the peephole and, on silent feet, leaves the room. Below, in the kitchen, he approaches Kish, who is preparing himself a late night feast. "Mother and Fain are upstairs in his room," he says. "They're making funny sounds."

He rushes toward the disguised Fain and Skallon. "I have found him!" he cries. "It is your enemy! I have seen him with my own eyes!"

He used simple Vertil to lure the black-robed assassin into the forbidden hall. Fain should know this but, in the fury of the chase, fails to reflect. Since first hearing of Alvea, he has admired the assassin caste above all others. Terrible in legend, they never act. That is the contradiction and that, for him, is also the beauty.

While Fain and Skallon hurry into the Great Hall to

confront their enemy, he climbs a stone spike and regards the shifting mob in the plaza beneath. They are like frantic insects driven madly about on the gray smooth belly of some rotting beast. What will happen now? Will Fain kill the black-robed one? Will Skallon? Will the man escape and initiate a chase or will he perhaps kill Fain or Skallon or even both? That is why his plans are never truly plans. Consciously, he leaves many options, alternatives. No moment is ever certain. Chance is welcome. When the assassin at last appears, streaking across the gray pavement, he feels nothing. Fain and Skallon follow. His plan has succeeded but he feels no satisfaction. Can a fisherman feel proud of the fish he has caught? No, correctly he cannot, for the One has long since elected to let the fish exist. So it is with his plans of chaos. He is an agent, never a creator.

Descending, he tells Fain where the assassin has gone. He takes part in the ensuing pursuit, knowing where—if not how—it must end. The assassin is trapped. Fain says, "The kid and I are waiting. He'll let me know if the Changeling comes out his way and I'll cover the street. I've decided we're going to do it your way, Skallon—no cold-blooded murder. You go back to the hotel, get Scorpio, and bring him here."

Scorpio! From his place at the rear of the building, he smiles. An unexpected wrinkle in his plan. Briefly, he envisions yet another alternate future: the dog arrives, sniffs out Danon as the Changeling. Fain, drawing his heatgun, kills the boy. Returning to the hotel, saying nothing, he has sex with Joane before returning in triumph to Earth.

But, when the dog arrives, he is too clever to come dangerously near it. The alternate future is erased from the slate of possibilities. Instead, the assassin is caught with ease. He fails to die, as Fain discovers the

subterfuge of the Vertil too quickly. Anger follows, a
great explosion of rage. Fain knows he has been
taunted, frustrated, made a fool of.

He remembers how on the homeworld he saw a motion picture film, created long ago in antique American Earth, that was brought to the planet by the original philosophers, as a sacred token of all that they
knew and believed. Among a people for whom art
could not exist—for art is merely a fruitless attempt by
the blind to forge order from the molten flux of
chaos—the film enjoyed a vast popularity. The story
told how, on a serene and ordinary day, those most
gentle and passive of all creatures, the birds, rose up
in mass to destroy their human masters. Watching in a
crowd, he laughed with the others, for to him the humor lay in the ceaseless efforts of the Earthers to devise some sort of explanation for a series of events that
were, of course, utterly senseless. Watching the film,
he was filled with a great sense of joy, comprehending
its truth and admiring the genius of those who had
also known it so many centuries ago. But he also remembers how he saw the film a second time and how,
that time, he was filled not with joy but with terror.
He stood and he screamed. He attempted to destroy
the print and was stopped only by force. *It is the
same*, he shouted to them. Each image, each frame,
each spoken word of dialogue. A description of chaos
told in the most orderly manner conceivable. The
madness of that contradiction terrified him. Since
then, he has steadfastly refused to see that film or any
other.

And he is frightened now, too. For similar, if not
identical reasons. His skipping, skimming Dance to
destroy Fain works too well. Each moment is like the
frozen frame in a finished film. Only the conclusion,

the denouement, the final revelation of victory or defeat, lies in real doubt. A merging, singing doubt. Now, for the first time, he begins to fear that, too. Everything proceeds too well, too certainly. When he acts, obvious events occur:

—While Fain and Skallon are busy attempting to lure the Changeling within range of the dog, he moves among the surging city crowds, planting in conspiratorial whispers the possibility of Earth infiltrators within the city. Using his remaining supply of Vertil with care, he captures a number of agents and sends them out to spread similar rumors.

—For the remainder of the afternoon, he rests quietly in his room. The following hours will be crucial, he knows, and already hesitancy and fear are beginning to affect him. He naps briefly but is awakened by the usual bad dreams. Hearing his cries, Joane comes to soothe him. He slides into her arms and places his head upon her soft breasts. Muzzy, warm, and dumb they are, singing graces, giving, yes.

—That night he drugs Skallon's ale with a mild euphoric purchased from a local street peddler. Before this, he has especially enjoyed listening to Fain's discussion of Changelings. Yet, when Skallon says, "The whole thing about Changelings is that they don't follow patterns. They're pure intuition," he is momentarily frightened. Skallon speaks only the truth, but he is aware by now that his current plan, by its success, is violating this precept. A premonition of future failure and ultimate death visits him. He drives the thought away. In chaos, the future can never be foretold. Only the One may glimpse what soon will be, and the One, if forced to tell, would only lie.

—Leaving the hotel, he enters the streets. Coming across an angry crowd discussing the possibility of Earth infiltrators at loose in Kalic, he uses his Vertil to create an even angrier disturbance. Then back to the hotel. He tells Skallon, "Something's happening a few blocks away. I can hear the noise. A crowd." He speaks breathlessly, with excitement, voice high and skittering not all of it feigned. Skallon, made compliant by the drugged ale, comes away with him. As they approach the crowd, he whispers, makes suggestions. Skallon nods, agreeing to everything. In the mob, Skallon reveals his true identity. But Fain arrives. With the help of his own supply of Vertil, Fain disperses the mob. Fain pilots Skallon through the mad sea. He grabs Fain by the sleeve and points. "This way. I know a place where we can hide Skallon."

"Where?" Fain still lacks trust.

"The hotel."

Fain shakes his head. "No, too obvious. Someone may have recognized him—or me. We'll have to get out of the city entirely."

But he has previously considered this objection—and found a devious way around it. "I do not mean within the hotel—I mean beneath it."

"Come again," says Fain.

On the homeworld, during his initial studies of the planet Alvea, he came across references to the existence of a system of underground caverns located beneath the major cities. Since his arrival here, he has explored these caverns on several occasions. Already he has chosen the perfect place in which to hide Skallon. Fain hesitates, then nods, lacking any real alternative. They return to the hotel and take Skallon below. Fain looks upon the room at the end of the tunnel and purses his thin lips. "This may do." He paces. "Are you sure there's no other way in or out?" He opens the closet door, studies the interior. "I want it so there's no way anyone or anything can sneak up on you and Skallon."

"There is no way."

"And you will stay with Skallon? I want to get back to the hotel and see what's up. He's been doped. I can't leave him alone."

"I will gladly stay."

"I'll tell your mother you're here."

Alone, as Danon, he stares at Skallon's slumbering form and contemplates the possibility of sudden murder. Jittering, jittering, let it come. The One. Approaching the bed, he crouches. His hands descend slowly. Suddenly, Skallon is awake. He stares. "Danon. Where—where am I? What—what—?"

Softly, he pushes Skallon down. "This is a safe place. You must not fear. Everything will be all right with you."

"But Fain—he—"

"Fain will return. I am to watch you. Be trusting, Skallon. Are we not good friends?"

Skallon soon sleeps again. He glides away from the bed, stands at the tunnel mouth. Beneath his gown there is the heatgun, but he will not use it. Fain is his enemy—Fain and his dog—but not Skallon. Left alone, Skallon will do nothing to prevent the proper triumph of chaos upon this world. Fain and his dog must die, but Skallon shall live.

Patiently, he awaits the invisible onrush of dawn.

Events now occur with the precision of successive snapshots:

Click. He fetches Skallon's breakfast.

Click. He lures Fain and Scorpio below.

Click. He awakens Skallon, ties him up, assumes his identity, hides him in the closet.

Click. He speaks with Fain, taunting him a final time.

Click. He hastens away, sprinting the length of the narrow tunnel.

Click.

Better, far better, that Skallon live a few ticks of time longer. Until this moment it has killed whenever possible. Death is, to Norms, disorder. But letting Skallon live deepens the Dance and will confuse Fain still more.

Ah—the leaping joy as it thinks of Fain. To have Fain at last, to destroy him in the deepest sense—that is a consummation. The moment comes now, presses forward. All else has bloomed properly in these last blessed hours: the Earthers are known, the Alveans rage. This Norm planet teeters, will soon fall, must shatter itself on the One.

A fever seizes it. The end is now merely waiting, prepared. A few moments, perhaps. But beyond the wreck of the furious delusion that is Norm Alvea, lies the consummation the One finally must demand. Fain himself must be crushed in a new way, a final and total way. Not by simple defeat. Not by returning, beaten, to Earth. Not by serene and sudden death. No. The One will be brought to fullness only if Fain finally sees himself as a fool, sees his order dissolve. The Changeling must whirl Fain through more stumbling Dances to make the man see. He must come ever closer to him, dancing nearer, until in some consuming moment Fain's eyes widen in surprise and fear and the One crashes through him, shatters, brings completion and death. There is danger for the Changeling in this, but the drumming leaping singing song of the One demands it. Each moment slides into the next, bringing fresh worlds, new paths. The Changeling knows that Fain is too important, has killed too many

Changelings, has imposed a vast sick tide of order. So
Fain must be done in the correct way, must meet his
end as he faces the One. The Changeling's quicksilver
mind flashes over rivulets of possibility. Its world is
unblocked by the Earthers' left-hemisphere dominance. It sees what is, what is real, what is One. No
mere words lead it, no babbling of tongues deceives
it. It can speak, can seem like a Norm, but the intuition that is in and of the One leaps high, commands
the mere word. Whatever must come, will—that is the
One. And here in the tunnels, in the blessed blackness, in the cloaking silence, here Fain the great killer
of Changelings comes.

2

Fain stopped. No, he thought, this won't do. The calm
sureness inside spoke through his building rage,
pressed a cool palm to his brow. *No need to care.
Nothing is final, son.* His hands trembled. He stood
stock still in the narrow tunnel and let his anger flow
over him, in him, through him, out of him. He could
wait. He would be calm. He would think. He had
done too much, fought too hard, to let this Changeling
trip him up now. There was an elaborate game going
on here. If he could keep up the dumb act for a while,
and sucker the Changeling in further, maybe there
was a solution possible. But it was hard to keep things
straight. For a brief moment the Changeling had be-

come Skallon. It was damned good, to do that, and so fast. And long before that, it had been Danon. Everything was clearing now. But now he had to think about the present, not the past.

"Scorpio!" he called, moving forward again. His hands brushed the slick tunnel walls and only then did he recall the flashlight in his gown. He clicked it on and felt relieved by its yellow pool. "Scorpio!" The dog would be waiting somewhere ahead, standing guard. Fain had no way of knowing how far he had come in his initial frantic rush. Not far enough; Scorpio wasn't answering.

Could the Changeling, disguised as Skallon, have caught Scorpio unaware?

Some of Fain's haste returned. The sure center faded. He trotted forward, watching for the end of the tunnel. He shouted Scorpio's name, paused briefly to give the dog time to reply. Finally, he thought he heard something—distantly—his own name. Now he ran again. It seemed as if he ought to have reached the end of this tunnel many times over. But time and distance were elastic quantities, easily stretched by darkness and fear. "Scorpio!" He stopped. "Scorpio, can you hear me?"

"Fain." He heard it clearly this time—a voice—yes, Scorpio's voice.

Fain ran. He ran until the air burned at his lungs, then stopped again. He struggled to shout. "Scorpio, listen."

"I. Hear. You. Fain." The voice was much more distinct this time. He must be close to the end of the tunnel.

"Scorpio, have you see anyone? Has anyone or anything gone past you?"

"Just. One. Thing."

"Who? What?"

"It. Was. Skallon."

"How long ago?"

"Shortly."

"Can you still see him? Or hear him? Scorpio, can you possibly pick up his scent? Skallon is the Changeling. Do you understand? That was the Changeling who went past."

"I. Will. Try. Fain." The voice showed no surprise. But, of course, it wouldn't—it couldn't. That was an advantage Scorpio would always possess over any mere human. The ways of the universe never disturbed him. Never knowing what to expect, he was never surprised.

Fain trotted again. The tunnel came to an abrupt end and all at once he experienced a tremendous sensation of open space. He staggered and nearly dropped the flash. Then he shined it all around. "Scorpio, where are you?"

"Here. Fain. Here. I. Smell. Changeling."

Fain turned his flash in the direction of the voice and caught the faint motion of a shadow. "Follow it. I'm coming." He kept his heatgun aimed at the darkness ahead. "If we hurry, we just might have it this time."

The path Scorpio took did not seem to lead back in the direction of the hotel. Fain tried not to think about that. It might mean anything—a different hideaway, perhaps a new identity. He ordered Scorpio to move quickly and broke into a quick walk. His feet kept wanting to run but he refused, knowing the need to conserve his strength. Occasionally, in the wider caverns, he caught glimpses of Scorpio darting ahead. They kept in contact by voice alone. Scorpio thought he was drawing closer. Fain halted and listened but heard no footsteps. The scent was strong down here. There were no other odors to confuse the dog.

Fain came to a blank wall and stopped. He shined his light, seeing two tunnels opening on opposite ends of the wall. He called, "Scorpio!"

"Here. Fain. Here."

The tunnel to the left.

Fain went that way.

The Changeling, clearly, knew where it was going. Fain wished he shared that knowledge. Already, he was hopelessly lost. The trail he covered in Scorpio's wake zigged and zagged crazily. It could have been random—the Changeling desperately struggling to escape—but Fain didn't think so. The Changeling had been given too much time. Disguised as Danon, it had had no reason to fear Fain. Every moment it knew exactly what he was up to. Fain blamed himself. He should have known. Danon had feared the dog too much. Danon had been present at every Changeling incident. Danon had had easy access to the city streets and the Great Hall. Fain should have known—and he had not. Was it too late now to recover what his failure had cost? Clearly, the Changeling thought it was. It had revealed itself, when it could have stayed hidden. It had laughed at Fain and taunted him openly. The riots in the city above. The explosion of hatred directed toward Earth. The apparent failure of the Central Assembly. The Changeling thought it had won, but Fain himself was less convinced. He thought there might be a chance. If he could catch the Changeling now, kill it, then Skallon—or someone—might possibly rebuild what had been destroyed. As a chance, it was slim, but at least he would have the pleasure of seeing his enemy dead. The last laugh. It was something.

"Fain. Here. This. Way." He followed the dog's voice, slipping underneath a low arch and then crossing a bridge above a narrow stream.

"Scorpio," he called, "how close are we?"

"Very close, Fain. Very close indeed."

He stopped. The voice this time wasn't Scorpio's . It belonged to someone else—someone he didn't know.

"Scorpio, what's wrong?"

Silence.

"Scorpio, are you there?"

Then he shined his light. The last few seconds, just before he'd first called out to the dog, he'd been aware of a certain feeling of familiarity: he'd been this way before.

Now, in the circle of light cast off from the flash, he saw the round mouth of the tunnel down which he had hidden Skallon.

He also saw the high nook where he'd ordered Scorpio to wait.

And he saw, hanging down from that nook, a paw. A dog's paw. Scorpio's paw.

Fain went over, shined his light, looked up. The red, charred hole in the dog's side was big enough to fit a post. The eyes were open but saw nothing. Dead, Fain felt the cold fur. And dead some time.

Which meant, all this time, zigging and zagging through tunnels and caverns, stumbling like a fool, he had been following the Changeling—and only the Changeling.

Inside Fain something welled up, flowed over. He forgot about Skallon bound and gagged in the cell, forgot about the flashlight swinging in his hand. Scorpio. Scorpio. Fain tripped. He fell. Crashed full face into a solid wall. Splashed waist-deep through a reeking pool. He had to get out, away from this darkness. He had to find the Changeling.

3

Skallon struggled against the bonds holding him. A shadowed figure loomed over him. Liquid eyes flicked here, there, studying. Skallon squinted, looking into the light. The man oozed, creaking. The head shifted subtly, the posture straightened, ears rounded off, nose tilted downward. The room whirled; Skallon fought to cling to consciousness. The dark figure above him was changing now, grunting with effort, joints popping, skin oozing into new folds and hollows. The drug clutched at Skallon and he saw suddenly into the world of this strange twisting shape. To the Changeling the world must seem fixed, stolid, barren. The shifting face smiled down at Skallon, plucking strings of memory. It was enjoying this process, reveling in it, radiating a burning joy. A certainty, an inner grace, crossed the flexing face. Its chin tucked in with a smooth flow. *To be like that,* Skallon thought. *To be able to make yourself over whole. My God, what a blessing! To live like that—! No wonder the Changelings were said not to fear death. To merge with the universe so well that you could flow into it, become a part of whatever the moment needed . . .* Skallon felt strange emotions fork like lightning through him. To live in the moment, to not fear death. Immortality. More than the pale promise of Gommerset—though now, instantly, Skallon saw in the rip-

pling, groaning form of the Changeling the proof that
Gommerset was right, had to be right. The panting
Changeling writhed in the stark light. *It is crucifying
itself,* Skallon thought. *Agony and torment and ec-
stasy. Crucifying itself to be what it must. Rapture.
Revelation. Bliss of motion. Consuming and devouring
dance of life.* What men spoke of and groped for and
called immortality, this being experienced directly.
The moment as forever. The infinite sliding grace of
the world. Alien it was, yes, something beyond man.
Perhaps in the end it was right that men hunted these
things, these creatures man's technology had created.
To allow them to live would be too great a contrast
for men to bear. *They would eclipse all our marble
monuments and passing glory. They would swallow
up our strainings, our vain building. They would end
us as men, forever.*

The Changeling stretched, grimaced, settled. It
gazed down. Skallon felt his eyes widen in surprise.
The face was his own. And Changelings killed
whoever they replaced.

Skallon tried to twist away, but the Changeling
moved with supple grace. The shadowy bulk came
between him and the light. Skallon knew what was
coming.

4

Fain blundered through the narrow tunnels, seeing nothing. Images of his father floated before him, seeming to grow out of the tunnel walls. Father . . . the calm center he had once had . . . Everything was slipping away from Fain now. His plans of coaxing the Changeling nearer and nearer, of playing a subtle game . . . all gone. His inner sureness had evaporated, too, leaving only the face of his father and the echo of his steps as he stumbled onward and, inside, a dull burning.

When he reached the trap door beneath the hotel, he kicked Kish's boxed supplies aside and clawed the door open.

Joane was alone in the kitchen. Fain's appearance must have startled her. She put her hand to her mouth and drew back. "Fain, what happened to you?" Her eyes went wide with fright.

He gripped her arm tightly. "Skallon. Did . . . ?" He swallowed, trying to force the words past his dry lips. "Skallon or Danon? Have you seen either of them? Did they or anyone come up out of that hole before me?"

She said, "Yes," nodding her head much too quickly. "I wanted to tell you. A man came. A man I did not know."

"How was he dressed?"

"As a Doubluth. As are you."

"Skallon's robes?"

"I do not know. They could have been—but I . . .
I . . ."

He let her go, knowing her fear would not help him.
His thoughts seemed to come with amazing clarity
now, but his rage had in no way lessened. He thought
of dead Scorpio. Poor, kind, dumb, gentle beast. Of no
harm to anyone or anything. "Did he leave the hotel?
Can I still catch him? Where did he go after he left
here?"

She pointed past him—outside. "He ran away very
fast. I tried to stop him, as you told me, but it was as
if he did not see me. His face was twisted, distorted.
And he was laughing. All the time laughing. It was
very frightening, Fain."

"But you saw where he went?"

"Not I, no. I—"

He slammed his fist against the wall. So it was useless—pointless—a failure. The Changeling had got
cleanly away and, without Scorpio to assist in the
chase, would not be caught again. The thin wood of
the wall cracked and bent beneath the force of Fain's
blow. His knuckles went numb. He sucked blood. His
hand might well be broken. The same as Scorpio's life.
By his own stupidity. His blindness in the face of what
should have been obvious.

Joane held his sleeve. "Fain, he did not get away.
Why didn't you let me tell you? I sent Kish after him.
Kish saw him leave the door and followed him."

Fain dropped his hand, ignoring the pain which had
now started to build. "Where—where did he go?"

She shook her head. "I would not know that. He'll
send a messenger when he can. You can wait, can't
you?"

Fain knew that he couldn't. He started to explain to

Joane but, just then, a young boy entered the kitchen.
He looked at Joane, then at Fain, and, his eyes growing big, started to back away. Fain reached out,
grabbed, and held the boy.

"Kish sent you here. From where? Where is Kish
now?"

Squirming in Fain's good hand, the boy stammered,
unable to utter a word. Fain shook him hard, but the
boy still refused to speak. Joane touched Fain's arm.
"Let me speak to him," she said.

Fain nodded and released the boy.

Joane crouched down. From a pocket in her gown
she drew forth three golden coins, which she placed in
the boy's hand. "I am Joane," she said. "Did Kish ask
you to speak with me?"

The boy nodded, glancing fearfully at Fain. "Kish is
waiting at the Hall of the Tagras. He said to tell you
the one you seek has gone there. A meeting of the
Doubluths is being convened. Kish waits outside."

Fain shook his head. The Changeling was wasting
no time—but why should it? Changelings did not
mourn the ones they murdered. "Where is this Hall of
the Tagras?" he asked the boy.

"It is all right to tell him," said Joane, when the boy
hesitated.

The boy spoke, but Fain did not understand. Even
after all these days the streets of Kalic were like a
maze to him. He missed Skallon—and Scorpio.

"I can take you there," said Joane.

"No. Let the boy do it. I think you ought to go below. Skallon is still down there, tied up. He—he can tell
you what's happened." Fain hesitated because he had
remembered something. He wasn't the only one to
mourn. The Changeling had also killed Danon. Joane
would have to know.

She nodded and spoke softly to the boy, promising

him additional coins if he led Fain to Kish. Then,
standing, she came over to Fain. "But first let me
straighten your robes and clean them. Your hand must
be bandaged. You frightened this boy, Fain. You cannot go out looking this way."

He nodded, knowing she was right. He intended to
kill the Changeling, but would that help her? Danon
was dead. Fain knew he bore as much of the guilt for
that as the Changeling itself. Could he ever explain to
her?

"Now you are fine," she said, pushing him back.
"You go to Kish, and I will go to Skallon."

The streets were even more crowded than usual.
Fain and the boy pushed and shoved, struggling to
hurry. There was no open violence, no loud speeches.
But he could feel the hate. It hung in the air like the
hard orange sun above. Kalic was a keg of powder.
The Changeling, clearly, intended to provide the final
fuse.

Kish waited outside a flat-roofed, single-storied
wooden building. When he saw Fain, he stepped forward. "Who is this crazy man who was hiding under
my home, Fain?"

"He's in there?" said Fain.

"I saw him enter with my own eyes and there is
only one way out. Is he your enemy, Fain? The one
you call the Changeling?"

Fain saw no reason to lie. "He is." Stepping close to
the building, he peered through a clouded window.
Within, he saw approximately two dozen Doubluths
seated in chairs. One old man—the new senior—stood,
addressing the others. "Which one is he?"

Kish, leaning past Fain's shoulder, laughed. "You
expect me to tell you that? They all have purple
robes, Fain. I followed the robes."

"You didn't see his face?"

"Not clearly, no. He was laughing all the time when he ran past me—a crazy man—but that may have stopped. Joane saw him better. Shall I bring her?"

Fain shook his head slowly. There would be no time for that, especially if Joane had gone below to Skallon. He knew, if he intended to act, he would have to move immediately. If the meeting ended and the Doubluths dispersed, he couldn't follow thirty men at once. If one man came out and went away, he couldn't afford to follow him, either; the Changeling might still be behind.

"I'm going in there," Fain said.

Kish shrugged and pointed to the door. "They will not stop you. You are a Doubluth. Of the high caste. I am a mere innkeeper."

Fain wasn't interested in Kish's envy—or his sarcasm. He thought of Scorpio with a hole burned in his side. He said, "Wait here. I'll be out shortly."

Then he went into the Hall of the Tagras. No one looked up or paid him any particular mind. The senior went on with his talk. He denounced the Earth as an insidious force. He accused the Consortium of deliberately starting the plagues. Fain found a spot at the rear of the hall where he could see everyone gathered inside. The senior might well be right. Fain knew the Earth Consortium well. It was not opposed to chaos as such, only to Changeling chaos.

Of course, the speaker might well be the Changeling.

Him—or any of the others. The monstrously gross—even for an Alvean—man in the front row. Or the smooth-faced young Doubluth near the middle of the hall. Or the bald-headed man beside him. Or the aged, wrinkled man. The one who was fast asleep.

The Changeling might be any one of the thirty men gathered in this hall.

And Fain knew he had no way of finding out for sure which one it was.

That was the joke. He had the Changeling trapped, penned, caught. And he was utterly helpless to act.

Fain turned to leave. What else could he do? As he moved toward the door, a flash of motion caught his eye. Glancing at the floor, he saw a slim fuzzy bug—some local version of a centipede—scurrying past his feet. Automatically, Fain raised his boot. He brought the heel swiftly down and squashed the bug. It was nothing important. It was an instinctive, almost subconscious act. But when he did it—the instant the bug died—everything became for Fain amazingly, startlingly, abundantly clear. The cold, bare, clear place at the core of his being suddenly opened and showed him what it was.

Fain laughed aloud.

He stood frozen in the hall on Alvea but he saw much farther.

—the hollow roar of a flame gun had filled the house, impacted sound, swallowing everything as the man covered his face with twisting hands and rocked backwards, the scream shrill and high as the flames washed him, cleansing him a last time, preparing him for—and then the tortured look, the riveting call that lanced between them as his father screamed, trying to form a last word, an unnecessary word now as Fain understood, the crushed insect writhing and feeling its burning insect acids spill out, and Fain felt sure the core of him split, surface, the two final blackening moments converging so that Fain saw, beyond all facts, that what was real and mattered was the streaming through the swelling series of events, the eternal sway and rhythm of the seconds moments days, that mattered, that Fain should do as was his nature, as his life had made him to do, act as the true dark spirit of Fain dictated, pit himself against the shapeshifter, end it here, the knowledge of what he must do suddenly both horrible and comforting, for it was in the flowing moment that all joy and pain came laughing liquid—

He dropped a hand to his waist. He must have cried out, he saw, because the assembled Alveans turned, startled. He drew the gun. His hand shook and he had to steady it, use the two-handed hold, legs braced, arms straight but supple. He blinked, his eyes wet, and clicked over to automatic fire. Someone cried out. A man came forward, running. The Changeling? Perhaps. A yawning moment—

Fain fired. An orange stabbing, bright as a star.

He cut a man in half. And swung the gun smoothly.

Screams, horrible screams.

Slicing and scorching. Billowing, acrid smoke.

Shrieks. And whimpering, silenced by the roaring, carving flame.

Men died. Thirty Alveans burned alive. Thirty of them—and one Changeling. Fain swung the gun around the hall once, then again; he wanted to be sure no one lived in unnecessary agony.

Fain, the merciful.

Fain, the preserver.

Fain, the destroyer.

Was there any difference?

Licking, snapping flames.

Fain dropped the gun. The reek of charred flesh sickened him.

He leaned over and vomited between his feet. *Scorpio*, he thought seneslessly, *you are avenged.*

At the core of him a cold vacuum spread outward, numbing his toes and fingers.

Fain turned and stumbled out the door.

Insect and father and shapechanger, all equal now.

Part
Five

1

Skallon ran through the streets of Kalic as fast as he dared. The soft air, heavy with moisture and the drifting, spiced smoke of cooking, rasped at his throat. Cowled figures turned to watch him, people looked at each other and murmured, but he pressed on, knowing that anything faster than a walk would excite interest, so he might as well run and perhaps outdistance anyone who was suspicious.

He had to find Fain. With Scorpio dead, things were desperate. Together they might still find the Changeling in time, but separated they would surely die. The Changeling had shown his hand; the thing was far smarter than Skallon had thought possible. How could belief in chaos give a being such power?

Sweat filmed his eyes. Ahead he caught sight of fretted stonework, elaborate red draperies. The Hall of the Tagras. A crowd sat in its cool shadow, awaiting possible aid or dispensations. Boys hawked fresh berries from the countryside. A woman sobbed against a ruined stone wall. Then he noticed something else.

The roaring came rolling out of the Hall windows. It sounded like the hollow voice of a furnace. There was a long moment when it seemed to go on forever and Skallon, jogging to a halt in the foreyard of the

Hall, suddenly realized that he was hearing a flame-gun on full bore.

Blinking, gasping, he stopped. The great ceremonial door edged open and Fain came out, tucking a hand-gun into his waist.

"What . . . what have you . . ." Skallon began.

"I got him," Fain said thickly. He tried to brush past Skallon.

"Got him? The Changeling? How?"

"Go see."

Fain stood panting while Skallon walked to the huge door and shouldered it open. Figures clustered at the edges of the foreyard, jabbering to each other but not daring to approach.

Skallon stood looking for a long moment at the Hall, now awash in blood and scorched deeply in the walls. Quite calmly and clearly he thought about the riot, about what he had done under the drugs. That was bad. A destabilizing event, to be sure; he needed no sociometric study of Kalic to know what the presence of Earthers, concealed Earthers, had done.

The effects could have been damped. With delicate tuning, with care, he could have healed the disunion he had caused.

But this . . .

There was no solution now. Alvea would tip over into a new sociometric phase. The castes might survive, the crude outlines of what Alvean culture had meant . . . but all would be altered by this destruction of an entire caste leadership. Alvea was beyond Earth's tinkering now.

Somewhere in that mess of disembowled bodies was the Changeling. Fain had done it, yes. But the Changeling had won. There would be a mad rage in Kalic now, a chaos that would spread throughout the countryside. Nothing he or Fain could do would stop that.

"Come on," Fain said at Skallon's shoulder. "Let's go back to the hotel."

"No," Skallon said. He turned, shrugging off the man's hand, and walked away into the milling, cowled crowd, into the yawning streets of Kalic.

Skallon found he was walking aimlessly, adrift in the scattered outskirts of Kalic. He grunted up a hill, slipping on gravel, banging a knee painfully. The hill looked down steeply on a flank of the city. Images slipped randomly through his mind. Joane, Fain, the blurred and flickering faces of so many Alveans, the riot, a hot brittle breath of incense and oil, a wan ruby light. His mind spun in its vacuum.

He heard a distant thudding. As he lurched upward he saw a woman lying on a bed. A brass bed, sheet and cover and blanket scrupulously in place, tucked in, neat. The woman lay looking at the sky. He saw beside her a tiny girl, her eyes mirroring the pale blue above. Neither moved or noticed his crunching footsteps. They had a look of waiting, of being at rest. He saw them breathing, long shallow breaths.

Suddenly, at the rim of the hill, a boy rose out of the ground.

"Where did you come from?" Skallon's voice rasped.

"Out of the earth," the boy said, beaming with his secret.

"I saw."

"My mother and sister are waiting for us to hollow out the first room."

The boy stepped back, scattering stones, and showed him the brow of a hole. A cave. From inside came the thumping Skallon had heard.

A man crawled out. He pulled behind him a pail of

dirt and rocks. The man looked at Skallon and said nothing. "Our home," the boy said proudly.

"But . . . why dig a cave? The plague . . . there are plenty of abandoned houses in the city. You could . . ."

"They are diseased places."

"It makes no difference. Few of the diseases can be communicated."

"*Ah*," the man said disparagingly.

"No, really."

"Can anyone be sure?" the man said with his grating voice. He glowered at Skallon fiercely. Embarrassed, Skallon stepped back a pace.

"Not, not totally, no. But most are surely genetic deficiencies . . ."

"We live here. Stay away from the houses of the dead."

The boy nodded gravely. "The way the old ones did. Before all this," he said in a piping voice. "Beneath the earth. In shelter."

Skallon watched numbly. The man fetched the pail out with knotted arms and pitched the rock down the hill, making a brown slash on the land.

"One room. Then another."

Skallon saw that the man had no legs, only stumps. A successful amputation, to stop a disease.

The man and then the boy crawled back in the lip of the hole. Skallon watched the woman and the slim, still girl. A silent, exhausted patience, older than centuries.

Rain began to fall, the first Skallon had seen on Alvea. The figures on the bed lay still, letting it fall on them in soft, persistent sheets. The thumping began again under the earth.

*   *   *

Now that the Changeling was gone, Skallon allowed his mind to summon up the images of it again. The rustling, creaking way it moved. The groans as its flesh shifted and arranged itself. The awful knowing smile. Skallon's own smile.

The creature was deadly and frightening, far more frightening than he had ever feared. But it was fascinating, too. For a moment Skallon had gotten a glimmer of what the thing felt, how it saw the world.

Walking, Skallon frowned, trying to recall the subtle impressions. He had gotten from the Changeling not ideas, but rather feelings, senses, emotions. Something about dancing, living lightly, moving through time like a ship on a still sea, gliding. And immortality. That Gommerset made some sort of sense, after all. There was some distant affinity of the Changeling for Alvea, he was certain.

But all the same, the creature—so like a man in so many ways, yet so fundamentally different—had tried to destroy the ancient culture of Alvea. *Had* destroyed Alvea now. It was a vile and yet fascinating thing, the Changeling. Skallon shivered. Perhaps he couldn't truly blame Fain for killing it. All the time, Danon had been the Changeling. The thing had been beside him, mocking. In the square, in the long meetings, during the chase through the Kalic streets. It was always laughing. Always there. And in the end, even when dead, it had won.

The Changeling was not dead.

Joseph Fain sat on the bed in his room in the hotel, sounds of chaos welling up from the street below, and stared at the dark stain on the floor beside his feet. He had just squashed a bug with his boot and now, for the second time in his life, he understood everything.

The Changeling had not been among those who died in the hall. He was as certain of that fact as he had ever been of anything.

To kill a thing, one must know it. The Changeling knew Fain. And with that knowledge, it would never have allowed him to catch it unaware.

Fain understood what the Changeling had intended. Sensing the presence of Fain's cool center, instinctively comprehending the source of his strength, it had set out to destroy that core.

This was meant to be the end: the realization that he had murdered a roomful of innocents should have pushed him over the brink.

Fain smiled tightly. A dead bug had saved him. He felt nothing—only a sheer, total, overwhelming peace. Not remorse. Not shame. Not guilt.

The Changeling had been far too successful. By obliterating the cool core within him, it had unloosened the knowledge to set Fain free, to make all concerns of life and death absurd and pointless.

At long last Fain truly understood the Changeling.

And he could kill it.

When he found it.

And that, he knew, would be soon.

Skallon drifted, light-headed and vague, through the clogged streets of Kalic. The discord he had envisioned now rose, in response to some unheard pulse. Gangs of small boys fought each other with sticks and dirt clods. Men ran breathless on frantic errands. Carts nudged their way through dusty streets, loaded with skimpy household provisions, their owners leaving the city before nightfall. The city gave off a soft, growling sound of doubt and bewilderment.

He reached the hotel by staying in the back streets, avoiding inquiring eyes. He had things to say to Fain but that could wait. He wanted rest, time to think. He slipped in the rear entrance and made his way through the dim hallway to his room.

Joane was lying on the bed. "You are safe!"

Skallon nodded. "Fain . . . he came back . . . he said the thing is dead."

"Revenge for the creature, the dog. And for Danon," she said simply.

"Yes, I suppose."

They sat for a while on the bed, not touching. Skallon wondered how grief came out, with Alveans. Joane's face was not streaked with tears, as nearly as he could tell in the faint light. She sat idly folding and unfolding her hands. A silence hung between them.

"Fain . . . he said he had to kill many . . ." Joane seemed to be searching for something to say. Small talk. Fain would have hated it.

Skallon nodded. "What did he tell you? Did he say it was his job? He didn't like to do it, but he had to?"

"He . . . something like that."

Skallon felt an overwhelming weariness. "Right. Right."

"You . . . will be going now?"

"Fain has probably called the orbiter already."

"Tomorrow, then?"

"No. Not tomorrow, not ever. I'm not going."

Her eyes widened. "Why?"

"If I went back I'd get stuck in a dorm somewhere, training for another planet, sopping up its culture. I don't want to. I know Alvea. Hell, I probably know it better than I know Earth. Nobody gets to see much of Earth anymore. It's all preserves and farmland. No room to move anymore."

"But to stay here . . . what you told me before . . ."

"Did I tell you that? Yeah, I guess I did. Earthmen can't live out a normal lifespan here. That's why

you're different from me. You've had your genes
pruned."

"You will die?"

"Not right away. I just won't recover fully, if I get
sick. Some damned nonadaptation will eat away at
me."

"How . . . terrible."

Skallon made a thin smile. "Somebody's got to try to
fix up what we've done here. And there's the Gommerset business. I'd like to get to the bottom of that."

Joane frowned. "You were not responsible for the
. . . for killing so many."

"I was a fool. The Changeling played us like pup-
pets. We never knew what was happening. I should
have seen . . ."

"But the deaths came out of the . . . disorder."

"No, it was my fault. And Fain's," he added sharply.

"When evil occurs, it expresses the whole of the universe. It is the same when good occurs. They both
come out of the random workings of . . . of the Sum-
mation."

"How can you believe in Gommerset if you . . .
well, maybe there's more to Alvea than I thought."

"What you think of as good and evil are not your
ideas. They are what they *are*."

"So?" said Skallon, musing.

"You should yield to them. Do not try to change
them."

"Everything you say just makes me more sure I'm
doing the right thing. I want to *know* Alvea. To truly
understand what you're saying. Do you understand
that, Joane?"

He could not read her expression. Dusk was gathering outside and the room had become dim. Skallon
was tired, his joints ached, and his throat felt tight
and dry.

"I do not know . . . Do you want to . . . ?" She lay back and lifted her hips, pulling the hem of her long dress up. "I will receive you."

"Why . . . no, no, I . . . am tired." Skallon was taken aback at this directness. Even as he said the words he watched her shadowed, fleshy thighs part and thought of finding some relief there. But no, he really wasn't in the mood. "I think I'll rest. Perhaps later."

She nodded and got up, her movements jerky. "I will return."

As Skallon lay back and tugged off his boots he thought of her, trying to read her mood in these last few minutes. She was different, changed, a woman capable of deep and shifting currents, a woman as complex as Alvea was complex, in a way Earth would never be for him. Earth, where everything was planned and controlled, had been known for centuries, would be forever. Earth, a lattice with people as the nodal points, all arrayed and known and living in a box that limited what they could do and know and love. Nobody bled on Earth, nobody died. One day they were there and then next day they weren't, *zip*, that was it. Nobody dug into the ground for shelter—hell, they were already living underground, leaving the surface for crops and preserves—nobody faced plagues and slow crawling death, nobody really *lived*, not the way the Alveans did. Those people on the hill, they were the ones Skallon wanted to help, wanted to know. They would be cast adrift by the chaos to follow, without the guides the castes had provided, dropping like small birds before the gale that was coming. He had to help them.

He fell into a troubled sleep, his face pressed into a rumpled pillow.

* * *

He awoke with sandy eyes and a parched throat.
But more than water or rest, he wanted Joane. He had
to talk about what came next. He would have to tell
Fain. They would probably have to leave Kalic, he
and Joane—certainly she couldn't stay with Kish now,
they had nothing together—and take shelter in the
countryside. There was a whole new life to begin.

He lumbered down to the kitchen, his Doubluth
robes snagging in the halls. Joane was not there. Kish
looked up from peeling vegetables, nodded, and went
back to work, clearly not wanting conversation.

Skallon walked through the lower hotel rooms, looking for Joane. The hotel was deserted. Outside, Maraban Lane stirred and clattered with traffic. People
moved aimlessly, carrying packages and bags, their
faces drawn and hostile. Some passing knot of women
began a hopeful chant, but soon it lost cadence and
dribbled away. Feet stirred dust in the heavy air.

Skallon turned away from the filmy windows. Very
well, he would see Fain. The moment had to be faced.

When he knocked on Fain's door there was a pause,
a silence from inside. Suddenly the door jerked open.
Fain stood to the side, back pressed against the wall,
his heatgun covering the door.

Skallon frowned. "What're you—"

Then he saw the figure on the bed.

Joane.

A spreading brownness down her thighs, seeping
through the cloth.

Eyes rolled back, white.

A smoldering hole in her belly, now filling with
red.

Skallon turned, wooden. "You—"

He struck at Fain with the edge of his hand, a
downward chop at the gun arm. Fain turned. Skallon
missed, lost his balance. He butted against the wall

and rebounded, knee coming up in a kick. Fain danced away.

"You . . . killer . . . insane . . ." Skallon said between clenched teeth, feet finding balance, looking for an opening.

He lunged. Fain stepped aside. Skallon tripped on Fain's outstretched boot and Fain clipped him cleanly on the back of the head. Skallon hit the floor and the world turned dark, dark and flecked with buzzing white spots. "Why . . . I . . ." he began.

"I didn't kill Joane, Skallon," Fain said, puffing. "That's the Changeling."

2

Joseph Fain held the woman in his arms and pressed her to him.

Something was wrong.

He drew her down on the bed. She was half-clothed. He kissed her.

It still wasn't right.

Something was missing. A yearning, a need.

Before Joane had seemed outwardly calculating, even casual. But the touch of her was warm and smooth; his hands seemed to hum as they moved over her. Some quality of her skin gave off a radiance of its own. Her need to be loved—loved by these Earthers, these strange and exotic men from the stars—came through.

Now there was something different. Had the deaths chilled the essence in her? Had Kish finally drawn some boundary, brought his masculine pride to bear?

He shifted his hands. She clenched him firmly and yet there was a quality in the embrace of holding back. She was hard, unyielding. Her tongue entered his mouth. Her fist, clenched hard, hugged tight between his legs. It was all there, the same as before, but something in her had shifted.

Fain moved mechanically, putting aside the confusion that now swarmed in his mind, and tried to focus on her. He remembered how she had come to him. After returning from the streets, still battered by the surfacing images of his father, of Scorpio, of days now dead, he had stopped at her room only long enough to say that the Changeling was dead. Her lined face was full of Danon's death and he went away. In his own room, shucking his robes, tired, he had signaled the orbiter to be ready for their return. Tomorrow. It would not be too soon. He intended to spend the remainder of the day resting and trying to find in the chaos swirling around some measure of genuine triumph. She could have left him that way. She could have stayed in her own room until he had gone. If she had done that, he would never have known. Was it because she (it) needed her (its) triumph, too?

She'd said, "Skallon asked me to tell you he has returned."

"Where is he?" He lay on the bed, peering up at her. She seemed strangely tall and elongated, but it was only the angle of his vision.

"He went to his room."

"Without seeing me?"

"I think he hates you, Fain. He said he will stay on Alvea."

"With you, I suppose."

"He wants it that way."

"I won't let him."

"It would be foolish if you did."

"He'd die."

"I know."

Then she removed some of her clothes. Fain took off what remained of his. They hugged. Kissed. Something was wrong—missing—and then he had known.

Fain pulled his lips away from hers and rolled aside. He fought to be calm, to control his disgust. The taste of that thing was like a foul musk upon his lips. He felt too numb, too dead to really care. In a normal voice, he said, "I thought I heard something outside."

She laughed and tried to draw him close again. "It's just Kish."

"No." He slipped away from her and whispered. "It might be Skallon. He could go over the edge. Stay here." He got his heatgun and opened the door. He could have killed her right then but he had to be sure. He had been wrong once. He had massacred a roomful of innocent men because of his mistake. The hallway was empty. He heard her moving nervously on the bed and quickly jammed the inject of Vertil he had palmed into the taut muscle of his forearm. He wasn't really thinking now. He was acting instinctively. A roomful of burned men. A half-naked woman on his own bed. A Changeling. No, he wouldn't think about any of it.

Breathing heavily, he went back into the room and closed the door. "I guess I'm spooked." He went to the bed, leaned over. She rose up to meet his lips. He drew back before they touched. "Stand on your head and clap your hands," he said. At the same time, he raised his heatgun out of sight behind his thigh where she couldn't see it coming.

She laughed and shook her head, letting long hair flutter like spores on the breeze. "Fain, you're always crazy."

"Am I?"

Then he shot her—it—through the belly.

3

—the bolt plunges searing burning into my oh God I fold around it trying to squeeze past its pressure and slip free as the fire thrusts into me taking claiming scorching blood and bile from me oh it won't stop I can't get—I—and the rushing darkness comes toward me now telling me again this part is ended—I have Danced too near—I was so close to a perfect form, a lush pinnacle—but pride takes—a bubble of blood bursts in my mouth as liquids evaporate licking hot from my guts and my intestines tumble out though my hands clutch at them, slimy things knotted tubes squeezing out between my warped fingers—slop and ooze—the shooting fierce pains—I spatter on the floor—pitching forward—dull ache, numbness works through my chest—I was a woman, a man, wanted too much, to be all and consume it, move through it—my self like worms twisting, headless, on the floor—the darkness—I shit myself in agony—the darkness rushes up through my legs—it—tightness—again I go into that place—another Dance—vessels burst—floor rising and rushing darkness—lancing pain—flame—shadows—I—

Skallon sobbed soundlessly, his chest heaving, and Fain knew there was no way to make him stop. So he talked. Fain had always hated people who talked when they couldn't think of anything else to do, and now he was one of them.

"Look," he said, "it's not Joane. Remember, when I was chasing the Changeling underground like an idiot? When it killed Scorpio. And came up through the kitchen. Well, it must have had more time than we thought. It must have killed Joane then, hidden the body. And assumed her identity. Sloughed away some body mass, somehow. Shaped itself. Made itself from man to woman. Christ, I don't know . . ." His mouth sagged, and then he caught himself. "Somehow. Somehow. By the time I finally made it back to the surface, the thing was ready. It sent Kish chasing some innocent Doubluth and then had me follow. It knew . . . what I'd do. It set me up. Set me up to massacre the high castes, and it was laughing all the time. To it, life is a joke. Danon. Joane. You and me. The whole damned universe. But the Changelings are wrong, Skallon. It's . . ."

Skallon wasn't listening. He stood over the body of the Changeling and wept. Skallon's problem was that he cared. The Changeling didn't. Fain didn't. But Skallon did. So who was the better?

Fain placed a hand gently on Skallon's shoulder, thinking of flame and madness. "We're going home tomorrow," he said.

5

Two men in purple robes stood in a secluded meadow on the outskirts of Kalic. They peered at the sky. One clutched a signaling device in his hand. He told the other: "The ship is well programmed in the event of any emergency. It'll just send down a smaller capsule, one I can pilot alone."

"Then there's no problem," Skallon said.

"Not really," Fain said. "But I think you'd better be damned sure. Once I'm gone, there'll be no going back. If you do stay here, you'll die, Skallon."

"I know." Skallon shrugged listlessly. "But when? Five Earth years, ten? Who knows? I might well live to see another new year, another Fest."

"You'll retain your disguise, I hope. Don't do anything stupid like letting them know you're from Earth. They'll tear you apart."

Skallon shook his head. "I don't want to live another lie."

"You'd rather die?"

"I'm going to do that anyway, aren't I?"

"Yes, yes, I suppose so." Fain listened to the beeping of the signaling device in his hand. There was something clean and pure—something reassuring—in its steady rhythm: *beep, beep, beep* . . .

"Look, Fain," Skallon said, "it's not that I haven't thought about this. I won't stay in Kalic. I would have, but Joane's dead, so there's no reason. I'll find another place, a small village, one where they'll accept me for what I am. Then I'll work. I'll live. I'll write. I'll study. What would I do on Earth? The same thing. But here at least I can be free."

"And alone. They won't like you, Skallon—you'll never be one of them. It's not easy being that much alone. It hurts, and what's much worse, it soon starts to hurt so much that you quit being able to hurt at all."

"That's you, Fain—it isn't me."

"I hope so. But you did love her, didn't you? Joane?"

"I slept with her, if that's what you mean."

"You know it's not what I mean."

"Then what is? That you slept with her, too? I know that—I knew it all along."

"Then you're wrong. Joane never slept with me."

"I don't believe that."

"I tried—sure, I tried—I'm only human. She turned me down. Believe her if you don't believe me. She wouldn't lie to you."

"What do you know about it?" But the anger had left Skallon's voice—the lingering bitterness. Maybe he did believe Joane. "You could stay, too, Fain."

He started to laugh, but Skallon wasn't being funny. The idea was something he had never considered. Stay here? Among these pseudos? Sure, and do what? Work? Marry? Relax? Live? "It's a sweet idea, Skallon, but it's not for me. This is your world, but mine's up there—the old blue Earth. Besides, if we both disappear, somebody's going to wonder. I can go back and cover for you. I can tell the necessary lies."

"Then what do you do? Hunt more Changelings?"

He hadn't thought about that. Slowly, Fain shook his head. "I don't think so. I think I'm finished doing that. When I get back, maybe I'll just retire."

"If they'll let you."

"There is that, but . . . here, wait a minute, Skallon. Let me tell you something. It's incredible, but . . . well, I didn't know it until yesterday. I knew it, but I didn't know that I did. I killed a bug. Squashed it with my foot. I don't know why that did it. Maybe it was seeing such an insignificant creature dead and knowing that it was just as important—just as complete—as any human being. It was a life, a soul, and I had killed it."

Fain paused. He knew he wasn't making sense and, feeling a muddy confusion, reached instinctively inward, groping for the center he had always carried. It was gone. This time there was no reassuring cold presence from deep within. The calm, serene center had dispersed, broken, spilled its contents into his conscious mind.

Fain shook his head. The musky odor of Alvea teased his nostrils, drawing his attention back to Skallon and the alien landscape surrounding them. "I had a father once. He was an exec VP in the research arm of the Consortium."

"Is he disappointed in how you turned out?"

"He probably would be, if he could, but he's dead. They killed him. That's what I want to tell you about. He was a geneticist, a damned good one. He discovered something. He believed in Consortium Equilibrium, too. So when he got this result he came immediately to the levels above him and told them. He expected praise, promotions, the works. Instead, they said he was wrong. They said he hadn't done his work well enough. A special scientific panel nailed him for it. They slapped him on the wrist, lightly, and sent him home."

"I see."

"That wasn't the end of it. He didn't quit the way they said he should. He checked his figures. Repeated his experiments. And he was right. He was positive he was right. And he told them so again."

"Told them what?"

"One time they could tolerate, but not twice. Once is a mistake and twice is treason. That's what they called him—a traitor. He never got another hearing, no second panel, nothing. They burned him down in front of me. Flamed him. When I watched him dying, I knew why."

"But they didn't kill you."

"They didn't think I knew. And they still don't. All that information got tied off while I was in massive psychotherapy, recovering from watching my father die. They destroyed his notes, his papers, his comlogex files, so there's no way of proving it. To cover their public image, they took the surviving boy and paid to have him patched up. Later, they put him to work. The information was buried so deep ordinary scanners didn't pick it up. Some specialist did me a big favor, driving it down deep. He must have known that was the only way I could survive. So he took the pressure that knowledge generates, and he turned it into something that protected me, made me able to think like a machine when I had to, something that would keep me alive."

"And living is that important to you, Fain." A thread of contempt ran through Skallon's voice.

"You misunderstand. Living isn't of the slightest importance to me. When Scorpio died, the old walls inside me started to crumble, and when I squashed that bug, they broke. The knowledge drifted up into my mind, out of my gut. I found out I'd been using that knowledge all along. Now I know *why* I believed. I knew then—and I know now—that life and death are utterly meaningless phenomena. I know what my father discovered and proved. He rechecked all the old data. He made new computations of his own. He used mathematics and genetics and he got data nobody had ever thought of looking for. He found out that crazy old Gommerset was right. So my father was burned down, knowing that it didn't mean a damn thing. I know that, too. When a man dies he is certain to be born again."

"Fain, you can't . . ." Skallon clutched Fain's robe, as if to draw the truth out of him.

Gently, Fain pushed Skallon back. "It's the truth, Skallon. Believe it. Believe me."

"Then you must tell others. Men have to *know*, Fain. You and I can . . . I've sensed it, too. We've got to tell."

"No." Fain studied the colors around them. He felt strangely serene, drained. "Nobody deserves to know that. Look at me. Look at this planet. Once you know what we know, nothing else is important. Nothing. It doesn't matter for you. You're staying here." He looked straight at Skallon. "And you're going to die. For the rest of them . . . well, aren't they going to find out soon enough?"

In the musky, heavy air the lines around Fain's eyes softened. The world was a thin film suspended over one vast fact. It was amazing, really, that humans could skate so surely over that thin layer. They seldom broke through, seldom discovered the abyss of certainty that lay under all the noise and distractions. And perhaps that was what the random dance of the Changeling meant. To cherish the lush chaos of the world, to spin and swoop through it. Because beneath it lay a sureness that rubbed away all the awful illusions. The Changelings remembered, so only the Changelings could embrace delicious death.

Fain laughed hollowly. He gave Skallon a last affectionate shove. "You'd better go."

He looked up. Above, a sleek bullet broke through ripe, knotted clouds. It gleamed. Mother was right on time.

CRADLE

Arthur C. Clarke and Gentry Lee

In a mind-blowing mix of scientific speculation and thriller, two seemingly unconnected events trigger off the discovery of nothing less than the secret of humanity's existence . . .

Written in conjunction with author and senior NASA scientist Gentry Lee, CRADLE is Arthur C. Clarke's latest masterpiece. It reaffirms his clearsighted vision of past, present and future, and will become a classic to rank with 2001: A SPACE ODYSSEY, RENDEZVOUS WITH RAMA and CHILDHOOD'S END.

AN ORBIT BOOK
SCIENCE FICTION
0 7088 8319 2

THE FUGITIVE WORLDS

Bob Shaw

The opening of THE FUGITIVE WORLDS finds
Toller Maraquine II – grandson of the hero of THE
RAGGED ASTRONAUTS and THE WOODEN
SPACESHIPS – bemoaning the fact that life on the twin
planets of Land and Overland has become dull and
uneventful compared to the stirring times in which his
illustrious forebear lived. Then, while on a balloon flight
between the worlds, he makes an astonishing discovery –
a rapidly growing crystal disc, many miles across, is
creating a barrier between Land and Overland.
Precipitated for personal reasons into investigating the
enigmatic disc, Toller – armed with only his sword and
boundless courage – becomes a pivotal figure in events
which will decide the future of entire planets and their
civilisations.

AN ORBIT BOOK
SCIENCE FICTION
0 7088 4874 5

FOOTFALL

Larry Niven and Jerry Pournelle

It was big all right, far bigger than any craft any human had seen. Now it was heading for Earth.

The best brains in the business reckoned that any spacecraft nearing the end of its journey would just *have* to be friendly.

But they were wrong! Catastrophically wrong!

The most successful collaborative team in the history of science fiction has combined again to produce a devastating and totally convincing novel of alien invasion.

FOOTFALL – the ultimate disaster.

0 7221 6339 8
GENERAL FICTION

FOUR HUNDRED BILLION STARS

Paul J McAuley

Dorthy Yoshida is a telepath and an astronomer. Because of her talent she is sent to investigate the mystery of a small planet orbiting a red dwarf star. Although it appears to have been planoformed, shaped by intelligent life, its only advanced life-forms are creatures called herders. They are known to possess primitive intelligence, while the slug-like herbivores they shepherd have only a rudimentary nervous system.

Could these life-forms really be connected with The Enemy, the unknown entity which fights a savage war with mankind in deep space?

It didn't seem likely. Until Dorthy landed, when her mind immediately detected a dazzling intellect, the intensity of which she had never before felt . . .

'Excellent science, grittily convincing human relationships, precision prose'
Lewis Shiner

LEGACY OF HEOROT

Larry Niven, Jerry Pournelle and Steven Barnes

Civilisation on Earth was rich, comfortable – and overcrowded. Millions applied for the voyage but only the best were chosen to settle on Tau Ceti Four. The Colony was a success. The silver rivers and golden fields of Camelot overflowed with food and sport nurtured by the colonists' eco-sensitive hands. It was an idyll, the stuff of dreams.

Just one man, Cadmann Weyland, insisted on perimeter defences: electric fence, minefield, barbed wire. Against what? Surely humans are the most destructive creatures in the universe? Surely the planet is friendly? Surely it's safe to walk in the fields after dark?

And beyond the perimeter the nightmare began to chatter . . .

'A version of ALIENS by writers who know the difference between Hollywood science fiction and the Real Stuff'
TIME OUT

0 7221 6407 6
SCIENCE FICTION

All Orbit Books are available at your bookshop or newsagent, or can be ordered from the following address:

Futura Books,
Cash Sales Department,
P.O. Box 11,
Falmouth,
Cornwall TR10 9EN.

Alternatively you may fax your order to the above address. Fax No. 0326 76423.

Payments can be made as follows: Cheque, postal order (payable to Macdonald & Co (Publishers) Ltd) or by credit cards, Visa/Access. Do not send cash or currency. UK customers: please send a cheque or postal order (no currency) and allow 80p for postage and packing for the first book plus 20p for each additional book up to a maximum charge of £2.00.

B.F.P.O. customers please allow 80p for the first book plus 20p for each additional book.

Overseas customers including Ireland, please allow £1.50 for postage and packing for the first book, £1.00 for the second book, and 30p for each additional book.

NAME (Block Letters) ....

ADDRESS ....

....

☐ I enclose my remittance for _____

☐ I wish to pay by Access/Visa Card

Number ☐☐☐☐☐☐☐☐☐☐☐☐☐☐☐☐

Card Expiry Date ☐☐☐☐

interzone

SCIENCE FICTION AND FANTASY

Monthly   £1.95

- *Interzone* is the leading British magazine which specializes in SF and new fantastic writing. We have published:

BRIAN ALDISS	GARRY KILWORTH
J.G. BALLARD	DAVID LANGFORD
IAIN BANKS	MICHAEL MOORCOCK
BARRINGTON BAYLEY	RACHEL POLLACK
GREGORY BENFORD	KEITH ROBERTS
MICHAEL BISHOP	GEOFF RYMAN
DAVID BRIN	JOSEPHINE SAXTON
RAMSEY CAMPBELL	BOB SHAW
ANGELA CARTER	JOHN SHIRLEY
RICHARD COWPER	JOHN SLADEK
JOHN CROWLEY	BRIAN STABLEFORD
PHILIP K. DICK	BRUCE STERLING
THOMAS M. DISCH	LISA TUTTLE
MARY GENTLE	IAN WATSON
WILLIAM GIBSON	CHERRY WILDER
M. JOHN HARRISON	GENE WOLFE

- *Interzone* has also published many excellent new writers; illustrations, articles, interviews, film and book reviews, news, etc.

- *Interzone* is available from good bookshops, or by subscription. For six issues, send £12 (outside UK, £13). For twelve issues send £23, (outside UK, £25). Single copies: £2.30 inc p&p (outside UK, £2.50).

- American subscribers may send $22 ($26 if you want delivery by air mail) for six issues; or $40 ($48 air mail) for twelve issues. Single copies: $4 ($5 air mail).

- -

To: **interzone** 124 Osborne Road, Brighton, BN1 6LU, UK.

Please send me six/twelve issues of *Interzone*, beginning with the current issue. I enclose a cheque / p.o. / international money order, made payable to *Interzone* (Delete as applicable.)

Name _____

Address _____

_____